WITHDRAWN
FROM THE RECORDS OF THE
MID-CONTINENT PUBLIC LIBRARY

LARGE
PRINT

F
Handeland, Lori.
The daddy quest

JUL 1 0 2006

MID-CONTINENT PUBLIC LIBRARY
Riverside Branch
2700 N.W. Vivion Road
Riverside, MO 64150

RS

The Daddy Quest

*Also by Lori Handeland
in Large Print:*

The Farmer's Wife

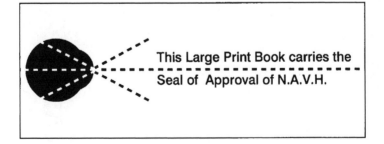

This Large Print Book carries the
Seal of Approval of N.A.V.H.

The Daddy Quest

Lori Handeland

Thorndike Press • Waterville, Maine

MID-CONTINENT PUBLIC LIBRARY
Riverside Branch
2700 N.W. Vivion Road
Riverside, MO 64150
RS

MID-CONTINENT PUBLIC LIBRARY

3 0000 12706714 2

Copyright © 2003 by Lori Handeland.
The Luchetti Brothers Series.

All rights reserved.

All characters in this book have no existence outside the imagination of the author and have no relation whatsoever to anyone bearing the same name or names. They are not even distantly inspired by any individual known or unknown to the author, and all incidents are pure invention.

Published in 2005 by arrangement with Harlequin Books S.A.

Thorndike Press® Large Print Romance.

The tree indicium is a trademark of Thorndike Press.

The text of this Large Print edition is unabridged.
Other aspects of the book may vary from the original edition.

Set in 16 pt. Plantin by Minnie B. Raven.

Printed in the United States on permanent paper.

Library of Congress Cataloging-in-Publication Data

Handeland, Lori.
     The daddy quest / by Lori Handeland. — Large print ed.
        p. cm. — (Thorndike Press large print romance)
     Originally published: Toronto : Harlequin, 2003.
     ISBN 0-7862-8141-3 (lg. print : hc : alk. paper)
     1. Mothers and daughters — Fiction.   2. Large type
books.   I. Title.   II. Thorndike Press large print romance
series.
     PS3558.A4625245D33 2005
        813′.54—dc22   2005022111

For Laverne and Sandra Michael
Everyone should have an
uncle and aunt just like you.

National Association for Visually Handicapped
serving the partially seeing

As the Founder/CEO of NAVH, the only national health agency solely devoted to those who, although not totally blind, have an eye disease which could lead to serious visual impairment, I am pleased to recognize Thorndike Press* as one of the leading publishers in the large print field.

Founded in 1954 in San Francisco to prepare large print textbooks for partially seeing children, NAVH became the pioneer and standard setting agency in the preparation of large type.

Today, those publishers who meet our standards carry the prestigious "Seal of Approval" indicating high quality large print. We are delighted that Thorndike Press is one of the publishers whose titles meet these standards. We are also pleased to recognize the significant contribution Thorndike Press is making in this important and growing field.

Lorraine H. Marchi, L.H.D.
Founder/CEO
NAVH

* Thorndike Press encompasses the following imprints: Thorndike, Wheeler, Walker and Large Print Press.

Dear Reader,

Thank you to everyone who wrote to me after reading *The Farmer's Wife*. Many of you requested books about the Luchetti brothers. I'm happy to say that *The Daddy Quest* is the first of those books.

Aaron Luchetti had his life all planned out. He would finish college, go to the seminary and become a priest. Since childhood he'd known that helping people was what he'd been put on earth to do. But on a mission trip to Las Vegas he meets Nicole Houston — a runaway who has turned to exotic dancing to stay alive. One night with her and everything Aaron believes about himself becomes muddled and confused. He leaves Las Vegas, college and his dreams behind, returning to the family farm for the next fourteen years.

Until a phone call from Nicole drags him back to Las Vegas and the child he left behind.

The Daddy Quest is the story of family, love and responsibility, a tale of how one man deals with the loss of a dream and the discovery that sometimes the wrong path was the right one all along.

I've created another cast of quirky characters — Janet, the ex-nun who keeps her halfway house running with profits from a comic-book series called *The Angel of Light.* Tim, a runaway who is looking for a daddy and finds one in a very unlikely man. And a few dalmatians with quirks of their own.

I hope you enjoy *The Daddy Quest* as much as I did.

Lori Handeland

For more information check out my Web site at www.lorihandeland.com

Chapter One

She found him in an alley, shivering behind a garbage can like so many other throwaways. But Rayne Houston had spent her life with strays and rejects. She knew just what to do.

No fast moves. No loud voices. Patience did the trick — and a little bit of food.

He was tougher than most. Took a few days to coax him out. But he didn't disappear. When she came by every day after school, he was waiting.

She began talking to him, pouring out all the horrors of being thirteen and different, of school and boys and of living at the halfway house and how embarrassing *that* was.

"As if I could bring my friends to a place called Mercy House," she mumbled.

As if she *had* any friends besides her mom, Janet and the parade of women who passed through their lives. Though, to be honest, Rayne hadn't been friendly with anyone lately. She snapped at her mom, ignored everyone else and spent a lot of time alone in her room. She felt . . . weird.

Grown-up but still a kid. Confident yet uncertain. Easily annoyed and just as easily thrilled. She wasn't sure what was wrong with her. Maybe it was just one of those phases she kept hearing about.

Rayne had never been interested in the stupid girly nonsense that went on at school. She saw real, live nonsense at home and on the streets of Las Vegas every single day. Stuff that made the silly dramas of seventh grade seem like a joke.

Still, one friend would have been nice. But all the kids thought she was a freak because she didn't dye her hair, or pierce her nose, or wear clothes that were three sizes too big whenever she wasn't wearing things that were at least a size too small.

Rayne glanced down at her favorite outfit — bell-bottoms and a flowing floral top she'd discovered in a secondhand shop that specialized in hippy clothes. She'd even found a matching scarf, which she'd tied around her forehead.

Sometimes kids sneered, "Make love, not war," when she walked by and gave her the peace sign.

"I'd rather be taken for an Austin Powers groupie than a hooker any day," she muttered.

The kid was a good listener, his big, blue eyes soft and sympathetic. Rayne considered how she could lure him home to stay and how she'd keep him a secret. Because at Mercy House there were no men allowed — only reformed prostitutes, drug addicts and exotic dancers.

"One big happy family."

The boy's head went up when she spoke, and his mouth formed the word *family,* but no sound came out. Rayne leaned forward, but at her movement he skittered back into the shadows again.

Darn. The kid was squirrelier than a browbeaten dog and twice as skinny. Someone had dumped him for sure, but not before they'd smacked him around a bit.

Rayne had seen too many people who'd been hit not to know what they looked like even when the bruises were gone. There was something in the eyes that screamed, "Don't!" Something in the way they held their bodies still and kept their voices quiet, as if trying with all they had not to be noticed.

The kid had a classic case of the don't-hit-me's, and just watching him made Rayne so mad she wanted to pound on whoever had done it.

Of course, violence never solved any-thing — or so Janet always said. But then she was an ex-nun. What else *could* she say? In Rayne's opinion some people only understood a good smack upside their stupid heads.

"Hey, kid, what's your name?"

She figured he wouldn't answer again — but a moment later a scratchy whisper split the silence. "Rat."

Rayne jumped to her feet. "Rat? Where?"

"No. Name's Rat."

She narrowed her eyes. Yep, some people definitely needed to be smacked. "They called you Rat?"

"Rug Rat, mostly. I like Rat better."

"I am *not* going to call you Rat."

He inched out of the shadows and into the fading light. His shrug only emphasized the boniness of his shoulders. The kid was so scrawny he made Rayne's teeth ache.

"It's my name," he said simply.

"How old are you? Five? Six?"

His face crinkled in thought. "I dunno."

Well, she couldn't leave a five- or six-year-old boy alone in the dark one more night. "Come on." She held out her hand. "I'll take you to my house."

He stiffened, staring at her hand as if it

were something more horrible than a rat. "No!"

His gaze darted from side to side as if he meant to run. However, Rayne blocked the only exit.

"Relax, kid." She refused to call him Rat. She just couldn't.

"Don't want to go back."

"Where?"

"The bad place."

"What bad place?"

"I dunno. But nobody liked me."

Rayne could relate. She tilted her head. "I like you."

He studied her for a nanosecond, before his lower lip jutted out. "Still not goin'."

"How about this?" she offered. "You can stay in the storage room. No one goes there."

Courtesy of the desert sand, basements were almost nonexistent in Las Vegas. Therefore, the storage space beneath the stairs at Mercy House was large enough to house another bedroom. If the maze of old furniture and boxes hadn't clogged it up. But the mess also made the room into a very good hiding place.

"Nuh-uh." The boy shook his head for emphasis.

"Listen, kid, I can't leave you here. It's

not right. You're going to come and stay at my place, and that's that."

"Don't like tall people."

"You mean grown-ups?"

He gave a short, sharp nod. "They hit."

"Not all of them."

"*All* of them."

"Believe me, the people at my house wouldn't hit you if you paid them."

He didn't look convinced, and Rayne couldn't blame him. But she had to get him off the street. Once she took him to Mercy House, let him settle down and see from a safe distance that the people who lived there were okay, he'd come out on his own.

Then she could worry about the no men rule. If she was lucky it might not apply to little boys.

"My mom would never send you back to the bad place," Rayne promised.

"How come?"

"Cause she was in a few herself."

Interest lit his eyes. She had him now.

When Rayne left the alley, the kid followed her all the way home. She hid him in the storage space, just as she'd promised, and went to her room with a smile. She'd always wanted a pet, but she could settle for a little brother.

14

★ ★ ★

Every night Nicole Houston climbed the stairs to the roof and watched the bright canvas of Las Vegas burst to life. First the sandy shaded hills receded as bright, white dots sprang up like popcorn across the horizon. Then, as darkness descended, the hills would deepen to blue midnight behind the flare of the electric lights.

Nicole watched so she would never forget how she'd gotten here in the first place.

Blinded by neon, lured to the music, the money, the vice — what lonely, orphaned, pretty girl wouldn't be? She'd been luckier than most, to find a place, a life, some hope. But it was because of where she'd started that she was able to be any good at what she did at all.

Nicole sighed and turned away. By night the city appeared downright beautiful — on the surface. By day it was always hard to believe a less attractive spot could exist. There weren't enough colored lights, sequins and glitter to cover the ugliness that thrived in certain corners of the world.

"Nicky? You up there?"

Thuds and mumbles preceded the arrival of the woman Nicole admired more than anyone. Pushing seventy, Janet Bristol

15

still moved as if she weren't a day over fifty-five. Her fading, flowing, waist-length red hair, willowy six-foot frame and tendency to dress as if she were an extra in a commando movie belied her original vocation. For nearly forty years Janet had been known as Sister Martha Grace.

"Here." Janet shoved a plastic cup into Nicole's hand, then collapsed into the only chair available, of the ancient lawn variety, frayed and listing.

In deference to the late-May heat of Nevada, which was positively balmy when one considered the desert oasis could top out at 110 degrees in the summer, Janet wore camouflage shorts and an army-green tank top. She'd left her combat boots downstairs, but her ankle-high black socks were still in place. Residents of Las Vegas referred to Janet as a one-woman army of God, and they were right.

Nicole glanced into her cup, which appeared to be filled with red wine. She knew better. In this house no drugs, no alcohol, no sex might as well be etched on the front door, which was just fine with her. She'd had enough of all three before she turned sixteen.

"To another job well done." Janet lifted a second cup and after Nicole tapped hers against it, they drank. This time the liquid inside was grape juice, but they'd performed the same toast countless times with countless other liquids. What was in the cup did not matter, what the cup symbolized did.

They'd saved another lost soul. Chalk one up for the good guys.

Lately, though, Nicole hadn't felt like much of a superhero. Perhaps because she was the mother of a teenaged daughter and had somehow morphed into the most boring person on the planet.

Nicole sighed. Janet's sharp gray eyes narrowed. "What?"

"Nothing."

"Nothing always means something."

How a woman who'd spent half her life as a nun could be the next best thing to Mother of the Year was beyond Nicole. Of course, Janet had seen more than the average nun. She had refused to be pressed into the teacher-nurse mold and boldly gone where few sisters had gone before. Straight to the belly of the beast. Viva Las Vegas!

In the end, despite all the women she'd helped and the lives she'd saved, Janet had been told to toe the line or get out. Still, she refused to be bitter.

"If everything goes our way in life, how would we ever learn anything at all?" she often said.

Nicole wished she were half the woman Janet was, but she never could be.

"Spill it," Janet pressed. "What did the girl do or say this time?"

Nicole smiled. Janet knew her so well, and she knew Rayne even better. What would Nicole have done nearly fourteen years ago if not for Janet?

She'd arrived on the doorstep of Mercy House, a sixteen-year-old pregnant stripper with a page torn from the yellow pages still clutched in her hand.

Better make that ex-stripper. Once she'd started to show, Nicole had been out on her tassels. But she was taken into Mercy House without question, and she'd been here ever since. This was home now, Janet and Rayne the only family she'd ever had, or would have.

"Rayne's hiding something," Nicole admitted.

The cell phone on Janet's belt shrilled. "Sorry." She lifted a finger. "Hold that thought."

With a scoop of the hand and a flick of the wrist that would make a CEO envious, Janet answered her phone. "Hello? What?"

She scowled. "No, I don't think it's all right to steal from a casino."

She listened, then shook her head. "Jesus threw the money changers out of the temple, he *didn't* take their money." Another pause. "Yes, I realize you're not Jesus. I'm not sure what tipped me off."

Janet rolled her eyes, and Nicole fought the urge to laugh. Her friend's cell number was common knowledge on the lower rungs of Vegas society — perhaps because Janet gave it out to anyone who asked and quite a few who did not.

As a result people called at all hours asking for advice, needing a kind word or a cool head, and Janet was there. Her no-nonsense style and comforting manner had become legend, but sometimes the questions were downright ridiculous, if not funny.

"Here's a thought," Janet continued. "*Thou shalt not steal.* Short, to the point, still relevant in today's society." She jabbed the end button with a practiced thumb. "I swear I'm going to get a 900 number. At least I'd get paid for all the advice I give."

"You'd never charge for advice."

"But I've got the perfect number, and I'd hate for it to go to waste."

"Okay." Nicole spread her hand in a

questioning gesture. "I'll bite. What's the number?"

"One-nine-hundred ask a nun."

Nicole quickly counted the letters and smirked. "Clever."

"That's me, clever old nun." Janet winked. "Now, why do you think Rayne is hiding something?"

Nicole let her mind wander back over the past few days. "She's jumpy. Missing sometimes. Late getting home when she's never been late before. Do you think she's got a boyfriend?"

"Ask her."

"I did. She just narrowed her eyes and looked at me like I was dumber than dirt."

"Kids." Janet made a tsking sound. "Can't live with 'em, can't put a shock collar on 'em."

"Gee, I see why people call from all over just to get your opinion."

"You're welcome." Unfazed by Nicole's sarcasm, Janet finished her juice. "Give the kid a break, Nicky. She lives in a halfway house with women. She's got no siblings, no father."

Nicole winced. Janet knew the truth about Rayne's father, but no one else did. Not even Rayne.

"All of the kids at her school have parents who are showgirls, magicians, black-jack dealers. This city is glamor on a shoe-string. She's got an ex-nun and a —"

Janet broke off, then stared into her cup as if expecting more grape juice to appear like a miracle. Janet was always expecting a miracle.

Nicole had learned over the years she had lived here that one thing separated a professional believer from the amateurs. One expected miracles, the other merely hoped for them. Nicole had lost hope long before she'd lost everything else.

"You think it's starting to bother her that I took my clothes off for a living? There are worse things."

"And we've seen quite a few of them. So has Rayne."

The familiar sense of guilt flickered. "Maybe now that she's older I shouldn't let her stay here. I could send her . . ."

"Where?"

Nicole lifted a brow. "Military school?"

Janet snorted. "Right. She's thirteen. She's supposed to be a pain in the ass. If she wasn't, I'd be worried."

Nicole sipped her juice. "Are you allowed to say *ass?*"

"I'm allowed to say anything I please. I own the joint. Or J. B. Grace does."

"And since you're one and the same . . ."

"Precisely." Janet got to her feet. "Now, if I want to pay the bills, J.B. had better get to work in the bat cave."

Janet's alter ego, J. B. Grace, comic book author, kept them in grape juice and various other sundries. Since Janet had left the church, then taken a few unpopular stands to protect her girls, much of their mission funding had dried up.

Several years ago Nicole had come across a notebook. In it were extremely detailed drawings that illustrated the story of a crime fighter named the Angel of Light, who brought down Old Testament retribution on a host of bad guys tearing up the streets of a fictional city that appeared very Vegas-like.

When Nicole had confronted Janet, she'd admitted to writing them to ease her frustration with all evil in the world. She'd brought out more, and Nicole had recognized many of the horrible tales they'd heard from some of the women who had passed through Mercy House. But in the realm of the Angel of Light, the bad guys always paid — often quite horribly. Nicole was hooked.

So were a lot of other people. The *Angel of Light* comic books had drawn a cult following and netted them enough money to buy Mercy House, ensuring they wouldn't be out on the street some month when the rent came due and they had nothing.

"Would you like to decide who gets Carolina's room?"

Nicole blinked and stared at Janet, who hovered in the doorway, one foot on the step leading down, another still anchored to the roof.

"Huh?"

"Pick a new recruit, Nicky. I'm busy."

"But — but —"

Janet always chose the women who would live at Mercy House. She seemed to have a sixth sense about those on the verge of change.

Carolina, whom they'd just toasted, had come to them from one of the party houses outside of Vegas. She'd been here eight months and left that morning for her new life as an assistant to the assistant chef of a ritzy restaurant in San Francisco.

Women who were ready to start new, but had no idea how, got the chance at Mercy House. But they had to want that chance deep down inside in order to succeed. Janet had always been the expert at seeing through the bravado and the toughness to the woman within. Nicole wasn't sure if she could. What if she chose wrong?

"Choose," Janet insisted. "Just because you've made some poor decisions in the past doesn't mean you're incapable of making a good one now. Unless, of course, you refuse to make any at all."

"The decisions I made at sixteen hardly count."

"I wasn't talking about when you were sixteen."

Her heart gave a hard, painful thud against the wall of her chest. "You promised never to bring that up."

"I did? I'm forgetting all sorts of things in my old age."

"No, you aren't."

Though Nicole's voice was cool and her face calm, her palms had gone damp as her pulse fluttered faster and faster. She could not talk about the past. She would not talk about *him.*

"Where's Rayne?" she asked sharply.

Janet's lips thinned. She knew what Nicole was doing, since she had done it a thousand times before. When conversation turned to . . . him . . . Nicole changed the subject. Rayne was always a handy subject to choose.

"She was shading one of my sketches."

"And her homework?"

"Done. Or so she said."

"Right." Nicole strode toward the steps. "I prefer to see it before I believe it."

Janet refused to move out of her way. Since Nicole didn't want to go hand to hand with the amazon warrior goddess, she was forced to stop and listen.

"Nicky, you can't avoid everything that hurt you in the past. Every mistake you made. It's not healthy. For you or for Rayne."

"I'm not avoiding anything. I just don't want to make another mistake."

"Also not healthy."

"I don't like to screw up. So sue me."

"There's a difference between wanting to do well and being so afraid of making a mistake you do nothing at all."

"I do plenty. You act like I'm some pathetic recluse who never leaves the house."

Janet gave her a bland look.

"I leave the house!"

"You're more of a nun than I ever was."

"Am not."

"Oh, that's tellin' me. You're twenty-nine years old and you haven't had a date in . . . What? Help me out here."

Nicole sniffed. "I don't date."

"Not healthy."

"So I'll eat more broccoli."

Janet raised a brow. "I'm starting to think you don't like men."

"What's to like?"

"You have no one to blame but yourself. If you'd told him about Rayne, he'd have come back."

"And denied everything he was, everything he'd ever wanted to be. I wasn't going to ruin his life."

"Don't you think that was his choice to make?"

"No. Because he'd have made the wrong one."

"Who are you to say what's wrong and right? Walked on any water lately?"

Nicole threw up her hands. There was just no arguing with a nun. "What's done is done. I can't change it now."

"You never should have told her he was dead. That is *so* gonna bite you on the butt."

"You've been spending too much time with Rayne. You're starting to talk like her."

"And you keep changing the subject."

"I never said he was dead. I said he was gone. He is."

"You're going to have to tell her sometime. Then she's going to —"

"Hate me."

"I was going to say, want to meet him."

Which was exactly what Nicole was afraid of.

Rayne didn't mean to snoop. But who hid secrets in the Bible anyway. Wasn't that some kind of sin?

She'd come to her mom's room as she did every day before supper. Sometimes Mom was there waiting, other times, like today, she was up on the roof thinking or talking to Janet.

Rayne should probably run downstairs and check on the kid, but she would have to feed him later, and she didn't want to disappear too often. Eventually someone would wonder what was going on and come searching for her.

So Rayne flopped onto the bed to wait, but in minutes she was bored. The only book near enough to touch was the Bible, and when Rayne shuffled the pristine pages, just look what popped out.

Her father's phone number.

The sight of a dead man's handwriting made her fingers shake. She smoothed her thumb over the letters and the numbers, imagined him writing the words, handing Mom the note, kissing her goodbye. Then walking out of their lives and dying too young.

Rayne wasn't exactly sure why he had left or how he had died. Her mom always got weird whenever Rayne asked about her dad — fidgeting, twitching and becoming all teary eyed. Eventually Rayne had stopped bringing him up at all.

She sighed dramatically. Her mom had had a rough time. No doubt about it. She'd been abandoned on the steps of Saint Nicholas Church in Houston when she was just a baby. Hence her name, Nicole Houston.

She'd been shuffled from foster home to foster home until one of her "brothers" had tried to be more than brotherly.

"Creep," Rayne muttered. Someone else who needed a good whack — with a two-by-four.

Nicole had then hopped a Greyhound for Vegas and done her best to get a real job, but she was a teenage runaway. However, she was a very pretty runaway, with long blond hair, big blue eyes and creamy skin over a whole lot of curves. She'd ended up dancing exotically in places where they weren't too particular about proof of age.

Rayne's mom had been bluntly honest about what she'd done, how awful it had been, and the steps that had led to each mistake. She had always been downright chatty about everything — except Rayne's dad.

"I guess it would really suck to have your boyfriend get himself dead and leave you holding the baby," Rayne muttered.

They didn't even have a picture. All Rayne knew was her father's name and that he had dark hair, blue eyes and came from Illinois. She'd always figured she must look like him since she didn't look anything at all like her mom.

Black hair, green eyes — where those had come from she'd probably never know — and . . .

Rayne snorted in disgust at the thought of her impish, heart-shaped face, minibody and nonexistent breasts. It frustrated her to be the shortest, flattest, cutest girl in school. Especially when thirteen-year-old boys referred to her mom as a "hottie."

"Damn it!" Rayne sat up, then hunched her shoulders in expectation of a roar of Biblical proportions if Janet heard her. But even Janet couldn't hear through a closed bedroom door, though sometimes Rayne wondered.

She had just reached out to put the note back where she'd found it, when a little voice made her hesitate.

Why not call the number and see what happens?

Rayne tilted her head, considered, then shrugged. "Yeah, why not?"

She grabbed her mother's phone and punched in the number. Five rings later a man answered. "Hello?"

Suddenly Rayne had no idea what to say. Who was she calling? Where was she calling? And why?

"Hey, I hear you breathing. Is this Zsa Zsa?" The man made a sound of disgust and then called out, "The baby's using the speed dial again."

"Uh, no, I, uh —"

"Hello?"

Rayne's mouth opened, then closed. She glanced down at the paper in her hand and blurted, "Aaron Luchetti."

"Oh, sorry. Thought my sister's baby was at it again. Aaron's not here right now. Message?"

Not there *right now?* Rayne froze.

"Hey? You still there?"

She had to shake her head, hard, to make the buzzing in her ears go away. Was the room spinning?

"Um, yeah. I mean no. No message, thanks."

Rayne clapped the phone back into the

30

cradle, then stared at the thing as if it might reach out and bite her.

Her mother's lie certainly had.

Chapter Two

Rayne wasn't waiting in Nicole's room and that in itself made Nicole itchy. The girl was up to something and Nicole meant to find out what. But first she had to find Rayne.

She wasn't in Janet's room or her own. The four women in residence hadn't seen her, either. The kitchen was empty, as were each of the three bathrooms. Where could she be?

Mercy House had once been a boarding facility for dealers who worked in the casinos downtown. Back when Glitter Gulch was run by the mob, Fremont Street was the center of all the action. However, those days were done.

Now the Strip drew the tourists. Located only a few miles away, the newer casinos had been built as amusement parks for adults with plenty of disposable income.

The city had done its best to draw folks back downtown by building *The Fremont Street Experience* — a light show that ran nightly on a screen permanently affixed above Glitter Gulch. They had succeeded to a small degree. But the show had become a joke to the locals, a kitschy bit of tourism that once seen did not ever need to be seen again.

Mercy House was located several streets over from Fremont, at the edge of an iffy section of town. However, it was where they needed to be to help those who most needed helping.

Nicole opened the storage room door and shouted, "Rayne?" into the jumble of crap stacked all the way to the ceiling.

Something skittered in the back, and she slammed the door shut. A few days locked in a dingy basement when she was eight had made Nicole wary of tight, dark places. Just another little phobia. Call the psychiatrist.

Making her way back to her room, Nicole considered the stray thought. She'd never gone to a psychiatrist, her innate distrust of anyone in authority making her wary. But perhaps she should. She knew she had problems. Big ones.

She wanted Rayne to grow up normal so badly the fear that she wouldn't kept Nicole awake at night. She was scared to death she'd screw up her kid because she'd never had a mom and had no idea how to be one.

Being shuffled from one foster home to the next had left Nicole clueless in family dynamics, as well. She had turned to books to fill the emotional gaps and come to the conclusion that their household was probably not the best example for an impressionable teenager. But it was the only one they had.

She had a good job here, one she enjoyed, one she was good at. They had a place to live and the support and friendship of Janet. Nicole and her daughter would continue to make do.

"Rayne?" Nicole pushed open her bedroom door once more.

Still empty. But a closer look than the one she'd taken before made her uneasy. Something was different.

She had come here on a few other occasions and been struck by the feeling that someone had been touching her things. It usually meant one of the new girls had broken down and gone searching for a fix or the means to get one.

Since Nicole had nothing, never had, probably never would and didn't care, there was no harm done. She expected such things at Mercy House. What she didn't expect was to discover her Bible had been shifted from its position on the night stand.

Nicole and God had not been speaking for . . . oh, about forever, so the Bible that she'd been given upon entering Mercy House had not seen very much use. She hadn't opened it — except that one time — but she couldn't say that she hadn't bumped it recently, just enough to slide the cover a few inches through the slight layer of dust on the nightstand.

She couldn't say that she *had,* either. Nicole snatched the book, flipped through Eden to the flood, past the prophets and on to the disciples. Where had she put it? Certainly not in the letters to the "ians."

"Ephesians, Philippians. Nope." Several pages fluttered by and a slip of paper shot out, drifting to the carpet in a lazy dance. The sight soothed her unease. She glanced back at the Bible and snorted. "Revelation. Well, Janet continues to insist that God has a sense of humor. Hardy-har-har."

She leaned down and plucked the paper from the floor. Written in precise hand-writing was the information she'd received in lieu of goodbye.

Call if you need me. Aaron Luchetti.

The sight could still make her angry

nearly fourteen years after she'd read the note for the first time. He'd signed his last name as if she wouldn't know which Aaron he was.

As if she would ever forget the father of her child.

"I'll be back as soon as I find my father," Rayne whispered.

"No."

The kid, who never came near enough to touch, had practically leaped into Rayne's lap when her mom opened the storage room door and called out. But Rayne knew she would not venture in here. She didn't like dark, creepy places — or the truth, it seemed.

Anger swelled, choking her. That was the only reason Rayne felt like crying. The *only* reason. Because her mom had lied to her all of her life. Not because she didn't want to leave the Rug Rat behind.

"Whadda you mean *no?*" she demanded, the tension in her throat and body making the words louder and sharper than she'd intended.

He scuttled back behind the cardboard box where he slept, then peeked out. "You won't come back. No one I like ever does."

Rayne sighed. The kid was growing on

her. But she couldn't take him along. She *couldn't.*

Before she'd packed her bag and crept in here, Rayne had sneaked into the office and gone online. It hadn't taken her long to discover that the phone number from the Bible was for Gainsville, Illinois.

Rayne barely had enough money to get herself to the middle of nowhere; she certainly didn't have enough to take the kid along, too.

"It's a quest," she blurted. "You know what that is?"

"Nuh-uh."

"Like Indiana Jones looking for the Ark or the Grail or those weird glowing stones."

"Who?"

Rayne frowned. Poor kid. He'd probably seen one movie in his life, if that. "Never mind. Heroes or heroines go on quests to find something important that will change their lives forever. I'm going to find my father."

His whisper was filled with wonder. "Can you find me one, too?"

Rayne didn't know what to say, so she didn't say anything for a while. But even when she cleared her throat, a tickle remained.

"I've gotta go, kid. You'll be safe here. I promise."

"Promises." He shook his head and sighed. "Made to be broken."

Was he *trying* to make her feel like pond scum? Rayne took a step closer and peered at his innocent, dirty little face.

Oh, man, he was sucking his thumb. Now she *had* to take him along.

"All right." She gazed heavenward and shook her head. "You can go."

His thumb came loose with a wet plop as he grinned.

"But no thumb sucking, no whining, and we're going to have to hitch partway because I don't have enough money for two bus tickets to Illinois."

" 'Kay," he said. "But —" The boy stuck his hand into the pocket of his pants, then pulled it back out. "Is this enough?"

His grimy fist was full of money. Twenties and fifties.

"Where did you get that?" He hunched his shoulders and started to back away. "Never mind." Rayne really didn't want to know. "Hand it over."

He did.

"One more thing, kid. I am *not* calling you Rat, so pick a new name."

" 'Kay."

They crept out the front door without anyone seeing them. It wasn't hard since there was a curfew, and Rayne was breaking it.

The night had turned cool, as it always did once the sun disappeared into the desert. She glanced at the boy. He had nothing but the clothes on his back — pants that were too loose, too short, and a T-shirt that might have once been white, but was now pretty gray. He needed new clothes, but she'd save that problem for another day.

His thin shoulders shook. How could he look so pathetic and so cute at the same time?

Rayne paused. "Hold on."

She dug in her bag and found a sweatshirt, which she yanked over his head. At least he'd stopped flinching every time she went near him.

The sweatshirt reached to his knees. He touched the soft, wash-worn material with one finger. "Thanks," he breathed, as if she'd just given him the moon.

"Yeah, well, if you catch cold, you'll hold me up."

Rayne dug in her bag some more, pulled out an old UNLV cap and stuffed her hair beneath it. She'd dressed in old, boring

39

clothes — no life, no style, no color. She hated them, but she needed to blend in as much as possible. She didn't want to be dragged back home before she'd even begun the journey.

The bus station was located on Main Street, not too far from Mercy House. In the lobby a considerable crowd hung out. Only a few faces turned their way, but none of them were interested. One thing about Vegas, all the bright lights, clanging bells and jackpot promises deadened people pretty fast to everything but their own troubles.

Another plus, the bus station was nearly as busy as the airport. Quite a few visitors ended up traveling home super economy after a few days spent losing their shirts and anything else that wasn't tied down. Tonight, no one was going to look at them twice, let alone remember them.

Her mom thought Rayne couldn't handle herself in the big, wide, scary world, but Rayne was going to prove her wrong. She was going to meet her father. She was going to find out the truth.

Did he know she existed? Would he care? Who was the bad guy? The mother she had always trusted or the father she had never known?

Nicole didn't panic until midnight. By then she'd called everyone Rayne knew and a few people she didn't. The entire house was in an uproar. The girls and Janet had dispersed to all corners of the city, but there was no sign of her daughter.

Two policemen arrived at 1:00 a.m. They asked the usual questions.

"Did you and your daughter argue?"

"No."

"Would she run away?"

"No."

"Does she have a boyfriend?"

"No."

"Where would she go?"

"I have no idea."

The officers exchanged knowing looks and Nicole ground her teeth. She could almost hear what they were thinking.

She didn't pay attention. She didn't know her child. Her daughter had run wild, and now she had run off. But they couldn't be farther from the truth.

If anything, Nicole paid too much attention, attempting to fill the role of two parents instead of one. And she knew everything about Rayne. Or at least she'd believed she had — until tonight.

"We'll check around, Ms. Houston. You

let us know if she gets in touch with you, okay?"

"That's it?" Nicole stared at them incredulously. "My thirteen-year-old daughter is — is —"

She moved her hands helplessly. She couldn't speak anymore. She couldn't think any further. If she didn't say it, then maybe it wouldn't be true. Her daughter hadn't disappeared; she was just temporarily misplaced.

Nicole took a deep breath, swallowed and tried again. "She's out there alone, and all you're going to do is check around?"

"There's not much else to do, ma'am." The officers shuffled their feet, shifted their shoulders, stared anywhere but at her. "We have no indication of kidnapping or foul play. That she took all her money and some of her clothes screams runaway. She'll show up on her own. Most of them do."

However it was the ghosts of the ones who didn't that kept Nicole awake all through the night. Or maybe it was the two pots of coffee she and Janet drank after her friend returned from her search.

"That's it," Janet said when dawn tinted the sky and Rayne still hadn't come home.

"You're going to bed and so am I."

"No. I can't."

"You have to lie down or you'll fall down, and that isn't going to help Rayne."

"But what if I'm sleeping while she's —"

"Don't!" Janet ordered. "Don't borrow trouble. Until we know any differently, Rayne's in a snit over something — "

"Rayne doesn't get into snits," Nicole interrupted.

"She didn't use to."

Nicole sighed. Her friend was right. Rayne *was* different, and Nicole had a hard time reconciling the emotional outbursts her daughter had been capable of lately with the calm, peaceful, always helpful child she'd known.

"Times change," Janet continued. "Who knows what might have set her off. She's thirteen."

"You keep saying that as if she was replaced by an alien when we weren't looking."

"That's what the teen years are like. Or so I hear."

"Terrific."

Janet patted Nicole on the back. "She'll show up soon. She will then be grounded for life and lose all privileges into infinity.

Which is what will happen to you if you don't lie down."

Nicole managed a wan smile. "Okay. But only for an hour. Then I'm going to go back out and search for her."

"I'll be right behind you."

They parted at the door of Nicole's room. She stepped inside and the first thing she saw was the Bible on the bed. She recalled her earlier feeling that someone had been in the room. What if that someone had been Rayne? What if — ?

Nicole crossed the floor, sat on the bed and opened the Bible to the Book of Revelation, which wasn't so funny anymore. She stared at the note and she wondered.

Even if Rayne had seen this, so what? She knew her father's name. But what if — ?

Nicole cursed and dialed the number.

Aaron Luchetti had just finished his morning chores and was walking into the house intent on breakfast when the phone rang. He didn't wonder if the call was for him. Ezra, the only friend he had, had closed up his tavern in Gainsville and gone off to Costa Rica to build an orphanage. Since Ezra was always doing things like that, Aaron had shrugged and wished him

44

well. But it had cut the phone calls for Aaron down to nothing.

Dean, always the charmer, answered on the fourth ring. "Yeah."

Aaron listened to his brother with half an ear as he yanked off his boots and placed them on the porch. His parents might be in Tahiti, but that didn't mean his mother wouldn't know exactly who had left manure tracks on the floor.

He could just see her sitting up in bed in the middle of the night and muttering, "Aaron did it." The woman could be downright spooky at times.

"Who? Father? What? No, he's in Tahiti. You want to leave a message?"

The crash of the phone into the cradle was followed by a curse. Not that such behavior was out of the ordinary for his brother, still Aaron was curious.

Of the six Luchetti siblings, only Aaron and Dean continued to work the family dairy farm on a regular basis. Their youngest brother, Evan, hired out to other farms and did odd jobs wherever he was needed. Their kid sister, Kim, had been married over a year and was busy with her own farm, husband and daughter. The remaining two brothers were off God knew where, doing Lord knew what, which was always the case with Bobby and Colin.

Aaron strolled into the kitchen and snagged some coffee, then stole Dean's Pop-Tart from the toaster and took a bite while his brother searched the empty refrigerator for . . . anything.

"What was that all about?" he asked.

Dean turned, scowled and snatched the Pop-Tart back. Since he was a hell of a lot bigger, even though Aaron was several years older, Aaron let him keep it.

"Hey, you ate off this!" Dean tossed the pastry back in Aaron's face.

"Why should you care? You eat dog food."

"Not since I was four."

"You liked it."

"I liked you then, too, but I got over it."

Aaron hid his grin behind his coffee cup. Dean got on a lot of people's nerves, but Aaron had always welcomed his brother's honesty. Even when, more often than not, it was couched in sarcasm and profanity.

Aaron took a large swig of coffee, then a larger bite of the pastry. He'd been up before dawn. Even though their farm was equipped with a robotic milking apparatus, the very latest in high-tech dairy farming, old habits died hard. The Luchettis continued to supervise. While cows were smarter than they appeared, they still weren't the brightest beings on the planet. Besides, there were always pigs to feed, chickens, too, and any number of disgusting things to clean up.

Today was Aaron's day on, leaving Dean free to do whatever it was he did while Aaron slaved, and their parents free to take a long overdue trip to Tahiti. Which reminded him.

"Who was on the phone?"

"Got me. She hung up without saying."

Aaron frowned and set his coffee cup carefully back on the counter. "Who did *she* ask for?"

"Dad." Dean plucked at the end of the shiny silver package encasing another toaster pastry. "I think."

"You don't know?"

"She said she was looking for Father Luchetti."

Aaron's heart stuttered. He dropped what was left of his breakfast on the floor.

Dean raised his gaze to Aaron's. "Do you think she meant you?"

"I'm not now, nor have I ever been, Father Luchetti."

"Right." His brother shrugged and returned to his food. "So she must have meant Dad."

"Must have," Aaron agreed, though deep down he knew better.

His gaze flicked to the phone. There was one way to find out. But he had to get his hands on that phone, in private, before someone else called. He glanced at his brother. "I get the shower."

Dean headed for the stairs. "Nope. Me first."

"I don't think so."

Aaron made a sudden move, as if he'd race past and claim the bathroom, then smirked when Dean ran, tossing the usual taunt over his shoulder. "You snooze, you lose!"

Seconds later, the bathroom door slammed. The sound of running water soon followed.

If Aaron hadn't felt as if he were spinning out of control and directly into his past, he would have laughed at how easy it still was to manipulate his little brother.

He crossed the kitchen in three quick steps, picked up the receiver and dialed *69. She answered before the second ring, as if she'd been sitting right next to the phone.

"Mercy House. Hello?"

Even though he'd known it had to be her

— who else would call the house and ask for Father Luchetti? — still Aaron's heart skipped at the sound of her voice after so many years.

Not that he hadn't heard the husky, sexy twang a thousand times in his dreams, but he hadn't spoken to her since leaving Las Vegas nearly fourteen years ago.

He'd waited for her call, hoped, even prayed for it. But when month after month passed, then year after year, he'd stopped jumping whenever the phone rang.

"Nic," he said, and her breath caught, the sound reminding him of twisted sheets, naked bodies, the first time he'd ever been with a woman.

"Aaron, wh-why are you calling me?"

"Because you called me."

"N-no I didn't."

"I star-sixty-nined the phone, Nic, and you answered."

She cursed. "I thought you were in Tahiti."

"That's my father."

"Oh."

The line buzzed with distance, the silence heavy with things that had never been said. So he said something — stupid.

"How are you?"

"Fine. And you?"

49

"Swell," Aaron muttered.

He couldn't believe they were having this inane conversation, even if he had started it. How many times had he played out what he would say to her if she ever called? Too many to count.

But right now, all the things he wanted to say stuck in his throat. How could he speak about the way she still haunted him — day in, day out? He remembered the smooth, creamy texture of her skin, the spicy scent of it, the sweet taste of her laughter and the salt of her tears.

She'd been the most beautiful woman he'd ever seen, voluptuous, tempting, with a sadness in her eyes and a neediness in her heart that had bewitched him.

"Why did you ask for Father Luchetti?"

"As far as I know, priests are still addressed as *Father,* or has that changed?"

"I'm not a priest."

He waited for the inevitable questions. Instead, all he heard was the sharp click of the phone when she hung up.

Aaron stared at the receiver in his hand until the line began to buzz. He could call back, but he doubted she'd answer.

And he wanted her to answer, not just the phone, but a single, very important question.

Why had she called him now?

Star-sixty-nine wouldn't give him the answer this time. But a quick trip to Vegas would.

Chapter Three

Aaron Luchetti wasn't a priest? Since when?

Nicole glared at the phone as if the appliance were at the root of all her troubles. She shouldn't have hung up until she learned the truth, but the shock had been too much for her.

Her hands were ice-cold and shaking. How could the mere sound of his voice after all these years make her feel as if he'd first kissed her only yesterday?

Because their first kiss had been a true first, something she dreamed about to this day. The first kiss she had welcomed, the first gentle, arousing embrace she had ever known.

Exhaustion caused bright lights to flash before her eyes. Nicole lay back on her bed and allowed herself to remember.

She'd been a stripper — make that exotic dancer — for nearly three months. Nicole snorted. The only thing exotic about the place where she'd worked had been the lack of rats in the dressing room. For a strip club, the Kitty Kat was almost classy.

She had no longer felt any embarrassment over shedding her clothes. Since the alternative was hooking, Nicole had thanked her lucky stars she could make enough to survive — barely — by dancing. Others weren't so fortunate.

Lack of money had been a blessing in one respect. It had nipped her drug use in the bud. Many of the girls needed something to help them forget what was going on in their lives, and Nicole had been no different. But she'd decided she'd rather give up the drugs, face the music and the leers straight, than sell her soul, live on the street or go back to where she had been.

When she first noticed the young man sitting in the front row every night, Nicole couldn't say. It seemed as if he'd always been there. Yet he was different from the others.

He didn't pound back the required two-drink minimum, then signal for more without taking his eyes from the stage, from her. Instead, he ordered the cocktails and let them sit, the condensation sliding down the glass, pooling in puddles, spreading across the table before dripping onto the floor.

He never touched those drinks. Not once.

He never looked at her body, either. Instead he stared at her face with a soft, warm, nonthreatening smile. He was downright strange, and he began to unnerve her.

At the time her self-worth had been tied up with her body, her success measured in the money she earned by revealing it. When the young man in the front row refused to so much as glance below her neck, she feared she was losing her appeal. If she did, what then? Her body was the only thing of value that she had. She'd never finished school. She didn't have a skill. She had nothing.

So Nicole danced faster, flipped her hair harder, shimmied closer. She made it her mission to get him to stare at something other than her face. But time after time, he would not.

Then one night he was waiting for her outside the Kitty Kat Klub, and she discovered why he was there.

"I'm on a mission from God," he said.

She laughed right in his face. What amazed her was that he laughed, too.

"I know. I sound like an old movie. But it's true."

She stared at him, shocked. "What are you, some kind of priest?"

54

"Not yet. But someday."

He seemed to glow with joy and purpose. Nicole didn't know what to make of someone totally devoted to God. That a man like Aaron — young, strong, obviously intelligent, with no visible warts — would want to spend his life alone both amazed and intrigued her. Though she should have run and kept on running, instead she'd stayed. And fallen in love with him.

Her first mistake. But what was one out of so very many?

Rayne had suspected all along that there was something not quite right with the kid. Otherwise why had he been dumped?

After an hour on a bus with him, she started to catch a clue as to what it was. He couldn't sit still.

He wiggled and he twitched. His toe tapped; his leg jiggled; his fingers were all over everything.

She tried to keep him entertained by playing the name game, though his attention often wandered to the window, another passenger, a fly on the seat.

Rayne would draw him back each time with the suggestion of a new name. Most of them were pretty silly, and he rejected every one with a smile or a giggle. Beneath the grime, the kid was inches away from adorable.

She was going to have to clean him up soon because people were starting to stare, although maybe the looks and raised eyebrows had more to do with his nonstop movement than the muddy streaks on his face, the dust-gray shade of his hair or the tangy scent of unwashed feet that followed wherever he went.

"Luigi?" she asked. "Pascal? I know. Ludwig!"

He snorted and kicked the back of the chair in front of them for about the seventh time. The lady sitting there turned around and snapped, "Can't you give him a pill?"

"A pill?"

"He's obviously hyper. They have pills for that, you know."

"He's not —"

"There's something wrong with him." She narrowed her eyes at the boy, who scooted closer to Rayne. "He's twitching for crying out loud. He's one of them drug babies, isn't he? You should be ashamed."

Rayne's mouth fell open. The woman thought the kid was hers, and that she'd taken drugs while pregnant with him.

However, that wasn't what shocked Rayne the most. What shocked her was that anyone would say something so nasty to a stranger, in public and in front of a child. The world was just full of wonders.

A snuffle drew Rayne's attention from angry eyes to a teary blue gaze. "I don't take drugs, Rayne. Promise. Drugs are the baddest of the bad things."

"I know you don't." She lifted his tattered sneakers into her lap so he couldn't kick the chair anymore, then turned a bland gaze to the woman. "Proud of yourself?"

She tossed her head and turned away.

"Never mind her," Rayne whispered.

He was sucking his thumb again and didn't answer. Rayne contemplated the seat in front of them, tempted to kick it herself. But what kind of example would that set? Rayne glanced out the window. Bein' a mom was no fun at all.

The miles rolled past as did the night. The kid fell asleep eventually, but he kept waking her up when he jerked and mumbled and thrashed.

There was something wrong with him, probably exactly what the nasty, big-mouthed woman had said. Rayne knew other kids who were hyper. Except they called it ADHD these days, though she wasn't exactly sure what all the letters meant.

But even if he did have ADHD, it wasn't his fault, and Rayne didn't plan to let anyone make the boy's eyes well with tears again.

Her mom had affectionately called Rayne Dudley Do Gooder for as long as Rayne could recall. She'd spent her life observing how a little kindness went a long, long way. So when kids were mean — and they usually were — Rayne stood up for the little guy, the fat boy, the weird dude. Someone had to.

In an attempt to stay one step ahead of any possible pursuit, Rayne had bought them one-way tickets to Albuquerque. She did the same to Oklahoma City. This turned out to be the best thing she could have done since the kid did better if they got off the bus and walked around for a few hours. To be honest, so did Rayne.

On the road to Little Rock, she ran out of ideas for the name game and still he answered only to Rat. Something had to be done about that.

"Didn't you ever hear a name that you thought was so perfect you wanted it for your very own?" she asked.

"Like what?"

"I don't know. I always wanted to be Katie or Amanda."

His nose wrinkled. "What for?"

"They're normal names. A lot of girls have them."

"B-o-o-o-ring," he sang. "Rayne's pretty. Like rain from the sky. Smells good, makes a rainbow."

She smiled. How many times had she wished her name was Rain or Rainbow? At least her name would match her taste in clothes. But she was stuck with the spelling she had.

"Rayne means queen or ruler according to my mom. She wanted me to be strong and brave. In charge."

"You are. I wanna strong, brave name, too. How about that hero name? Indiana Jones."

Rayne crooked a brow. "That's not really a name, kid. More of a nickname. And I think, it was what they called the dog."

"Then who's the strongest, biggest, baddest, bravest guy you ever heard of? Guy who don't take nothin' offa no one."

"Arnold Schwarzenegger?" Rayne said dryly.

"Who?"

She kept forgetting the kid was cinematically challenged. "He's an actor. Was in this great movie called *The Terminator.* Very mean and nasty."

"That's my name then. The Timinator."

Rayne laughed. "We can probably come up with something better."

"I like it. I want it."

Well, anything was better than Rat, kid or boy. "How about we call you Tim for short?"

" 'Kay."

The bus tour continued to Saint Louis where they bought Tim new clothes to go along with his new name. Before she let him put them on Rayne sneaked Tim into the women's room and scrubbed him as clean as he could get with a sponge bath.

"I was right," she said when he was dry and dressed.

"Huh?" He glanced up from a serious study of his unusually large tennies. He might be shorter and skinnier than average, but if he ever grew into those feet he would give the real Terminator something to worry about.

Rayne winked. "I *thought* there was a little boy under all that dirt. And I was right. You sure clean up pretty."

His sweet face scrunched like a raisin. "*Pretty* ain't for boys, Rayne."

"Handsome, then." She tweaked the

strand of light-brown hair that fell past his eyes and flopped over a freckled nose. She should put his hair in a ponytail, but that would probably be more of a battle than it was worth.

His smile revealed an endearing gap in the top row of his teeth, which reminded her. He needed a toothbrush. Immediately.

Being a mom — even for a little while — was a never-ending job. How had hers managed?

Rayne shoved the sympathetic notion out of her head. She was still mad, and would be for quite a while, if not forever. Some things were hard to forgive.

Tim slid his hand into hers. "You'll never leave me, will ya, Rayne? 'Kay? I'll be good. I'll listen. I won't eat much, or talk, neither, and I'll try my hardest not to wiggle. But sometimes I forget. Just don't —"

He broke off and his lip trembled.

"Don't what?"

"Don't take me somewhere and tell me you'll be back and then leave me all alone." He squinted at her between his bangs. "I really hate it when that happens."

"That happens to you a lot?"

"A lot, a lot."

"Your mom do that?"

61

"I dunno. Can't really remember which lady was her. Maybe none of 'em." He shrugged. "But you're the best there ever was. You don't yell, or pinch, or hit."

Rayne sighed and counted to ten. Right now she wanted to hit something — or someone — yell and pinch, too. If she ever had the misfortune to meet Tim's mom she might shake the woman until she rattled. Lucky for them both that wasn't likely to happen. Rayne had a feeling Tim's mother was long gone and never coming back. Which suited Rayne just fine.

She squeezed his hand. "I won't leave you. We're on a quest, remember?"

"That's right." He smiled at her with complete trust and perfect innocence. "The daddy quest."

"The daddy quest," Rayne murmured. "I kinda like that."

Aaron stared out the window as his plane prepared to land. A neon oasis rose out of the desert. Or at least that was what it looked like from the sky.

He'd never been a fanciful man — farm boys who aspired to the priesthood, then ended up farmers, weren't known for their imaginations. But it had been so long since he'd seen a city composed of bright lights, he couldn't help but be enthralled by them.

From a very young age, Aaron had felt a bond with the church. He'd loved the music, the candles, the tapestries and the gold. He even loved the Latin. The church was history come to life, the sense that what was ancient survived. He had belonged there.

So after graduating from Gainsville High, he'd trotted off to a private Catholic college in Missouri. He'd been so certain he knew what he wanted, where he belonged, so arrogant in his belief that he was God's chosen.

His first mission trip to Vegas had shown him the truth. It was easy to be pious when you'd never been tempted.

He'd taken one look at the city of sin and seen a thousand possibilities. There was so much to be done and so many people who needed him. Aaron was intrigued by the smoke, the booze, the money. But what really drew him in was the women — or should he say woman?

"Please remain seated until the aircraft has come to a complete stop at the gate."

The voice of the flight attendant, followed by the immediate scrambling of everyone on the plane for the front door, brought Aaron out of his reverie. They'd landed while he'd been mooning over the past.

He waited until everyone else had left before he retrieved his single bag and followed. Several people from his flight had already hit the slot machines stationed just past the gate.

Aaron shook his head. He'd never understood the allure of gambling. There was so much more to be done with money than throw it away.

He walked straight through the terminal and out the front door, pausing only to hail a cab. "Mercy House," he said. "Near Fremont."

The cabbie nodded and Aaron was thankful he didn't have to elaborate. He hadn't wanted to call Nic again for fear she'd bolt if she knew he was coming to town, so he'd gotten the directions off the Internet, and he wasn't completely certain where the place was.

The Web site had identified Mercy House, owned by a former nun — how was that for coincidence? — as a halfway facility for women who wanted to start over.

Guilt pulsed to the beat of his heart. Fourteen years and Nic was just now starting over? Had she been stripping, or worse, since he'd left her behind?

It was long past time he faced her. Long past time he apologized for betraying her trust.

But he'd taken one look at her up on that stage and everything he'd ever known about himself and his future had gotten tangled. Because he'd taken one look at Nic and he'd wanted her with all his heart and soul.

Something a would-be priest had no business wanting.

So he'd made his first mistake. Rather than asking for a different assignment he'd decided to prove to anyone who might be interested that he could resist temptation.

He'd learned that only a moron spit in Satan's eye.

He'd thought he could save her. Instead he'd lost himself.

The doorbell rang at 10:00 p.m., over twenty-four hours since Rayne had turned up missing. Nicole was dead on her feet, but she still flew down the steps and yanked open the door.

Aaron Luchetti stood on the porch.

For a single instant, joy at the mere sight of him consumed her. Then panic set in.

But the one moment of hesitation was all

he needed. For a slow-talking, laid-back farm boy, he had always moved quicker than a lizard through the sand. His big, hard hand hit the door before she could slam it in his face.

"Nic," he murmured, staring into her eyes in the same way he always had. As if he could see into her mind, her heart, her soul, as if she were someone he'd like to know.

Aaron had been the first person to look at her in such a way. He'd made her believe he wouldn't be the last. For that alone she could not hate him, though there were a few other incidents that strained her good-will.

"What the hell are you doing here, Aaron?" She gave up trying to close the door and turned away, walking into the living room where she could be closer to the phone.

"What do you think?"

"I have no idea."

Why *was* he here? He couldn't know about Rayne or he wouldn't be so calm. Not that she'd ever seen Aaron anything but calm.

No, she took that back. Once he'd been over the edge of reason, but then so had she.

Nicole shook off the memory. She would

not dwell on the only night of passionate love she'd ever experienced while the man she'd experienced it with stood so close she could touch him.

That she wanted to touch him, desperately, made her clench her hands until her fingernails bit into her palms and brought her back to what sense she had left.

"You called me, Nic. Why?"

"I found your number." She shrugged, hoping to make him believe the phone call had meant nothing, just as he had. She needed time to think, and with him so near she couldn't. "There was a moment of foolish nostalgia. That's all. You didn't have to run all the way out here."

"I gave you that number to call if you needed me. I promised to come if you called."

She glanced at him sharply. "I don't remember any promises."

His lips tightened and he closed his eyes. "I promised myself."

Nicole went still. If she had called him fourteen years ago, he would have come. She'd always known that, which was why she had not called.

Aaron had pledged his life to God, and because she had loved him, she couldn't take that away. For years she'd lived with the belief that the only man for her was a man she could not have, and in keeping their child a secret she had given him a gift equal to the one he had given her.

Now she knew that her sacrifice had been in vain. And it pissed her off. She had to tell him about Rayne, but first she had to know why everything she'd believed to be true suddenly wasn't.

"Why aren't you a priest?"

His eyes snapped open. "How could I be after I failed the only test I'd ever been given?"

"There was a test?"

"You, Nic." His smile was so sad, so Aaron, she actually took one step toward him before she caught herself. "You were my temptation, and I failed miserably."

Nicole gaped. He was serious. "You're telling me God's sitting up there with a scorecard? Pass. Fail. A, B, C on the old temptation test? I don't believe that."

"I didn't think you believed in God."

"Oh, I believe. I believe he's got it out for me."

"Nic," he began, but she didn't want to hear the same old argument. God loved her. He had a funny way of showing it.

"You gave up the only thing you'd ever wanted because of one night?"

"I betrayed your trust and all that I stood for."

"How can love be a betrayal?"

He shoved his fingers through his wavy, dark hair and turned away, as if he couldn't bear to look at her any longer. "That night wasn't about love, it was about lust."

Nicole was glad he wasn't looking at her. Then he didn't see her flinch at his words. What for her had been the only love she'd ever known had been for him a corruption of everything he believed. And she'd called *him* an idiot.

She couldn't tell him about Rayne. Her child deserved better than a father who would see her as nothing more than the result of an itch being scratched. How could she have been so foolish as to think that just because she loved him, he would love her?

"I'm sorry, Nic," he continued. "I was supposed to be helping, and instead I left you to fend for yourself. I can't tell you how happy I am to see you're finally getting out."

Nicole gaped, then she started to laugh. Aaron faced her with a frown. "What?"

"You think I just got out of the life now?"

"Well, yes. Isn't that why you're here?"

69

In truth, she probably wouldn't have gotten out if not for Rayne. Nicole had trusted no one back then. She'd had enough people try to help her then hurt her instead. She never would have set foot in a place like Mercy House if not for the baby inside her.

"I live here," she answered. "I've been working here for almost thirteen years. You can lay aside your hair shirt, Aaron. I got out right after you left. I didn't need any help from you."

He blinked. "Good. Great." Then he glanced around the room as if at a loss for what to say or do next. Which made two of them.

"Well, thanks for stopping by." Nicole started for the front door. "I'm sure if you head right back to the airport, you can catch a plane out tonight."

As she passed him, he grabbed her arm. Her momentum going one way, when he held on she stumbled. Immediately his grasp gentled as he steadied her.

For one second she leaned on him and it was good. He smelled the same, like a cool summer breeze in the desert. He felt the same, too, taut skin over sinew and muscles, work-hardened palms and a height just enough over her own so she could rest her head on his shoulder with ease.

His breath brushed her temple; time rushed back so fast she went dizzy with the memory of a love that had only been lust.

The momentary softness and warmth turned to a hard cold knot in her chest. She tried to pull away. He wouldn't let her go. But when Nicole glanced into his face, he stared past her, skin as pale as the fluffy white clouds they used to watch while they shared their days and his dreams.

"Where did you get that?" His voice was hoarse; his expression confused.

This time when Nicole pulled away, he let her go, and she followed the line of his gaze to the photograph of Rayne on the table next to the phone. A chill ran over Nicole and she hugged herself.

Trapped. Now what?

"Where?" he repeated. "Where did you get that?"

The way he continued to refer to Rayne as *that* cracked what was left of her self-control. *"That,"* she snapped, "was all I got from you."

Aaron continued to stare at the picture of his sister when she was maybe twelve or thirteen. Except he couldn't recall Kim ever dressing like a hippie. She wouldn't be caught dead in something so retro. Kim was a new millennium fashion plate, which made for some mighty amusing situations since she was now a farmer's wife.

Even her daughter, Glory, had been born with a penchant for the finer things. So much so that she'd earned the nickname Zsa Zsa because she gravitated to fancy clothes and saucy hats.

Aaron shook his head and the photograph of Kim wavered, then reformed. Something wasn't right. That picture could not be Kim, no matter how much it looked like her.

The ground seemed to shift as he heard what Nic had said — all she'd gotten from him — and suddenly he understood who the girl in the picture was.

"I've gotta sit," he muttered, then did, on the floor. He put his head between his knees. It didn't help. He still thought he might throw up — or pass out.

Nic didn't speak, which was good because what in hell could she say to explain this? She'd had his baby, and she'd never told him.

He had to know why, but when he opened his mouth a different question came out entirely. "Where is she? I want to see her."

"You and me both."

"What?" Aaron managed to raise his head.

"She's gone." Nic glanced at the photograph and her mouth trembled. "You want to know why I called? Because my daughter disappeared last night without a word or a trace."

"You mean *our* daughter."

Her eyes met his, clear blue and haunted. He knew the truth but he wanted her to say it. She waited several long, tense moments before she did.

"Our daughter."

How could he be filled with both joy and terror at her words? Because he'd been given a gift, only to have it snatched away in the next instant.

Aaron stood, then touched Nicole's shoulder. She shuddered beneath his hand. She was scared, too, and the Nicole he'd once known had never been scared of anything.

"I'll find her, Nic."

"Promise?"

Aaron hesitated. Every promise, every vow he'd ever made he'd broken, so he'd stopped making them a long time ago. But he could tell she needed something to hold on to, so he nodded.

"Promise."

Chapter Four

"What's going on here?"

At the sound of Janet's voice, Nicole leaped away from Aaron's touch. He'd only been resting his hand on her shoulder, but she'd felt him in her heart. She had to remember that her foolish dreams of a love denied were merely that. Foolish.

Nicole spun to face Janet, who stood in the hall scowling at Aaron. There was no sign of the other girls, who must still be out searching for Rayne. Nicole's eyes burned.

Janet swung her gaze from Aaron to Nicole. "Who is he, Nicky, and what is he doing here?"

The no men rule. She hadn't forgotten. She'd just been too shocked by the sight of Aaron to apply it.

"*He* can speak for himself." Aaron moved Nicole aside and held out his hand. "I'm Aaron Luchetti."

Nicole held her breath. Janet knew all her secrets and she'd never learned tact.

Her friend raised her gaze from Aaron's

hand to his face and grinned. "It's about time."

Aaron blinked as Janet pumped his arm up and down with undue force. "Ma'am?"

"I assume you're here about the girl." She let go of Aaron and turned to Nicole. "I'm glad you finally told him."

"She didn't tell me anything."

Janet stilled and slowly turned back to Aaron. "Then how do you know?"

He gestured at the picture of Rayne on the table. "She could be my sister's twin. It wasn't hard to figure out."

"Hmm." The older woman glanced at the photo. "The Lord certainly works in mysterious ways."

"I'll say," Nicole murmured dryly.

Both Aaron and Janet ignored her.

"If you didn't know about the girl until you saw the picture, then what are you doing here?"

"Nic called. I came."

"That's not exactly true —" Nicole began. Janet cut her off with an imperial wave of her hand.

"She should have called you long ago. You have a daughter. Time to pay the piper."

Janet's eyes narrowed. When she'd been a nun children had no doubt groveled and admitted every transgression when she turned that look on them. Aaron was no different.

"You're right, ma'am."

"Hmm." Janet tapped her lip and stared at Aaron a moment longer. "Call me Janet. I take it you were able to get away from your congregation for a while."

"I have no congregation. I'm a farmer."

Janet turned "the look" in Nicole's direction, and she had a mad urge to admit everything. But there was nothing left to tell. She'd spilled her guts to Janet long ago.

"You'd better catch me up, Nicky."

"Yeah, *Nicky,* catch her up," Aaron drawled. "And while you're at it, catch me up, too. I want to know why you didn't call me as soon as you knew you were having my child."

Nicole opened her mouth, then shut it again. She glanced first at Janet, who raised her eyebrows and shrugged, then at Aaron who just glared.

"Maybe I'd better leave you two alone," Janet murmured. "We can talk later."

She disappeared, leaving Nicole alone with the one person she should not be alone with. He crossed his arms over his chest. She found herself inordinately fascinated with the raised veins in his forearms that led down to his hands. They hadn't been there the last time she'd seen him. They made him appear rough, almost dangerous.

Nicole raised her gaze from his hands to his face. He didn't look dangerous; he looked angry. She'd never seen Aaron angry before, and while he had every reason to be, she had reason to be angry, too.

If he wasn't a priest, he'd had no excuse not to come back. Even if he hadn't loved her, she'd thought he respected her. His respect had given her confidence. But maybe that was as much of a lie as so many other things.

"What's her name?" he asked.

"Rayne. Rayne *Houston*," she emphasized.

He winced and she wanted to take the word back, but he didn't give her a chance.

"Does she even know I'm alive?"

"Not exactly."

"Not exactly? What does that mean? Either she does or she doesn't."

He stilled as a thought occurred to him, then rubbed his thumb between his eyes as if his head ached. It was a gesture Nicole remembered from the past. He was upset. Join the club.

Aaron dropped his hand. "Does she think I'm a priest?" He sighed and glanced away, murmuring, "What must that be like for her?"

Trust Aaron to worry about how difficult life was for everyone else. Nicole pushed aside the warm fuzzy feelings. They wouldn't do either one of them any good.

"She knows your name." Nicole took a deep breath. "She thinks you're dead. It was easier that way."

"For who? Damn it, Nic, why didn't you call me?"

"You left, Aaron. You didn't love me. You loved God. I didn't know you'd be an idiot and give him up, too."

He stared at her incredulously. "You didn't tell me about my child because I was going to be a priest?"

"Can you think of a better reason?"

"There's *no* reason to keep something like this from me."

"I wasn't going to ruin your life." She took a deep breath and glanced away. "But it seems I did anyway."

"No." He moved forward, hand outstretched, but stopped just short of touching her. Somehow that hurt more than anything else. Once he'd been unable to keep from touching her when he shouldn't. Now he wouldn't, even though he could.

Aaron let his arm fall back to his side, then put his hand into his pocket for good measure. He hunched his shoulders and stared at the ground. "My life is fine," he murmured. "You don't need to worry about me."

"You're lying." She knew it as surely as she knew her heart was broken.

He glanced at her sharply. "Why would you say that?"

"You wanted to help people. You were good at it. I doubt you're happy farming."

"I didn't say I was happy."

Her heart fluttered at the thought of his being unhappy. She had to stop feeling like this. One thing she could not do was let him know how much she had loved him. Things were bad enough without his pity.

"If you aren't happy, then why are you farming?"

"I don't know anything else."

Nicole sighed. "We really screwed up, didn't we?"

"Yeah."

"How are we going to fix it?"

He perked up at the idea of fixing things, and she smothered a smile. He was still the same Aaron, despite the disturbing lack of purpose in his eyes.

"We'll find Rayne. Then we'll deal with the rest."

"The rest?"

"Me. Her. You. Us."

A quiver rocked her belly when Aaron said *us*. But she knew he didn't mean it the way that she wanted him to.

"There isn't any us, Aaron."

"There'll always be an us because of Rayne."

She wanted to deny that, but truth was truth. Rayne was the best of them both.

"Do you have any idea where she went?" he asked.

"None."

"Did you two argue?"

"No. She just disappeared."

His gaze sharpened. "Could someone have taken her?"

"I thought that, too, until I checked her room. She packed a bag. Took all her money."

"You're sure she didn't know about me?"

Nicole had a sudden flash of her Bible, the Book of Revelation. Might that have been Rayne's idea of a joke rather than God's?

She tilted her head. "Did anyone call

81

your house asking for you besides me?"

"Not that I know of. But I can check."

He went to the phone, picked it up and dialed.

"Do you know what time it is?"

"Hello, Dean. I miss you, too."

"Eat dirt, big brother. I have to get up in three hours."

"Sorry."

Aaron *was* sorry, but he'd had to call. A thirteen-year-old child was missing, his child, and he didn't give a damn if it was 1:00 a.m. in Illinois.

"You left me alone here," Dean continued, sounding wide awake, not sleepy at all.

Aaron frowned. "Where's Evan?"

"Gone."

"Gone where?"

"Your guess is as good as mine. You know how he is."

Aaron did. Their little brother, who was bigger than both of them, had a habit of taking off for weeks on end. Sometimes it was a woman, just as often a job. Still —

"It isn't like him to disappear when he's needed at home."

"He wasn't needed. Not if I have the robotic milking system and you. But, *sur-*

prise, I come out of the shower this morning and no you."

"I left a note."

"Not where I could see."

Aaron glanced at Nic. She was studying a picture on the wall and pretending not to listen. He'd never told her about his family. They'd talked mostly about their hopes and their dreams. Or maybe he had. He couldn't recall anything about her dreams. Had she had any then? Did she have any now?

He pulled his attention from his past to his present. "I left it in the center of the kitchen table."

"I'm looking at the table."

Which only proved that Dean *had* been awake. The man needed less sleep than anyone Aaron had ever met.

His brother continued. "I've got dried jelly, ancient ketchup and enough coffee rings to form a kaleidoscope, but no note."

"You're going to have a fat lip if Mom comes home and sees that mess."

"I'll tell her you did it. Hey, wait." Dean clunked the phone onto the counter loud enough to make Aaron jump. A few seconds later he was back. "The note fell under the table." The sound of paper rustling traveled over the line. "Had to take a trip," he read aloud. "You call that a note? Where are you?"

Aaron hesitated. He didn't want to tell Dean he'd gone to Las Vegas. That would raise all kinds of questions he wasn't ready to answer. Not on the phone. Not yet.

"A friend needed help." Which was close enough to the truth to even sound like it.

Nic gave him a quick glance at the word *friend* before she went back to staring at the wall.

"Okay. You still haven't told me where you are."

Aaron ignored the implied question. He'd called to *ask* a question.

"Has anyone called for me lately?"

"What? You mean since you've been gone? No."

"I mean *lately*. In the last few days."

"No one ever calls for you, bro."

Aaron ground his teeth together. He loved his brother, but sometimes he wanted to knock Dean to the ground and hold his face in something disgusting — the way he always used to. He knew he had no life. Dean didn't have to rub it in.

"So no one's called and asked for me," he clarified.

"No. No one. Except for that Father Luchetti call, but you said —" He broke off and the line went silent. "Oh. I get it. Someone asks for Father Luchetti, then you do a Houdini. You *are* helping someone."

"What the hell did you think I was doing?"

"I hoped you were having some fun for a change."

Aaron glanced at Nic. She was the most fun he'd ever had.

"I'm not," he snapped, as much to himself as to his brother. "I don't know when I'll be back. I'll call when I have a number where you can reach me."

He hung up as Dean sputtered and growled. His brother could handle the farm alone. It wouldn't be easy, but he could do it. If he really needed help he could call their brother-in-law, and Dean's best friend, Brian Riley. Dean had helped Brian out last year when Brian had taken a nosedive off his roof at the sight of their sister — and wound up with two broken wrists. But that was another story.

Besides, their parents were due home from their second honeymoon any day now. Knowing their father, he was so bored of the sun and the surf he'd be arm wrestling Dean for possession of the chores within an hour of his return.

"You live with your mother?"

Aaron lifted his gaze from the phone to Nicole. He could imagine what she was thinking, though her expression was bland. He was a thirty-two-year-old, unmarried man who lived at home. He might just as well tattoo L-O-S-E-R on his forehead. But he wasn't going to deny the truth, either. He'd never been very good at it.

"With my mother, father and brother."

"Sounds nice."

For a second he thought she was making fun of him. But a glance at her face revealed she was wistful.

"I wish I had a big family. It would be good for Rayne to have someone besides me and Janet."

"She does," he said quietly.

The wistfulness disappeared, chased away by a touch of fear. She turned back to the picture on the wall. "I guess you're right."

Aaron crossed the room and stood next to her. "What's the matter?"

She hesitated, then all the words came tumbling out. "You deserve to see her and get to know her, but please, Aaron, don't take her away. She's all I have."

"Take her away?" he repeated.

Nicole twisted her hands, but she met

his gaze without flinching. "I'm sure the courts will think Rayne would be better off with you and your Midwestern farm family than with her ex-stripper mother and an ex-nun surrogate grandma."

"Courts?" He couldn't seem to stop repeating what she said, because he had no idea what she was talking about.

"Custody," she said slowly. "Of our daughter."

Suddenly he understood. "I wouldn't do that."

She snorted. "If I had a nickel for every father who said he wouldn't, then did, I'd be a rich woman."

"You know me better than that, Nic."

"Do I?" She stared into his eyes. "I don't think I know you at all."

He had a sudden urge to brush her blond hair away from her cheek, let his thumb trail over the skin beneath. She'd always had the softest skin imaginable, the creamy texture both torment and temptation. She had smelled exotic back then, a mixture of spicy and sweet, a scent he'd never been able to identify, but it had haunted him just the same.

Leaning forward, he sniffed. She smelled like . . . coconuts. That was new. It made him think of hot sand, hot sun, hot sex.

Aaron straightened. Blinked. She didn't know him at all? That only made two of them.

He forced himself to move away before his fantasy extended to touching her, kissing her and more. He didn't know if he'd be able to stop. It had been so long since he'd touched anyone, or anyone had touched him.

His attention was captured by the picture in front of them. He frowned at the artwork, which was out of place on a living room wall.

The focus of the pen-and-ink drawing was a figure whose face was cloaked in shadow. But instead of fear and trepidation, the picture emitted a sense of peace. Perhaps because the man's trench coat spread into the wind like an angel's wings, and a crucifix gleamed against his chest as if lit by an inner fire.

"The Angel of Light," he murmured.

Out of the corner of his eye he saw her glance at him quickly, then away. "You know the series?"

"I've been a fan from the beginning."

How could he not be? The Angel of Light was God's superhero — everything Aaron had once dreamed of being and then some.

"This is the original." Nicole let out a pent-up breath. "Whenever I'm upset I look at it and I feel better."

"An original?" He frowned. "That had to cost —"

"Nothing."

The question flitted through his mind — had she paid in something other than money? Anger burned the thought away. Both at himself for being such an ass — and at the idea of her being with any other man.

Foolishness. They'd been separated for fourteen years. There'd been other men for her. Just as there'd been other women for him. But suddenly she was the mother of his child, and that changed everything.

"I didn't do what you're thinking."

He glanced at her sharply. How did she know?

"Not that I haven't."

"What?"

"Gone down on someone for money."

He choked. "Nic, do you have to talk like that?"

She'd always been honest to a fault — about what she did, who she was. Until she'd had his child anyway.

"Why not say it?" She shrugged. "You were thinking it."

"No. I wasn't." Not *that,* at any rate.

"Please, Aaron. I'm not stupid."

No. She'd never been stupid. Desperate. Alone. Strong. Brave. But never stupid.

"That's the past."

"Is it? If you think about my past every time you see me, then it isn't the past."

He didn't know what to say, so he focused once more on the picture. "We have more important things to worry about right now than the mistakes we've made."

"True. But so you don't keep wondering . . ." She tapped a chewed-off fingernail against the frame on the wall. "Janet is J. B. Grace."

"She is?" He glanced at Nic, then back at the drawing. It was like finding out that Elvis was alive and in the building. "Did I say I'm a huge fan?"

She raised a brow. "Yeah, I think you did."

Aaron's cheeks heated. Trust him to drool and grovel and behave like a social reject. But she didn't seem to notice.

"Lucky for us a lot of people are fans. The Angel of Light keeps this place in toilet paper."

Nicole moved past him and into the hall. Aaron followed. "I'm going to get some sleep and then go out searching for Rayne again."

"Fine."

She opened the door, then looked at him expectantly. Aaron wasn't sure what she wanted until she swept her arm out in invitation.

"At Mercy House we have one particular rule and it's my favorite."

"What's that?"

"No men allowed. There's a motel four blocks that way." She gave him a little shove in the right direction. "I'll see you in the morning."

Chapter Five

"That wasn't very polite."

Nicole still leaned her head against the door, trying to forget the sight of his face.

She took a deep breath, gathered what was left of her composure and faced Janet, who stood at the top of the stairs in a camouflage nightie.

"Is there a soldier somewhere without a tent?" Nicole asked.

"Sarcasm won't make me forget the subject."

"Which is?"

"The father of your child."

Nicole winced. She really didn't want to talk about this.

"Get up here."

Janet turned and walked away. Nicole climbed the steps. What she wanted had little to do with it.

Stepping into Janet's room she was struck again by the austerity of the place. Janet might have left the church, but her decorating tastes still ran to cell block chic — bare walls and white sheets. Perhaps she exhausted her creativity on the Angel of Light, leaving little left over for interior decoration. Or maybe she had more important things to worry about than paint swatches and wallpaper samples.

"Sit." Janet pointed to the ladder-back chair in front of her desk.

Nicole did as she was told. Janet took a seat on the bed, folding her long legs beneath the skirt of her gown. "What happened?"

"You heard. I kicked him out."

"Before that."

Nicole opened her mouth, shut it, then shrugged. "I don't know where to start."

"Pick a place, any place. Why is he here? Why isn't he a priest? Why did you kick him out, when I could tell all you wanted him to do was stay?"

"Rules are rules. No men allowed."

"You could have gone with him."

Images of what might have happened if she had done just that filled Nicole's head. Instead of tempting her, they only made her sad.

Lust not love — she'd had plenty of that and she wanted nothing to do with it again. If she'd let him touch her the way that she wanted him to, the way he wanted to if the heat in his eyes was any indication, she'd lose the self that she'd found. She'd worked too hard, for too long, to go back to where she had been, and if she had sex without love, that was exactly where she'd be.

"No." Nicole took a breath and her chest hurt. "No, I couldn't go with him."

Janet reached over and laid her hand on top of Nicole's. "Spill it, Nicky. You'll feel better if you do."

Since Nicole had never been able to keep anything from her friend, she spilled it. Even the part where Aaron had said that he never loved her. When she was through, she didn't feel any better. In fact, she felt a whole lot worse.

Her daughter was still missing. She was scared. She was lonely. She was sad. She wanted everything to go back to the way it had been, but now it never would.

Janet flipped her long, thick braid over her back. "Secrets you keep, trouble you find."

"Do *not* start talking like Yoda. I hate it when you do that."

"Fun it is. Especially when mad you get."

Janet only did her Yoda impression when she wanted to lighten the mood. But there was no lightening this mood, so the best thing to do was ignore her. Bored she would get. Eventually.

"I take it this is your way of saying 'I told you so'?"

Janet sighed and gave up on dispensing Yoda wisdom. "It's my way of saying you should tell him that you loved him."

"Didn't you hear what I said? He never loved me. He wanted me. Like a hundred other guys."

Nicole fought the rising tide of despair. All she'd ever wanted was someone to love her. She'd spent nearly fourteen years dreaming that someone did. Now that dream was dead.

"The boy doesn't know what love is. I bet if you told him that you loved him then . . ." Janet eyed her thoughtfully. "That you love him now, he'd come around. Give him some time. Give him a chance."

Panic pulsed to the beat of Nicole's heart. The thought of telling Aaron that she loved him and having him say, "Thank you," or something equally mortifying, nearly reduced her to tears. She couldn't do it.

"I *don't* love him."

Janet snorted. "Right."

Nicole pressed her lips together so she wouldn't shout or sob. "He's not the same man I knew. I'm not the same woman."

"I'd say that was a good thing." Janet paused, considering. "Has he changed that much?"

"I don't know."

"You've been in love with an ideal. Now the real thing is here. Why don't you find out who he is? Who you are. Who you could be together."

The words were tempting, but there was one truth Nicole couldn't get past. "He'll never love me the way I need him to."

"Baby, nobody loves us the way we need them to." She tilted her head. "Except God."

Nicole rolled her eyes. "Do you get points every time you use the G-word?"

With a wink, Janet got to her feet. "Doesn't everyone?"

Aaron walked the streets of Vegas in the darkest hour of the night. He remembered again what had drawn him here. Everywhere there was someone in need.

He knew better than to hand out money. It would be used for alcohol, drugs or worse before he reached the next block. Instead, he stepped into a convenience store.

The clerk watched him warily. Aaron didn't think he looked menacing. Before leaving home he'd changed out of his usual attire — old T-shirt and even older jeans — into a new T-shirt and newer jeans. He'd even left his knee-high, manure-encrusted work boots behind and ferreted out his rarely worn athletic shoes. He looked average. But then the clerk had no doubt encountered his share of armed robbers who appeared average and harmless.

Several moments later Aaron carried all the packaged muffins, sandwiches, single-serving juice and milk containers that he could manage up to the counter. The man frowned at the array, but he didn't ask questions, and he removed his hand from beneath the counter where a pistol, shotgun, or maybe even both, resided.

Aaron didn't mind. Wasn't third-shift convenience store clerk the most dangerous job in America? A man did what he had to do to stay alive. But Aaron did experience a twinge of unease at the thought of his daughter living two blocks from a place where it was common practice to hold a gun on a customer.

He paid his bill then continued down the street, dropping food at the feet of everyone who could use a meal. He'd only walked a short way before his sack was empty.

Some would call him foolish. What good did a single meal do in the face of so many other problems? But he'd heard countless stories of one small incident of kindness turning someone's life around. He knew one thing for certain, a meal couldn't hurt.

Over the years Aaron had contributed to charities, served on mission boards and generally been the perfect example of a Christian farmer. But he hadn't done anything worthwhile with his own hands. He hadn't realized how much he'd missed the doing until he'd come back here.

Aaron crumpled the empty sack and tossed it into the garbage can in front of the motel before he stepped inside. The clerk contemplated him with a bored expression as he chewed on what was left of his cigar. "Whaddya need, bub?"

The office smelled of old food, old smoke, old beer — probably because that's what was lying around on every surface and floating through the air.

"A room. Maybe with a kitchen?"

"Nah. You don't want the kitchen. Believe me."

Considering the state of the office, Aaron took the man's word for it.

His room was opposite a flashing red neon sign that said otel California. Once in a while the missing *M* flickered, nearly came to life, then died again. Aaron couldn't decide if the name was a joke or a mistake.

He tossed his bag onto a chair and shut the door. His room was shaded in red. He hit the light. Now it was orange.

His mother would have a stroke if she saw the sheets. The bathroom was better, which only made it borderline disgusting. The carpet had stains he really didn't want to identify. The clerk had no doubt been right about the kitchen.

Aaron didn't care. He had to be close to Nicole.

She didn't want him here. He'd figured that out even before she'd shown him the door. But when she'd first seen him on the porch, for a single instant she'd looked at him as she had fourteen years ago, and he'd felt . . . special. It had been a very long time since he'd felt anything but lost.

Then the shadows had filled her eyes, and she'd become a stranger instead of the girl he'd known. Aaron couldn't blame her for wanting him gone. His presence must bring back a lot of bad memories. While the sight of her brought back only good ones for him.

He paced the room, picked up the television remote, then put it back down. He flopped onto the bed, but he was too wired to sleep. Too on edge to watch something as trite as television.

I have a daughter.

Aaron couldn't get his mind around the fact. It would be easier, perhaps, if his child were a child. But to find out he had a daughter he didn't even know about, then discover she was a young woman to boot . . .

Aaron stared at the water-marked ceiling but all he saw was Rayne's face.

This time yesterday he'd been sleeping peacefully in his bed. An unhappy, lonely man who lived with his mommy. Today he was the father of a missing child, and the panic that had consumed him since he'd learned first of her existence and then of her loss, would not allow him to rest.

He'd never met her; she didn't even know he was alive, but she was his child, and he could think of little else but finding her.

The doorbell rang at 7:00 a.m. It was with a sense of déjà vu that Nicole raced down the stairs.

Just like last night, Aaron stood on the porch. But the initial joy she'd experienced

100

at the sight of him then did not return this morning.

Her daughter had been missing for over thirty-six hours. She hadn't slept. She couldn't eat. She felt little to nothing at all.

Aaron stepped in without being asked, crowding Nicole back into the hall. She turned, intent on reaching the kitchen and the coffee, but he put his hand on her shoulder. The urge to lean on him was nearly overwhelming. And because it was, she forced herself to remain straight and still.

"You look exhausted."

She glanced at him. His eyes were glassy; he'd cut himself shaving; his skin was pale beneath the tan.

"You don't look much better. Coffee?"

He nodded and she slid away from his comforting hand. Moments later they sat on opposite sides of the kitchen table staring into steaming mugs.

She'd forgotten about the no-men rule again. But right now it felt so good not to be alone, she couldn't kick him out.

"I went out searching for her," he murmured.

"All night?"

His shrug was answer enough.

"Where?"

"Around. Here, there."

Nicole frowned. "Where exactly?"

"Past downtown. South of my hotel. Make that my otel." His lips twitched, but she didn't get the joke.

"It's not the best idea to be alone in certain places at night."

Vegas was a city that never slept — and that wasn't always a good thing.

"I know better than to go to West Las Vegas."

She gave an impatient sigh. "Just because most of the gang activity is there doesn't mean there aren't scary people closer to home. And guys with guns don't care how big or strong you are. Besides, Aaron, you've got *sucker* written all over you."

"Worried about me, Nic?"

Her lips tightened. "I always worry about fools and idiots. Call it my hobby."

He smiled, but the expression was sad and Nicole was struck again by the differences in him. Once he'd been full of joy and life and purpose, a bit annoying — true — especially when her life had been anything but joyful. But she'd smiled more when she was with him; she'd learned to laugh again. Aaron no longer seemed to laugh at all.

"Why did you go out alone?" she asked. "You could have been hurt."

His gaze was puzzled. "Why wouldn't I? Rayne's my daughter."

"Physically, yes. But you don't even know her."

"Knowing her has nothing to do with it. I'd search for any lost child, anywhere, but my child . . ." He shook his head. "I'm terrified I'll never see her, touch her, talk to her. I can hardly think straight. I certainly couldn't sleep."

A wave of longing washed over Nicole, and she pushed it down deep where all her buried longings lived. He was a good man, despite some foolish convictions and an overactive guilt gland. When he loved, he would do so with all his heart and all his soul.

She wanted Aaron's love for her daughter. If Nicole couldn't have him, at least Rayne could. If they could only find Rayne.

"Has anyone checked the Strip?" Aaron asked. "Or Glitter Gulch?"

"We did, even though she wouldn't be there."

"Why not?"

"You have to be twenty-one to go into a casino without a parent. Security is very anal about that. You saw Rayne's picture.

She looks younger than thirteen." Nicole blinked back a sudden rush of tears. "Makes her so mad."

Aaron nodded. "My sister hated it, too. Mom always said when she was forty, she'd be glad she looked thirty."

"Yeah, tell it to a teenager. Get your head chewed off."

"Is she . . ." Aaron's voice drifted off.

"What?"

"A pain in the butt?"

"Yep. And I wish she was being a pain in mine right now. I remember every time I complained about having a thirteen-year-old and —" Nicole swallowed the heat at the back of her throat.

"And what?"

"I hate myself."

Aaron patted her on the back. "We all say things we're sorry for. You can tell her when we find her."

If we find her, she thought.

"You're sure she couldn't hide in one of the casinos?" Aaron asked.

"Very sure. The guards would escort her right out the door before she took ten steps inside. And if she was wandering the streets for any amount of time alone, someone would notice. Janet has contacts all over this town."

So did Nicole. Which only made Rayne's disappearance all the more disturbing.

"Where on earth could she have gone?" Aaron murmured.

A thought teased at the back of Nicole's mind, wispy, unformed. She tilted her head, listened, strained to bring it forward.

"Nic?"

Holding up her hand to stall him, Nicole closed her eyes and saw a —

"Bus station," she blurted.

As she opened her eyes, Aaron swallowed the coffee in his mouth in one loud gulp. "Pardon me?"

"Between you, me, Janet and the girls, we've covered most of the town. No one's seen her."

He was nodding before she finished her sentence, and then he finished her thought. "So maybe she isn't in town." He stood. "Lead the way."

Ten minutes later they stepped into the bus station. It was every bit as depressing as Nicole remembered. She'd arrived in Vegas with stars in her eyes and fifty dollars in her pocket. Both had been gone within the week.

The thought of Rayne following the same path she had terrified Nicole. As if he sensed her distress, Aaron gave her shoulder a quick squeeze before striding up to the counter.

"We're looking for a girl."

"You, me and half the world, pal. You've come to the right town."

Nicole showed the man Rayne's picture. "This girl."

The guy barely glanced at it. "Never seen her before."

Nicole leaned forward. But before she could take the guy's head off, Aaron spoke, ever calm and always polite, his voice sanity in an insane world.

"She disappeared two days ago. We think she might have come here."

"Hundreds of people come here. I can't remember 'em all. And I ain't the only one who sells tickets."

Nicole sighed. "This is like finding a needle in a haystack."

"So we take the haystack apart strand by strand." Aaron returned his attention to the clerk. "Who else sells tickets and where can we find them?"

"Night shift just got off." The man pointed to the door. "He's leaving right now."

Nicole ran outside. "Hey, mister! Wait up, please."

The guy turned, took one look at her

and leered. "Anything for you, baby."

She gritted her teeth. No matter how many years it had been since she'd stopped taking off her clothes for money, she could still be jerked right back to the feelings she'd had then by a single leer and one "Hey, baby." Why did her blond hair and big chest make guys look at her and see candy just for them?

"I have a question."

"Me, too." He winked. "Are you a C cup, or is that a D?"

Nicole ignored him. Sometimes it even worked. "Have you seen this girl?"

He sidled close, pretending to stare at the picture. Instead, he pressed his forearm against the side of her breast and kept it there.

"I'd say a D. How much so I can find out for my — ?"

A fist slammed into the man's jaw, and he crumpled like a puppet whose strings had been cut.

Nicole could do nothing but stare as he lay at her feet, moaning and holding his chin. She glanced at Aaron. The fury in his eyes made her step between them. She placed her hand on his chest, felt him vibrating beneath her fingertips.

"Don't ever touch her again."

He didn't shout, but he didn't need to. The intense expression on his face, the size of his fists, the ferocity in his stance would have frightened anyone. Nicole would have been frightened, except she knew, as surely as she knew he didn't love her, that he would never physically hurt her.

As if to illustrate her thoughts, Aaron's fists relaxed and became the hands she still dreamed about, gentle and sure on her elbows as he moved her out of his way.

The man on the ground scrambled back, his gaze on Aaron's face. "I didn't know she was yours. How was I supposed to know?"

"Aaron," Nicole warned. He didn't even look at her.

"She isn't mine. She isn't anyone's but her own. How would you like it if someone grabbed you and asked what size your jock strap was?"

The guy considered the question, then got a big, dopey smile on his face. "I wouldn't mind."

Aaron made a disgusted sound. "Get up."

The smile became a pout. "So you can knock me down again? I don't think so."

Aaron hauled the guy to his feet by his shirt. He didn't let him go. Nicole found herself inordinately fascinated with the bulging muscles in Aaron's forearms. He hadn't had those fourteen years ago. She kind of liked them.

"Nic," he snapped. "Bring that picture over here."

She blinked, realized she'd been staring at Aaron's muscles and practically drooling. Shaking her head to clear it of the unfamiliar thoughts, Nicole hurried forward and held out the picture of Rayne.

Aaron snatched the photo and shoved it under the clerk's nose. "Seen her?"

The man frowned. "Not sure. There *was* a kid . . . but she had on a ball cap. Couldn't see her hair or her face too good. Hard to say."

"When was this?"

"Couple of nights ago maybe."

"Where did she go?" Aaron asked.

Nicole's heart raced and she held her breath.

The effort of thinking back all of a few days seemed to expend his meager brain power, because the guy let out a huge groan before saying, "New Mexico. Albuquerque, I think."

She released the breath she'd been holding as hope lightened her heart. The man dashed it with his next words. "Yeah. I'm pretty sure her and her little brother got on the bus to Albuquerque."

"Brother?" Aaron glanced at Nicole and she shook her head.

Aaron released the man's shirt. "Thanks for your help."

"Uh, yeah. Sure. Any time."

He jumped in his car and sped away. Aaron kept his back to Nicole, staring down the road.

"That wasn't Rayne," she said.

"No."

His head dropped between his shoulders. The movement pulled his T-shirt taut across his back. Nicole admired the way his body tapered from wide to slim. Was the skin underneath the shirt as tan as his arms? Would it be soft or hard? Would the muscles ripple beneath her fingers and against her mouth? Would he taste as great as he smelled?

Nicole tore her gaze from Aaron's back. What on earth was the matter with her? They were searching for Rayne, and all she could think about were the muscles Aaron had grown since the last time they'd touched.

Perhaps her inappropriate thoughts were some kind of defense mechanism. So she didn't surrender to all-out panic, where she would only wail and mumble in fear for her child, instead her mind sent her images of Aaron without a shirt. A sound of distress escaped her lips before she could snatch it back.

"What's the matter?" Aaron asked, though he didn't turn around.

"Nothing." Her voice was breathless, a bit hoarse, and his shoulders twitched at the sound. Nicole frowned. Why wouldn't he look at her?

She crossed the short distance and stepped in front of him. His eyes were closed, his expression one of inner torment.

Reaching out, she touched his arm. He jumped and opened his eyes. "What's the matter?" she echoed.

"I used to be a man of peace."

"And now you're not?"

"I decked that guy."

"I saw. It was great."

"Great?" He shook his head. "Hitting someone never solved anything."

"No? Well, it solved things very nicely for me."

She rubbed her palm up to his elbow, then down to his wrist. The hair on his forearm tickled her skin. A delicious tingle went from her hand all the way up the back of her neck.

"No one ever stood up for me before, Aaron. Thank you."

"But —"

"No buts. There are some people in this world who don't understand peace. He was one of them."

"So I should help him not hurt him. Teach him a better way instead of proving that violence solves anything."

Nicole snorted. "Right."

He pulled away, scrubbing his fingers through his hair, leaving it standing on end in several places. She wanted to smooth the stray strands back into place and because she did, Nicole put her hands behind her back and kept them there.

"When I saw him touching you," Aaron said, "when I heard what he was saying, I wanted to pound him into the ground. Then stomp on him a while."

"Me, too."

"I never felt like that before."

"Never?"

He shrugged. "I fought with my brothers. Hell, I have four, sometimes fighting was our main entertainment on a long summer night."

He had four brothers. She hadn't known that. What *had* she known about him? Only that he looked at her as no one else did. That he was sweet and kind. That he loved her, or so she'd thought.

Nicole sighed. She really needed to get over it.

"I never wanted to hurt anyone the way I wanted to hurt that guy," he murmured.

"You hit him once, Aaron. The world as we know it hasn't come to an end."

"No?"

She smiled. "No."

"I didn't scare you?"

Nicole almost laughed, but he was so serious, so concerned she couldn't. Instead she shook her head to keep from blurting out that she'd been far from scared, she'd been . . .

What?

Interested? Intrigued? Excited? Aroused?

She pushed those disturbing thoughts away. If Aaron knew his brute force had aroused her, he'd be holding an exorcism in a heartbeat.

"Of course you didn't scare me."

"You're sure?" he pressed.

"Aaron, how could you scare me with one punch into someone else's face? I've seen much worse. Been in the middle of it, too."

"Someone hit you?"

He was so aghast, the laugh she'd stifled

earlier broke free with a single, harsh bark. "A whole lot of someones."

Silence hung between them. His fingers curled into fists again. She wished she'd kept her mouth shut. Aaron's heart was too soft. Unlike hers.

Nicole placed her hand over his. "That was a long time ago. I don't think of it anymore. You shouldn't, either."

His fingers unclenched and entwined with hers. His other hand came up to cup her chin. His eyes, bright blue and intent, captured Nicole as they had once before.

"I don't want anyone to ever hurt you again."

Too late, her mind whispered as their lips met.

Chapter Six

She was still the most beautiful thing he'd ever seen. More dazzling than neon, warmer than the desert sand, her voice as sexy as a saxophone in the night. For Aaron, what he'd felt about Vegas and Nicole had always been tangled and confused.

Nothing had changed in that respect. Since he'd seen her standing in the doorway of Mercy House he'd wanted to kiss her and known he should not.

But the feelings he'd been fighting — the desire, the need — were now all jumbled with other feelings he couldn't fight. Tenderness, fear, possessiveness, pride. He gave up the battle and surrendered.

Cupping her chin, he marveled at the texture of her skin against his rough hands. Her eyelids fluttered closed, dark lashes forming a half moon against her cheeks. She swayed toward him, lips full and pale, reaching for his.

He couldn't stop. He had to taste her again, and it didn't matter that they were standing in a bus station parking lot beneath the ruthless desert sun. He could have cared less if fifty people were watching them. It didn't matter that the garbage bins were ripe. He barely heard the cars passing by. Aaron's mouth touched hers and everything and everyone disappeared.

The kiss began as comfort. He was never sure if he meant to comfort her, or if he needed her to comfort him.

Her lips were cold, but they warmed beneath his. Her breath brushed his cheek; he shivered though he was anything but chilled.

Gently he relearned the shape of her mouth, tasted the fullness of her lower lip, nibbled at the corners that so rarely smiled. She sighed and opened for him, her tongue sweeping out to meet his. And the kiss left comfort behind.

He hadn't realized that he'd lowered his hands to her hips, until she cupped hers at his elbows. They were no more than a whisper apart.

He'd always admired how they fit together. The top of her head came up to his eyes. He could kiss her for hours and never get a crick in the neck.

Her hips filled his hands. They were

fuller; he liked them like that. He especially enjoyed how her shirt rode up at the waist, allowing his thumbs beneath to stroke her stomach. The muscles fluttered and danced at his touch. Feelings awoke within him that had been sleeping for a very long time.

Her palms skimmed the hair on his arms and he shuddered. As if learning the contours of his skin she traced her thumbs down the veins in his arms, rolled over the ones that marred the backs of his hands. He could swear her pulse echoed the rhythm of his.

He pressed kisses from her mouth down the line of her jaw, to the soft hollow of her throat where that alluring pulse throbbed. He pressed his tongue to the beat and felt her . . . everywhere.

"Buddy? Hey, buddy?" Someone tugged on his shirt. "You got another sandwich on ya?"

Nicole gasped and spun out of his arms, glancing around the parking lot frantically. No one was there, except for the street guy yanking on Aaron's arm.

He shook his head, trying to clear it, but he couldn't stop thinking about how she'd tasted, how she'd smelled, how she'd opened her mouth, touched her tongue to his and made him remember everything he'd never truly wanted to forget.

"Sandwich?" he repeated stupidly.

"You know. Bread, meat." The guy pressed his palms together and lifted them to his mouth. "You eat it?"

"Oh." Aaron scratched his head. "I'll get you one. Wait here."

He headed for the bus station. Nicole stepped in his path. "What the hell are you doing?"

"You heard."

"You're just going to buy him food because he asked?"

"Can you think of a better reason?"

"He'll be asking you every time he sees you."

"And your point would be?"

She made a sound of frustration and stomped her foot. He could relate. Having their kiss interrupted made him want to growl and stomp, too. Seeing her mouth swollen from his, her cheeks pink, her shirt untucked . . . remembering the way her hips used to be and the way they were now because of him, because she'd had his child —

Aaron turned away as confusion made him dizzy. He wanted her in the same way he had before, perhaps more so, but she

118

was also the mother of his child and that made him feel . . . different, too.

Softer emotions swirled through him — affection, respect, admiration — yet none of them could curb the hunger that possessed him whenever she came near.

For years he'd believed he had his libido under control. Now he understood the desires hadn't gone away, they'd only been sleeping until he'd come back to her.

What he felt for Nicole he'd never felt for anyone else, and he didn't know what to think about that.

"How can she be so much like you without ever knowing you at all?" Nicole asked softly.

He froze. "What?"

"Rayne feeds people, too. She says sometimes it helps."

Aaron sighed. "Sometimes it does."

"Yeah, sometimes it does," the street guy said. "You mind, buddy? I'm starvin' here."

Aaron stepped around Nicole and headed for the door before he surrendered to the voice that insisted he take her back to the motel and keep her there for a week.

Nicole watched Aaron walk away. Maybe *walk* wasn't the right word. He was nearly running.

She wouldn't be surprised if he bought a ticket instead of a sandwich, then hopped the next bus to anywhere but here.

She turned away with a sigh. *He'd* kissed *her.* So why did she feel so guilty?

"Nice show," the street guy said. "You two oughta take that on the road. You could probably earn a bundle on the stage."

"What?"

"You and big boy. You can sure heat up a parking lot. I thought you were going to do it right here. If you don't mind an audience, and I guess you don't, you could make pretty decent money."

Nicole stared at him for a moment trying to figure out what he meant. Then it hit her. "There are places like that?"

"Honey, there are places like anything you want around here. You just have to know where to look."

Nicole had lived in Las Vegas for years, worked in dives most people wouldn't step foot in, dealt with women who'd known even worse and yet she was still amazed at the amount of things she did not know about this town. Perhaps that was one of its charms — if you could call such a place charming. Nicole certainly couldn't.

The man moved off, hovering around

the door, waiting for Aaron. He appeared harmless enough, but she kept an eye on him just in case. She wasn't going to let Aaron get knocked over the head and robbed in broad daylight. Not while she was around.

Since she couldn't stand still, Nicole paced the pavement. Ever since Aaron had kissed her, her skin had tingled, her body had throbbed, her mind had become tangled and torn. All she could think about was him.

Once she'd relished the closeness, the tenderness they'd shared. The best part of their single night together had been when it was finished and he'd held her, then murmured her name. She would have done anything for him. In fact, she had.

But, today, after he'd defended her, Nicole had experienced something entirely different than the wonder and the warmth. When his lips had touched hers she'd wanted nothing more than to lose herself in him. Yank off his restricting clothes, press her palms to his skin, then her mouth. Drop to her knees, taste him and have him taste her.

If he'd broken the embrace, then led her to his room, or even a secluded alley, she'd have gone gladly. Once again she'd have done anything. And that frightened her.

Was this lust? No wonder empires had fallen and worlds had been lost for one single taste of desire.

The door to the bus station opened. Her gaze was drawn to Aaron as he stepped into the sun. Just the sight of him made her heart thud harder, her breath come faster — until he glanced her way and then her breath stopped altogether.

Aaron handed the street guy the sandwich but continued to stare at her. The intensity in his blue eyes made her shiver. He'd always looked at her like that, and she'd always thought it meant love. Now she knew better.

But after today she had to wonder.

Had what she'd felt for *him* been lust all along?

"We're here!"

Tim leaped from the bus and hopped from foot to foot. Rayne joined him. "Do you have to go again?"

"No. I mean maybe. Yes."

Rayne hoisted her backpack onto one shoulder, then grabbed his hand and pulled him toward the gas station, which appeared to double as a bus station in Gainsville.

Tim hung back. Not to be stubborn, but because he was so interested in everything and everyone. Since he'd started to talk, he'd gained momentum every day and now he rarely stopped, asking questions as if he'd been wound up tight and left to run down on his own.

"Is your daddy here? Can we eat? What's the name of this place again?"

He never paused long enough for Rayne to answer, which was just as well, because she had no idea what the answers were to many of his questions. She almost missed the time when he hadn't spoken. *Almost.*

They were the only ones getting off in Gainsville. She wasn't surprised. For miles and miles all she'd seen were fields of indecipherable crops — except for the corn. She knew what that looked like.

A blast of cool air hit them in the face as they stepped into the station. The man behind the register scowled.

Before he could say a word, Tim slipped free of her grasp and ran up to the counter. "Are you my daddy?" he asked.

The guy blinked. "Huh?"

Rayne grabbed Tim and tugged him back to her side. "Shh," she admonished, and though he continued to do the pee dance, he did close his mouth.

Rayne couldn't believe he'd approached a stranger like that. Tim must want a daddy even more than he wanted to hide or maybe he knew she would never let anyone hurt him again.

The clerk's confused expression was replaced by another more ferocious scowl as he watched Tim squirm. "Bathrooms are for paying customers," he said before Rayne could even ask.

"You want the kid to go on the floor?"

"He should have gone on the bus."

As if in answer to the man's statement came the sound of gravel spraying every which way as the bus pulled out of the lot and left them behind.

"He should have done a lot of things, mister. But he's little and not quite house-trained yet."

Rayne squeezed Tim's hand. He danced faster and made a sad face. The guy rolled his eyes. "Oh, all right. But hurry up."

"Gee, thanks," Rayne muttered and followed Tim to the rear of the store.

"I'm watching you in my mirror. Don't stuff nothin' in your pocket, hear me?"

Rayne didn't bother to answer. She'd had the same treatment in every store and station across the country. It didn't matter that she'd paid her way; folks saw two scruffy kids on their own and labeled them thieves and runaways.

"I'll be right here," Rayne told Tim, taking her usual position directly outside the men's bathroom door. "Any trouble in there, you holler and I'll be inside in a flash."

Tim grinned. "And you'll kick their sorry ass!"

"Hey!" the clerk shouted. "Watch your language."

Tim slapped his hand over his mouth, and his eyes went wide. Rayne turned him toward the bathroom and gave him a little shove. "Never mind," she whispered.

Sometimes Tim forgot what were good words and what were bad. No doubt he'd heard them jumbled together so often he couldn't tell the difference.

He also had a teensie problem with his volume control. Rayne wasn't sure if his ADHD had busted it or if the inability to keep his voice on low was a boy thing. She'd seen plenty of little guys on the bus who had needed their volume control fixed, as well.

As she waited for Tim, Rayne stared out the window of the gas station. The late afternoon sunshine gleamed hot, sparking light off the hoods of parked cars and the glass fronts on the shops across the street.

Rayne had grown up in the desert, and for some reason she'd thought the rest of the country couldn't be as hot as Vegas. She'd learned differently. The first days of June in Illinois were not only scorching but muggy. She'd heard murmurs on the bus that such heat, so early, was unusual. But that didn't make it any easier to take.

Rayne studied the dreary buildings that comprised the town of Gainsville. White lumber, gray brick, a little red brick just to break up the monotony, not a trace of neon anywhere. How could they stand it? A wave of homesickness passed over her, so strong she felt a little dizzy.

Luckily Tim chose that moment to rocket out of the bathroom and give her a hug. How the kid could be so affectionate when he'd had too little affection in his life was beyond her.

Rayne passed her hand over his hair, ruffled it a bit, which made him giggle, then hugged him back. He turned his head and stared at the store clerk, who was glaring at them still.

"I hope he's not my daddy, Rayne. Nor yours, neither."

Her stomach lurched. What if her father turned out to be like this man — short-tempered and selfish? What if he had another family? What if he'd always known about her and didn't care? What if he slammed the door in her face?

She hugged Tim tighter and he started to squirm. She let him go, then grabbed the collar of his shirt and hauled him back before he scooted away and touched something he shouldn't. Another thing about Tim, he just couldn't keep his busy fingers to himself.

"What are we gonna do now?" he asked.

Rayne had no idea. Should she walk up to the front door of her father's house — wherever it was — and announce she was his daughter? Or hang around town a while and see what she could find out? All the questions without answers were driving her crazy.

"Hey, sister." Rayne glanced at the clerk. "You gonna settle in for the night?" He peered at her more closely than she liked, so she tugged her cap lower on her forehead and put the reflective sunglasses in her pocket back on her nose. "Say, aren't you a little young to be on a bus alone?"

"No," she answered.

"Someone supposed to be picking you up? Maybe I should call the chief."

Chief?

Rayne had visions of a guy in a big feathered headdress. Indians in Illinois? Well, she supposed they had some stashed somewhere — probably out of sight.

"They frown on vagrancy around here."

Oh. The light dawned. *Chief of* police.

"We're going." She tugged Tim toward the door.

In a tiny town like this, everyone knew everyone else's business. No one slept on the street or in a park. Obviously there wasn't any sleeping in the bus station, since they didn't have one. If anyone tried anything funny *the chief* would come and take them away. Where, Rayne wasn't sure.

Her thoughts of hanging out and asking around disappeared quicker than Tim's mama. Rayne doubted she'd be in town an hour before someone called the cops.

"Hey, mister?"

The clerk gave a long-suffering sigh. "What now?"

"You know anyone named Luchetti around here?"

"Luchetti?" He stood up straighter. "You here to visit them?"

Visit wasn't exactly the term she'd use, but it was close enough.

"Sure."

"You must be some kind of relative."

"Some kind."

He stared at her for a long minute and Rayne sighed. "Never mind. I'll ask someone else."

"Hold on there. John would have my a—" He stopped midcuss and glanced at Tim, who waved. "My head," he finished, "if I let his family walk out to his place."

Rayne had no idea who John was, but she liked him already since this guy seemed afraid of him.

"We don't mind."

"You don't know how far it is." He pointed out the front window. "Way down that county highway about five miles or so, then you gotta turn right and go another mile to reach their farm." He picked up the phone. "I'll just give them a call and let them know you're here."

"Them?"

"The Luchettis. All of 'em live on the same farm. Except for the girl. But then she's not a Luchetti anymore."

So much information for her to take in. There were a lot of Luchettis. They lived on a farm. And her quest was nearly at an end.

As the man dialed, Rayne inched toward the door. Her heart pounded faster; she couldn't think what to do. There was no way she was explaining who she was to some stranger so he could explain it over the phone.

But if she and Tim ran, *the chief* would be on them before they could get half a mile down that county highway. Since there were very few trees and the crops were no more than ankle high, they'd have nowhere to hide.

The guy scowled and slammed the phone back into the cradle. "Machine's on. They must be in the barn or the fields." He grabbed a ring of keys off his belt. "I'll have to close up and drive you out there."

"You can do that?" Rayne blurted.

"Why not? I own the joint."

She almost laughed when he used Janet's favorite excuse for having her way. Until the homesickness broadsided her, and she had to blink fast to make the tears disappear. No matter how hard it was, she had a quest to complete before she could go home.

The owner twisted a key in the register, then walked around the counter, switched the sign on the door from Open to Closed, made use of another key and motioned for them to follow him out the back door.

"But, Rayne," Tim whispered, though

his whisper was the volume of everyone else's everyday speech, "we can't get in a car with a *stranger.*"

He stared at the clerk as if the man were a monster. Considering Tim's life thus far, Rayne had to wonder who had told him about strangers.

"I'm Harvey," the guy said. "Harvey Griss. And you are . . . ?"

"The Timinator. No one messes with me."

Harvey's lips twitched. He very nearly smiled before he stopped himself, then glanced at Rayne.

"Rayne."

He waited expectantly for her last name. She stared at the floor and didn't supply it. She wasn't a complete idiot. If she wanted her mother to know where she was, she'd have told her herself.

Rayne had no doubt her mom had called the cops already. For all she knew, her face was plastered all over the news, though she didn't think so. This guy hadn't recognized her, and he'd been staring at her enough. No one else had, either. But she wasn't going to make it easy for everyone by blabbing her name.

"Fine," Harvey muttered. "Suit yourself. But since we're not strangers anymore, let's get a move on."

Moments later she and Tim were seated in his car and headed down the highway.

"Can't believe John would let any of his family loiter at the bus stop. Especially kids."

"Well, we weren't exactly sure when we'd get here. You know how bus schedules are."

Harvey just grunted. Rayne wasn't certain if he believed her or not.

"We're on a quest," Tim said, as he bounced up and down in the front seat. Thankfully the seat belt kept him from hitting the ceiling.

"Tim," Rayne warned.

" 'Kay." He stopped bouncing and shut his mouth. Seconds later his fingers tapped a tune on the window.

Harvey scowled. "What kind of quest?"

"It's a game," Rayne blurted before Tim could spill anything more about daddies. As it was, news of their arrival would probably be all over town in an hour. She didn't need strangers knowing more about her business than she did.

"Oh. Like travel bingo? For the bus?"

"Yeah. Like that."

Harvey glanced at Tim, who was still tapping but had started kicking the glove compartment, as well. Harvey's shoulders tensed and a tick fluttered under his right eye. "Knock that off," he barked.

Tim gasped, plastered himself against the door and held one busy hand in his lap with the other. He crossed his legs at the ankle.

Harvey cursed. "What's the matter with him?"

"Nothing."

Rayne berated herself for letting Tim sit up front. She should have kept him next to her so she could hold him down. As annoying as he was, he didn't deserve to be frightened. She hated it when he reverted to the quiet, scared little boy she'd found in the alley.

"Nothing? Right." Harvey shook his head. "Never mind, kid, I won't bite. I'm just not used to so much energy."

Tim glanced at Rayne and she shrugged. He unwound himself and scowled out the window, obviously concentrating all his brain power on remaining still. Rayne doubted the period of inactivity would last for long since Tim's thoughts were as scattered as his hairstyle.

"So how are you related to John?"

Since Rayne had no clue who John was, she had no trouble answering. "It's complicated."

"Cousins twice removed and such? I never did understand how that works."

"Me, neither."

She had no cousins. Or maybe she did. Aunts? Uncles? Grandparents? Half sisters or brothers? Her head spun and her anger at her mother returned. How could she have lied to her for so long?

"There it is." Harvey pointed out the front window.

Rayne followed his finger. Rising out of the flat, flat land were three silver silos. A stone farmhouse and various white-plank buildings dotted the countryside nearby. She recognized a barn but the rest were a mystery.

Tim started bouncing again. Harvey winced but he didn't say anything.

"Rayne, look." He pressed his face to the window, leaving a mouth-shaped wet splotch on the glass. "All sorts of different animals. Can I play with them?"

"We'll see."

He treated her to a sad face. "We'll see always means no."

She narrowed her eyes. He shut his mouth and quit bouncing.

Harvey stopped at the end of the long lane leading to the house. "I'm not gonna drive in since I gotta get back. No tellin' how many customers I lost. Tell John I dropped you off."

As soon as Rayne and Tim climbed out, Harvey left in a flurry of dust and gravel. The two of them turned and stared at the picture-perfect farmhouse and the green fields dotted with cows. How could a place appear so peaceful while Rayne's heart thundered and her stomach rolled?

"Is your daddy down there?" Tim asked.

Rayne took his hand. "Let's go find out."

Eleanor Luchetti was picking up the mess her sons had made while she and their father had been on a long overdue trip to Tahiti, when the dogs began to bark.

Figuring her daughter had arrived to welcome them back, she absently strolled to the front window. Two children were walking down the lane hand in hand.

Frowning, she dropped the dirty laundry into a chair. She was going to read the riot act to Dean as soon as he came in from the barn. Too bad Aaron and Evan had disappeared. By the time they returned she wouldn't be half as mad.

The thought made her frown even harder. Evan disappeared all the time. But Aaron? Never. Dean said he was helping a friend, which, considering Aaron, was probably true. But why all the secrecy?

Eleanor glanced up and down the road, trying to figure out how those kids had gotten here. All she saw was a little bit of dust headed back toward Gainsville.

"Strange," she murmured.

If they were selling cookies or fruit or candy for some school group their parents shouldn't just drop them off. Gainsville was safer than a lot of places. However, most of the children who were abducted had lived in safe places, too.

Eleanor shivered. What was the world coming to?

The kids reached the yard, and the farm dogs circled them, barking madly. The little boy shrank against the girl's side, and she pushed him behind her while she scowled at the animals. She said something, punctuating the words with a jab of her hand toward the barn.

Eleanor's frown turned to a smile as the dogs slunk away. Whoever the kid was, Eleanor liked her already.

The children continued toward the house. Eleanor couldn't see the girl's face as it was hidden by a baseball cap, but there was something familiar about the line of her jaw. She'd no doubt seen her in town at one time or another.

She moved to the front door and opened it before they could knock. "Hello," she said. "Can I help you?"

The little boy grinned, revealing holes where several teeth should be. "Hi. I'm the Timinator. But you can call me Tim."

"Hi, Tim. I'm Eleanor Luchetti."

He hopped from foot to foot. After raising five boys, she knew that dance. "Do you have to use the bathroom?"

"Yep."

She opened the door wide. "Down the hall and to the right."

The kid scampered away. Eleanor turned back to the girl and blinked. The face was still shadowed by the bill of her cap, but it was a face she knew very well.

Familiar green eyes stared into hers with determination. "I'm looking for my father."

Eleanor nodded. One of her sons needed his ass kicked. But which one? It could be any one of the five except —

"Aaron," the girl said. "My father is Aaron Luchetti."

Eleanor wondered if it was too early for a drink.

Chapter Seven

The lady, who said her name was Eleanor, put her hand against the door and swayed as if she might faint. "Didn't see that one coming," she muttered.

"Are you all right?"

"Yeah. Just give me a minute."

She took several deep breaths, yanked on the collar of her floral T-shirt and straightened as if pulling herself together from the inside out.

"You said Aaron, right?"

Rayne nodded. "Is he here?"

"You'd better come inside. . . ." Eleanor tilted her head and her long, white braid swayed out and then back to rest against her hip. "What's your name?"

"Rayne. Rayne Houston."

"Pretty. Come in and sit down. Let me get my husband."

"Aaron?"

Eleanor laughed. "That's the nicest thing anyone's said to me in ages. But even without this hair, I doubt I'd pass for the wife of a thirty-two-year-old man."

Rayne thought she looked pretty good. Her hair might be white, but it was long and thick, and the braid was cool. She was a big lady, not fat, but strong and solid. She wore jeans and her feet were bare. Her toenails were painted the same pink as the flowers in her shirt.

When Eleanor reached out and tugged on the bill of Rayne's cap gently, Rayne met eyes of the deepest blue. "I'm your gramma, honey."

"You believe me?" Rayne blurted. "Just like that?"

"Of course."

"Why?"

"Come on in here and I'll show you."

She stepped back and Rayne followed her into the hall, then into the living room. The place was old, but not junky old, though it was messier than she'd have expected from a woman like Eleanor. No, this house had been here a very long time and been loved by family after family.

"Sit, if you can find a clean spot. You'll have to excuse the house. I've been away and my sons are pigs."

Rayne blinked. Eleanor was blunt, kind of like Janet. She couldn't help but like the woman, even if she barely knew her.

"I — uh — need to find Tim. He

might —" Something crashed at the back of the house. Rayne sighed. "Do that."

"Don't worry about him. This place has lived through five boys and then some. He can't hurt anything that hasn't already been hurt a hundred times before."

"Thanks, but I still need to find him."

It made Rayne nervous to have Tim out of her sight for very long. She inched toward the hall.

"Is he your brother?"

"No, ma'am."

"You don't have to call me ma'am."

Rayne shrugged. She couldn't call her Gramma. Not yet.

As if sensing the dilemma, Eleanor smiled. "You can call me Ellie if you like. Everyone else does."

Rayne stepped into the hall just as Tim careened toward the living room. He bounced off her hip and slammed into the wall. A single picture jittered and nearly fell. Rayne grabbed for it, steadied it, stared at it.

She turned to Ellie in shock. Tim wrapped his arms around her waist. "Hey, Rayne," he shouted. "That's you."

"No," she managed. "It isn't."

The face was the same, the eyes and the hair, too. But the girl in the picture wore clothes from at least a decade past, and she was older than Rayne was now. The theme song from *The Twilight Zone* started up in Rayne's head.

"That's my daughter, Kim." Ellie straightened the photo and glanced at Rayne. "Senior prom. And this is Brian Riley." She pointed to the tall young man in the tuxedo. "They're married now. Live about five miles from here. They have a baby girl. Her name is Glory."

Rayne nodded numbly. An unknown number of uncles, an aunt, a cousin, two grandparents — the family she'd never known she had was multiplying so fast she couldn't keep track of them all.

"I need to sit," she said, untangling Tim's arms from her waist.

"You and me both."

Ellie walked back into the living room and pointed to the couch. "You two go ahead. I'm gonna call the others."

Rayne figured she meant call, as in telephone. She jumped when Ellie went to the window, threw up the sash and shouted, "John. Dean. Get in here!"

She turned and took in Rayne's shocked expression. "Sorry, honey. There's probably going to be a lot more noise around here than you're used to."

Rayne was used to quite a bit — though usually outside her house instead of in — screaming, fighting, sirens, the shattering of glass. Which reminded her.

"Tim? What was that crash I heard?"

His face scrunched up as he thought. "Dunno."

She put her hands on her hips. "Tim."

"Really. Don't remember no crash. 'Cept when I put the toilet seat back down — slipped and then it slammed. You said never, ever leave it up on penalty of death." He gave Ellie a solemn stare. "Girls hate it when you do that."

Ellie smirked. "You'll get no argument from me."

They sat and immediately Tim started to bounce up and down. Rayne put her arm around his shoulders and held him still. His leg began to jiggle. Ellie's gaze narrowed, and a speculative look came into her eye.

Rayne laid her hand on Tim's knee. What if he drove everyone here as crazy as he'd driven everyone they'd ever met? What if Ellie asked Tim to leave?

She lifted her chin and met Ellie's gaze straight on. Rayne would just have to go, too. Tim was hers now.

The older woman raised a brow. "You

think I like to kick puppies?"

"Huh?"

"Your pet there. I won't hurt him."

"I'm not a pet." Tim bounced once, real high, before Rayne pulled him back down. "I'm Tim. Me and Rayne, we're on the daddy quest. She's gonna find hers, then I'm gonna find me one, too."

"The daddy quest?" Ellie murmured. "Catchy."

"It was Tim's idea." Rayne hesitated, then gave up on being polite. She had to know. "Where's my father?"

"He's disappeared."

"Wh-what?"

"That's what I said."

Before Rayne could ask anything more, two men tromped through the front door.

"Boots off!" Ellie ordered without even glancing their way.

They grumbled all the way back out again. Seconds later they returned.

"Where's the fire, Ellie?" the older man asked.

His gaze swept over Rayne, moved on to Tim, then shot right back to her and stuck there. His mouth dropped open. Rayne glanced at the second, younger man. His expression was identical. After seeing the picture in the hall, she understood why they were staring, even if she had no idea who they were.

Tim leaped to his feet, and with expert dodging ability scooted past Rayne's grasping fingers. He ran straight up to the men and proclaimed, "Are you my daddy?"

Both snapped their mouths shut with an audible click of teeth and took a giant step back, staring at Tim as if he were a snake.

Rayne snickered. So did Ellie.

The older man raised his gaze and got it stuck on Rayne once more. "What's goin' on here?" he demanded.

"John." She put her hand on Rayne's shoulder. "Meet your granddaughter."

"Uh-oh," the younger man said. "Someone's in deep shit."

Tim threw his arms around the man's waist. "You *must* be my daddy."

The guy raised his hands up high, as if he were surrendering and stared down at Tim in horror. "What? Not me. Let go, kid."

"Dean, put a zip on your lip for once. Take Tim outside and let him play with Bull and Bear."

"A bull and a bear?" Rayne stood and walked toward Tim, pausing halfway between him and the couch. "I don't think so."

"The Dalmatians," John said. "They're harmless."

"If you don't mind a little dirt and slobber," Ellie muttered.

"What kid does?" John shot back, his eyes on Rayne all the while. "Do as your mother says, Dean."

"Fine." Dean pulled Tim's clinging fingers from around his waist. "But I'm not your daddy, kid. You're barking up the wrong tree there."

" 'Kay," Tim sang, happily sliding his hand into Dean's and skipping ahead of him toward the door. Rayne couldn't believe the changes in Tim since leaving Las Vegas. This trip had been good for him.

Dean paused, pulling back as Tim pulled forward. "Just tell me who's in deep sh—" His gaze flicked to his mother's, then back to Rayne. "Trouble," he finished.

"Aaron," Rayne answered before anyone could say differently. "My father is Aaron Luchetti."

Dean whistled through his teeth. "This is gonna be good."

"Get lost," John snapped.

Dean shrugged and let Tim pull him outside.

John Luchetti continued to stare at Rayne. He was very tall, very lean, his face tanned and lined, his eyes the same brilliant green as her own. He crossed the short distance that separated them, then lifted a hand traced with heavy veins and touched a finger to her cap. "Do you mind?"

She shrugged and he pulled the hat from her head. Rayne's long, dark hair tumbled down. He glanced at his wife. "It's uncanny."

"I'll say."

Returning his attention to Rayne, he winked. "Knock, knock."

"Not now," Ellie groaned.

Rayne glanced at her gramma in time to see her roll her eyes.

"Knock, knock," John repeated.

"Who's there?"

"Farmer."

"Farmer who?"

He waited a beat, then hit the punch line. "Farmer people here than there were yesterday."

Rayne snorted and John's grin spread from ear to ear as he nudged his wife with his elbow. "Even without the eyes, the hair, that face, I'd know she was one of ours."

"One of *yours*," Ellie grumbled.

"As you can tell," John spread his hands wide, "she doesn't like my jokes."

"I love knock-knocks," Rayne said.

"Stick with me, kid, I've got a million."

"And he means that. Literally." Ellie shook her head. "Who'd have ever thought a love of knock-knock jokes would be in the genes."

"Who'd have thought," John echoed. He indicated the couch with a flick of one long finger. "Now maybe we should all sit down and have a little chat."

Rayne's amusement vanished as her mind raced ahead, trying to figure out if she should tell them everything or nothing at all, wondering what it meant that her father had disappeared from here at the same time she had arrived.

They all sat down. No one spoke. What was there to say? Or maybe there was too much to say, they just didn't know where to start.

"Where are you from?" Ellie asked.

Rayne hesitated, uncertain. She didn't want them sending her back on the next plane. But she could hardly refuse to answer, and since she'd never been anywhere but Vegas, she couldn't exactly make up a whole new hometown.

"Las Vegas," she answered.

"Vegas?" Ellie blinked, then frowned. "Huh."

Silence pulsed for a few minutes more. Rayne could hear the tick of the clock on the wall.

"So you're Aaron's girl?"

Rayne jumped at the sudden question and glanced at John, her grandfather. She couldn't get her mind around that. When she nodded, his grin spread from ear to ear.

"That's great!"

Rayne frowned. "Great?"

What was *wrong* with these people? She didn't have much experience with families, but she could tell things were not progressing the way one would expect when folks discovered a thirteen-year-old granddaughter they'd never known they had.

"John," Ellie warned.

"What? I'm thrilled to discover my son is a father. What's wrong with that?"

"Nothing. I just know why you're so thrilled."

"Why?" Rayne asked.

Ellie pursed her lips and raised her eyebrows at John. Her expression shouted, *Nice job, numbskull!* without her saying anything at all.

"Uh, well, hmm." John cleared his throat. "How much do you know about your father?"

Rayne frowned. Was he a psychotic killer or something? Maybe he was in prison and that was why he wasn't here. Or maybe her imagination was running away with her. It wouldn't be the first time.

"I know his name and that he lives in Illinois."

"That's all?"

"Pretty much. Why? Is there something wrong with him?"

"Of course not," Ellie answered at the same time John said, "Not anymore."

"John!" Ellie snapped.

He spread his big, hard hands. "What?"

"I think you'd better tell me about him," Rayne interrupted.

After a final glare at her husband, Ellie turned to Rayne. "There's nothing to tell. Aaron is a good man. He lives here. He works on the farm."

"He's not married?"

"No. Never."

Rayne frowned. Even she knew that a thirty-two-year-old man who still lived at home and had never been married was a bit odd. In a small, conservative, midwestern town like Gainsville it was downright radical.

"Why not?"

"He . . . uh, well, he was —" Ellie broke

off and stared at her hands.

A thought burst into Rayne's mind and straight from her mouth. "Gay?"

"No!" John snapped, then looked sheepish. "I mean, obviously not since you're here."

The light dawned. Her grandfather had thought her father was gay. Which explained why he was so darned glad to meet her. But she still didn't understand what was making her gramma squirm.

"What, then?"

"He was going to be a priest," Ellie blurted.

Rayne blinked. "A what?"

John shrugged. "I wasn't so thrilled, either."

Rayne went silent, trying to take in this new information. "What happened?"

"We never knew. He went to college, then on a mission trip to Vegas."

"Uh-oh," Rayne said.

"Exactly. Before we could say Hail, Mary he'd quit school, moved home and gone to work without a word as to why. That was fourteen years ago." Ellie brushed Rayne's hair from her face. "How old are you, honey?"

"Thirteen."

"Bingo," John murmured.

"He didn't become a priest because of — ?" She pointed a finger at her chest.

"We'll have to wait until he comes home to find that out."

"Do you think he knew about me?" Her voice wavered. "That he didn't want me?"

"No."

Ellie touched her hair again. Rayne swallowed and fought the urge to throw herself into her gramma's arms and hold on tight. What kind of impression would that make?

"Aaron would never have a child and turn his back on her. He's not that kind of man." Ellie paused. "But tell me, Rayne, why did you ignore him?"

"Until last week I thought he was dead."

"Dead?" Ellie sat up straighter. "Why did you think that?"

"My mom said so."

"Oh." A flash of annoyance crossed her gramma's face. "And what does your mom say now?"

Rayne hesitated. She didn't want her mother to know she was here. Not yet. Because Nicole would come racing across the country to drag her back, and Rayne wasn't ready to go. Not until she met her father. Not until she got to know her family. Not until she learned where the lies ended and the truth began.

She didn't want to lie, either. Her mom had always insisted on the truth. To Nicole, lying was one of the worst things a person could do. Then why had she been lying to Rayne all of her life?

Anger bubbled, hot and blinding. At that moment, Rayne wanted to hurt her mom as her mom had hurt her, even though she knew it was wrong.

"She was mad when I found out the truth," Rayne blurted.

"How did you find out?"

"She had his phone number." Quickly Rayne explained what had happened when she called the Luchetti house.

Ellie frowned. "Dean didn't say anything about a phone call."

"Evan," John muttered. "He never leaves messages. I don't know why he bothers to answer the phone as he passes on through."

"Then what happened, Rayne?" Ellie asked.

"She put me on the bus. Said if I was so interested in my dad, maybe it was time I lived with him for a while."

Ellie's eyes widened. John's mouth became a thin line. They looked at each other, then back at Rayne. She could tell they thought her mom was a witch with a capital B, and Rayne nearly confessed.

Then Ellie gathered Rayne into her arms. "Maybe your mom was right."

And for the first time in months, Rayne felt as if she belonged somewhere. So she swallowed the truth and went with the lie.

"What's that?"
"Chicken."
"What's that?"
"Cow."
"What's that?"
"Pig."
"What's —"
"Kid," Dean interrupted gruffly, "haven't you ever seen animals before?"

"Nope. Or at least not animals like these. Seen birds. Pigeons mostly. And rats. Big as dogs and a hell of a lot meaner."

Dean raised his eyebrows at the casual curse word. The kid just kept on talking.

"Can't hug rats. Bad idea."

He threw his arms around Bear's neck and squeezed. The dog took the opportunity to lick the kid all over his face. Dean sighed. If his mom saw that she'd have a stroke. Lord knows where that mouth had been half an hour ago.

Bull, not to be left out, sidled up on the boy's other side and slobbered in his hair.

Tim collapsed onto the ground giggling. The Dalmatians took that as an invitation to fall all over him and grind him into the dirt.

Dean stood back and let them roll around. At least when the kid was playing with the dogs he wasn't asking questions and dancing on Dean's toes.

He'd never seen anyone so hyper, unless he counted the dogs. Dalmatians were high-strung, not the best pets in truth, but damn good farm dogs. They were relentless.

He glanced at the rolling ball of dogs and kid. Kind of like Tim here.

Dean hadn't been around too many children. His sister's daughter was nine months old. Zsa Zsa was cute, somewhat amusing and basically a pain in the behind. She needed to be fed and watered and cleaned up after. He didn't mind doing that for cows. He liked cows. But kids . . . ?

Dean shook his head. Not so much.

His gaze was drawn back to the boy. Where had he lived that he'd never seen anything but rats and birds?

Sympathy tugged at Dean in spite of himself. He gazed over the acres upon acres of Luchetti land and wondered what he'd do without it. He loved this farm, even if there were times, in the middle of all the sweat and the work, that he forgot how very lucky he was to be here.

Not everyone would agree. There were those who considered him a fool for staying, who thought him a failure because all he could do was farm.

Even if he'd had any interest in college, any hope in hell of getting into one, he wouldn't have gone. Dean wasn't a smart man. He knew that. He accepted it. There were worse things to be than average.

Or so he told himself over and over again when jealousy of his above average siblings threatened to overwhelm him. To be average in his family was to be part of the furniture.

Why he let it bother him he didn't understand. He'd never wanted to be anything but what he was. So why was he so unhappy?

The kid disentangled himself from the dogs in a single motion and took off running. Bull and Bear followed with barks of joyous pleasure. No one had ever been able to keep up with them — until now.

"Hey!" Dean shouted. "Where do you think you're going?"

Tim must not have heard him because he kept on running, disappearing around the corner of the barn. Dean wasn't worried. What could happen to the kid in the thirty seconds it took Dean to catch up?

When the dogs came running back in his direction, tails between their legs, Dean frowned. When he heard a low groan followed by a swoosh of air through flared nostrils, he ran. Before he turned the corner, he knew.

Tim had slipped through the fence, built to keep cattle in, not little kids out. He stood on one side of the corral, a Black Angus bull on the other.

"Nice cow," Tim said, his voice too loud to be soothing, even if Herby was in the mood to be soothed, which he never was.

Herby was a prize bull, an excellent stud and a very crabby hunk of beef. He didn't like animals. He didn't like people. He barely tolerated the cows. From the looks of things, he liked Tim least of all.

Dean didn't bother to shout a warning. He climbed the fence, vaulted over the top, then hit the ground running at the same time Herby trumpeted his fury and began to run, too. Fortunately Tim was nearer to Dean, and Herby was slowed down by the two-by-four hanging from the ring in his nose.

Tucking Tim under his arm like a football, Dean ran for the end zone. He reached the goal line, made that the fence, and climbed as fast as he could. Going up with the kid in his arms wasn't easy, but he made it, inches ahead of the bull.

They were perched at the top when Herby ran into the bottom. The fence shook, Tim wiggled, Dean lost his footing and they both tumbled down.

Luckily they landed in a pile of straw. Unluckily it was used straw.

"Shit," Dean muttered.

"Sure is." Tim sat right up, his bony knees knocking against Dean's ribs like tiny razor blades. Dean forgot all about the pain as wonder spread over Tim's face. "You saved me from the mean old cow."

"That wasn't a cow."

"But it was mean."

"Yeah. Very. Don't go in there again, okay?"

" 'Kay." He bounced a bit and Dean slid away from the knifelike kneecaps. "You're a hero. Just like Arnold Schwarzenator."

The way the kid mangled the name forced a laugh out of Dean. Tim tilted his head. His long hair swung across his face, and he brushed it away impatiently, leaving a smudge of slime on his cheek. In his eyes

Dean saw so many things — fear, awe, hope.

"You're *sure* you're not my daddy?"

For an instant, Dean wanted to be, and that worried him so much he snapped, "Damn sure."

The kid didn't flinch at the curse or the words. "If I could pick a daddy," he murmured, "I'd pick you."

No one had ever chosen Dean before. He wasn't sure what to do about it now. But when Tim snuggled against Dean's side and placed his head on Dean's shoulder, the knot of unhappiness that lived inside his heart loosened just a little.

Chapter Eight

Janet was waiting on the other side of the door when Nicole and Aaron returned to Mercy House. She must have been out searching for Rayne, too, because she still wore her combat boots and fatigue pants. Her only deference to the heat was a black tank top and camouflage visor.

"Did you find out anything?" Janet demanded.

"I'm afraid not." Aaron followed Nicole inside.

She had planned to thank him for his help and shut the door in his face. But Aaron, despite his amiable nature, had never been easy to push around.

Fourteen years working on a farm had strengthened his body, even though his heart appeared just as soft. As they'd walked the streets searching for Rayne, he'd blown every cent in his wallet on meals for the hungry.

She should write him off as a chump. Instead she found the contrast of strength and kindness far too endearing.

Being with Aaron today, after sharing a kiss that morning, had been one of the hardest things Nicole had ever done. She gave him a quick sideways glance as he shut the door behind them. He saw her looking and smiled. How could he be so nonchalant?

All day long her worry about her daughter had warred with the memory of his kiss. But he didn't seem to remember it at all.

Nicole stopped just inside the doorway and Aaron bumped into her back. His hands came up to rest on her shoulders, steadying her.

"Whoops," he murmured, and his breath brushed her ear.

She had to clench her teeth to resist the sudden urge to turn in his arms, press her cheek against his chest, breathe in his scent and savor his heat.

"My, aren't you two cozy?" Janet brushed past. "I didn't think you liked men, Nicky."

Nicole tensed and gave Janet a dirty look. But the older woman wasn't paying any attention. She was too busy causing trouble.

"Nic doesn't like men?" Aaron appeared confused.

"That's what she says."

"I'm too busy to date."

"Yeah, aren't we all?" Janet muttered.

Nicole glanced at Aaron in time to see his lips twitch. The idea of Janet dating *was* somewhat amusing.

"Sit," Janet ordered. "We need to talk."

They did as they were told. Nicole could tell Aaron wanted to ask more questions about her love life, but he wasn't sure how.

"The police called."

Nicole couldn't speak past the panic. She reached for Aaron's hand, and met his coming in the other direction. Their fingers linked and he held on tight.

"What did they say?" Aaron asked.

"There's no news." Janet lifted her gaze from their joined hands to Nicole's face. "What did you think they'd say, Nicky? They wouldn't *call* with bad news. They'd knock on the door. You know that."

Aaron glanced at Nicole. "*How* do you know that?"

"They've knocked quite a few times before."

"What kind of bad news would they bring here?"

He appeared genuinely confused. The man was so naive he made Nicole's head ache.

"Women come here because they want to change, but sometimes changing is too damned hard."

"I don't understand."

Nicole glanced at Janet helplessly. Janet took pity and explained.

"Addictions, be they drugs or booze or men, are difficult to give up even if you want to. And when you're lured back, you go back hard to make up for the time you lost."

A new thought made Nicole straighten and remove her hand from his. Was that the explanation for her reaction to Aaron? Nicole had never been addicted to men, but she'd become addicted to him — or at least to how he made her feel. She'd been lured back to those feelings, so she'd gone back hard.

The cure was simple. She had to go cold turkey. No more kissing, no more touching, no more dreaming of him. Too bad she couldn't get rid of temptation altogether.

Because Aaron was staying until they found Rayne. He'd promised, and while he didn't seem to think his promises were worth very much, Nicole did.

"Are you talking about overdoses?" Aaron asked.

"Among other things." Janet raised her hand to forestall further questions. "Whatever you can imagine, Aaron, worse things have happened. Let's leave it at that, hmm?"

Aaron went silent. His expression made Nicole want to gather him into her arms and stroke his hair. Because she shouldn't, she stood and moved to the window.

"I hate to think of Rayne seeing what she's seen," Aaron murmured.

Nicole spun around, angry words on her lips, but Aaron's face was so sad, she held them back. He wasn't criticizing, merely sympathizing.

"Rayne's a strong girl," Janet said. "She knows the streets. She knows people. She likes to help them, but her mama didn't raise any fool."

Janet favored Nicole with a fond smile. Warmth spread through Nicole as it always did when Janet gave her approval.

"If anyone's safe out there on her own, it's Rayne, and it's because of how she was raised."

"I wanted her to have what I never did," Nicole murmured.

Aaron's serious, concerned gaze shifted to her face. "What's that?"

"She knows that she's loved, and she knows what's right."

Rayne knew she was wrong, but as Janet always said, once you told a lie, it was kind of hard to go back to the truth.

So Rayne didn't. At least not about how she'd ended up in Illinois. She made up for her guilt over that lie by telling the truth about everything else. In fact, she blabbed all the secrets in her head.

"Mom was a runaway. A stripper. She sold her body. She had to eat."

Ellie's face paled with every revelation. John's turned red. Rayne discovered she couldn't shut up.

"We live with hookers, exotic dancers, a drug addict or two. I found Tim in an alley. Kept him in the storage room a while."

"Y-your mother kept him in a storage room?" Ellie reached for John's hand. "With the junk?"

Rayne shrugged. "She didn't know."

"She didn't know a child was living in her house?"

"No."

Ellie closed her eyes. Her mouth moved — as if she were praying, or perhaps counting to ten.

Tim's high-pitched laughter drew Rayne's attention. By the time it rose to a shriek, she was already running out the door.

She stopped dead on the porch. Tim, stripped to his Angel of Light underwear, danced beneath the spray of water from the hose in Dean's hand. The dogs wiggled and leaped in the sparkle of droplets turned gold by the setting sun. Several cows watched placidly from behind a fence while a bull with the biggest earring she'd ever seen in his nose bumped his head against the barn wall and bellowed. Nothing like this ever happened in Las Vegas.

"He's laughing." John's voice was full of wonder.

"Tim laughs a lot."

"I meant Dean. He never laughs at all."

"Never?"

Ellie sighed. "No."

"Why not?"

"Dean was never much of a yuckster," John answered. "He's a farmer."

"So are you."

John shrugged. "I find a lot in life that's funny."

"And Dean?"

"He finds a lot in life to bitch about."

"John!"

"What? Like she hasn't heard the word before?"

"She doesn't need to hear it any more." Ellie turned her back on her husband. "Dean? What's going on here?"

Rayne glanced at her uncle in time to see his smile disappear. Too bad. He was kind of cute when he smiled. In fact, most women would call him hot.

"Kid fell in the used straw. He needed to be hosed off."

"Hi, Rayne." Tim kept dancing as he waved. "Wanna come and play?"

"Not right now. I'd better find you some dry clothes."

Rayne went inside and searched through her backpack. John remained outside, while Ellie followed Rayne. "He's going to be tired."

"Not in this lifetime," Rayne muttered.

Silence settled over them, broken only by the continued sound of Tim's laughter, the low voices of the men and the shrill barking of the dogs.

"What's the matter with him?" Ellie asked.

Rayne glanced up quickly, Tim's spare shirt in her hand. "Nothing."

Ellie raised a brow. "I'm not saying my kids are perfect, but they're normal. Kind of."

"There's *nothing* wrong with Tim."

Rayne yanked a pair of shorts free. "He's adorable."

"He is."

"He won't bother you."

"I never said he bothered me. After raising six kids, five of them boys, very little does. What's wrong with him?"

"He's just a tiny bit hyper."

Ellie snorted. "That's like saying the Pope is a little bit Catholic." Rayne shrugged. "Isn't hyper politically incorrect these days?"

"What isn't?"

"You got that right."

Her gramma continued to stare at her, expecting an answer. Since she'd seen that look on both her mom and Janet's face, and knew Ellie would stay there until Rayne gave in, Rayne sighed and did. "I think he's got ADHD."

"I've heard of that. What did the doctor say?"

"Doctor? Right."

"You didn't go to the doctor?"

"Ellie, I found him behind a garbage can. There's no doctor for kids like him."

"Sure there is."

Rayne just shook her head. Ellie might have seen a lot, but she hadn't seen anything near to what Rayne had seen. She had no idea what life was like for people on the streets. Around here she probably never would, and maybe that wasn't so bad.

"You don't know for sure that he's got ADHD then," Ellie pressed.

The door flew open. Tim slid across the floor on his wet clown feet and caught himself with his hands before his face hit the wall. He turned, streaking mud across the white paint and did a dance in the puddle on the floor.

"Yeah," Rayne muttered. "I think I do."

Tim stared at the mess his feet and hands had made. His lip trembled and his eyes filled with tears. "Oops," he whispered.

"Never mind." Rayne pulled him close, then met her gramma's gaze. "We'll stay in the barn until my father comes."

"Don't insult me. You'll stay in Kim's old room."

"Insult you?"

"Honey, family doesn't stay in the barn."

Aaron stood outside Mercy House and stared at the stars. They were much dimmer here than at home. He hadn't noticed last time. Probably because he'd been too dazzled by all the other lights in the sky.

The door opened behind him and Aaron spun around. His smile faded at the sight of Janet.

"She's gone to bed. You get back in here." She walked away, leaving the door open, expecting him to follow. Janet didn't need the camouflage to mark her as a general.

Wondering what she could possibly want with him, Aaron went back into the house.

"Have a seat." Janet gestured to the chair opposite her couch. The computerized ring of a cell phone made them both jump.

"Excuse me." Janet's hand went to her hip with the speed of a gunslinger. She drew the phone, flipped open the top with a flick of her wrist and answered. "Hello?"

The pleasant, welcoming expression on her face folded into a frown. "No, I can't send the Angel of Light out to kick someone's . . . butt for you."

Aaron's lips twitched. He shouldn't eavesdrop, but he couldn't exactly help it.

"Because he's not real."

She listened for a moment. "He seems real to you? Have you been drinking? Smoking? Shooting up?" Janet sighed. "All of the above. Well, no wonder then. Listen, I'm going to give you a phone number. Call it and someone will come to get you."

"No." She shook her head. "Not the Angel of Light."

Janet recited a number slowly, several times, then hung up.

"Another fan?" Aaron asked.

"Kind of. As a writer I guess I should be flattered that he thought the Angel of Light would be available by phone."

"But?"

"But as a human being, it creeps me out. How can anyone think fiction is reality?"

"Because truth is stranger than fiction most of the time?"

She studied him as if he'd just said something very clever, though he'd only recited a cliché, then smiled and patted his hand. "I'd offer you a drink, but we don't do alcohol here."

"And I don't drink."

"Why not?"

He shrugged. "Never cared for the taste. I'd rather have iced tea any day."

"Don't have any of that, either."

"It's good that I don't want any then." He remained silent, waiting for her to speak. When she didn't he sighed and spread his hands. "You didn't ask me in for tea. I got that. So what *did* you ask me in for?"

"Answers."

"Okay."

"What are your intentions with Nicole?"

He blinked. "Uh, um, well — I —"

"It's not a tough question, Aaron."

It was for him. Aaron remembered their embrace, his nearly unquenchable intentions.

But ever since he'd kissed her she'd been different. She no longer looked him in the eye. She avoided any incidental contact. She acted as if she couldn't bear the sight of him, and while he couldn't say that he blamed her, he didn't understand it, either.

She'd responded to his kiss the same way she had all those years ago. Because of that, the instant his lips had touched hers he'd been dragged right back to the night he'd given her everything and taken it, too.

He should be horrified to discover he wanted her still. Had he learned nothing at all from his mistake?

Obviously not, since he wanted to make one again.

And where would be the harm? whispered an insidious voice. They were adults and single. He was a farmer; she was a . . . social worker — sort of. They could have sex until their eyes crossed and no one would mind.

Aaron sighed. Except him.

"Nicole and I, we —"

"You what?"

He searched for what he meant and found it in a simple statement. "We're strangers."

"Strangers who share a child."

"Yes. But that doesn't make us any less strangers."

"So get to know her. For the sake of that child."

Aaron was tempted. He wanted Nicole, always had, and he was beginning to think he always would.

But a day in her presence had not only reawakened the lust, it had made him more and more intrigued with the woman Nicole had become. As they'd trolled the streets of Las Vegas searching for their daughter he'd gotten a glimpse of her life, and it was his.

She might have sneered at him for handing out a sandwich, but she meted out sustenance, too. Nicole answered questions and listened to troubles, referring people to any number of associations for as many different problems.

She wasn't a bleeding heart. She had little patience for fools. But for those who truly needed and wanted help she was there. Nicole was living the life Aaron had dreamed of, back when he'd bothered to dream.

He found himself captivated by it and by her. Not just because he wanted to take her to bed and keep her there awhile, but he also wanted to spend time with her, be with her. And that confused him more than the desire had. There was something about Nicole that called to the man he had forgotten.

Aaron lifted his gaze to Janet's. Her scowl had disappeared. She was watching him with something akin to sympathy in her eyes.

"Spill it," she ordered.

So he did. "She's . . . different."

"You thought she'd stay the same?"

"In my mind she did."

"She was in your mind a lot?"

Yes. Usually at night.

Janet lifted a brow as if she'd heard his thoughts. They were probably all over his face.

"I thought of her," he admitted.

"But you never called. Never wrote. Didn't you ever consider that you might have left more than a memory behind?"

He hadn't. Not once.

Once again she read his face, or maybe his mind. "Why not?"

"I thought she had taken care of . . . that."

"That? You mean birth control?"

Aaron nodded. Embarrassed, miserable. He'd never been any good at talking about the personal, probably because he'd never had much personal to talk about. But discussing sex and birth control with a seventy-year-old former nun was pushing it, even for him.

"You didn't ask her?"

"I wasn't exactly well versed in the etiquette."

"A virgin."

He didn't bother to answer since she hadn't asked a question. Instead, unable to sit still any longer, Aaron got up and paced the carpet.

"Why her?" Janet pressed. "You were what? Twenty?"

"Eighteen."

"And you'd never touched anyone before Nicole. Why?"

"Never wanted to."

"But you wanted to touch her."

He paused at the window and stared out at the street. "More than anything I'd ever wanted before."

"Then how could you leave?"

Aaron turned his back on the moon, a

silver sheen that cut through the soft blue of the night like a knife. "Everything I'd ever believed about myself was a lie."

Janet stared at him for a long moment. "What did you believe?"

"That I was on the path God had chosen for me, and I wouldn't slip off. That I was incorruptible." He gave a self-deprecating laugh. "Invincible. Ready to save the world from itself."

"My, oh my. You were asking for it, weren't you?"

"I'm sorry?"

"No one's that perfect, Aaron."

"The Angel of Light is."

"He isn't real. You are." She gentled her voice. "You wanted to be a superhero, but you're just a man. That's okay. We aren't supposed to be perfect. We're supposed to live and learn and —" She made an annoyed sound. "Would you sit so I don't get a crick in my neck?"

Aaron sat, though it was difficult to keep still when he was so agitated.

"You need to move on with your life, Aaron."

"I have." Even as he said the words, Aaron knew they were a lie. He'd existed; he had not lived.

"You went backward instead of forward."

"You think I should have been a priest?"

"No. There are too many men who are who shouldn't be. But you could have done any number of other things instead. There are so many different paths we can take. Who knows when a wrong turn might actually be a right?"

"I don't understand."

"I can't tell you how many times I've thought I've chosen the wrong way, and down that road I discovered greater riches than I could ever have imagined."

"Like what?"

"The Angel of Light stories were my way of rebelling against all the evil I saw in the world. I hid them, embarrassed by how angry I was. But in the end, they were a gift and not a curse. I've reached people in this format I couldn't have reached any other way."

"I've never been very good at traveling a different path than the one I'm on. I stepped off once and look what happened."

Janet sighed. He felt that he'd disappointed her, but he wasn't sure how.

"Nicole said you liked to help people. That you were good at it. You never considered an occupation where you'd be able to use that gift?"

"Like what?"

"Social work. Police work. Teaching."

Aaron shook his head. "How could I help anyone when I couldn't even help myself?"

"What is it that you did that you think was so wrong?"

Since he'd been over and over and over again the tally of his sins in the night, Aaron had no problem listing them now.

"Pride that someone so beautiful would even talk to me, greed for more of the same, envy at her freedom, anger at myself for the lust I couldn't control, gluttony of the spirit and sloth ever since I left this place."

"The seven deadly sins. You are a bad boy."

His hands clenched. "It's not funny."

"You're right. It isn't, because I can see you actually believe what you're saying. And you hate yourself." She shook her head, reached over and placed her gnarled hand atop his clenched one. "But God loves you."

He knew that as surely as he knew his middle name was John. But God's love had never been the issue. He knew that God loved him. He just couldn't understand why.

"You buried yourself on a dairy farm for what?" Janet lifted her hand from his and slid back on the couch. "Penance?"

Aaron shrugged. He'd never analyzed his life. He'd just endured it. He hadn't realized how unhappy he was until he'd come back here, seen Nicole and felt . . . reborn.

He blinked at the revelation. Since he'd returned he felt alive again. He didn't want to go back to the way things had been.

"So you've punished yourself for your sins. But what about Nicole?"

"Nicole did nothing wrong," he snapped.

Janet raised a brow at his vehement defense. "I never said she did. But Nicole managed to move on."

"She did. She's fine now."

"But why?"

"What?"

"Why is Nicole fine?" She repeated her question slowly, as if speaking to an idiot. Perhaps that was what Aaron was since he couldn't quite figure out what she meant.

When he continued to stare at her, Janet shook her head and answered her own question. "Did you ever consider that your sin was her salvation?"

Chapter Nine

Aaron continued to stare at Janet. He had no idea what to say. Then Nicole walked into the room and he couldn't say anything at all.

"Janet, I was thinking —"

She stopped dead at the sight of him, and the skirt of her powder-blue night-gown swirled around her bare feet. All he could do was stare. She was so pretty.

The shade of the cotton made her eyes more blue. The lace at the yoke made her skin appear as fine as clover in a meadow, as soft as a snowflake drifting silently through the night.

While he should be appreciating how the thin material outlined the weight and shape of her breasts, trailed across the flat plane of her belly and over the spike of her hip, before draping down her long legs to stop at her ankles and allow the glint of a gold ankle bracelet to wink in the light, all he could think about was how it had felt to walk with her by his side all day.

She crossed the room, yanked an afghan

from a chair and tossed it over her shoulders, before turning to face him again. "What are you doing here?"

He forgot his conversation with Janet, the theological questions and implications. *Sin? Salvation? Who cares?* his mind whispered as pure joy spread through him at the sight of her.

"Aaron?"

"Hmm?" He grinned like a fool.

Janet snickered. Nicole shot her a glare that would have made his mother proud, then turned the same on him. "You. Here. Why?"

"Um . . ." A hint of her scent, and he couldn't quite recall.

"We were talking." Janet interjected.

Nicole's eyes narrowed suspiciously. "About what?"

Aaron's dreamy inertia fled. Bringing up the past with Nicole would only make her sad again. Or mad. He wanted to avoid both.

"Nothing." She raised an eyebrow. "Well, nothing in particular. We were just getting to know each other."

Janet coughed. "Yeah. What he said."

"I thought there were no men allowed."

"I make the rules." Janet stood and faced Nicole with her hands on her hips. "I

180

wanted to talk to Aaron, so I did."

"Dictator," Nicole muttered.

"You got that right."

"If you were this sarcastic and cranky as a nun, it's a wonder they didn't make you take a vow of silence."

"You try being called Martha for forty years and see how you like it."

"I always wondered where you got the name."

Janet smirked. "Martha was a cranky Bible chick."

"That explains it then."

Aaron glanced back and forth between the two of them. He'd been raised in a household comprised mostly of men. Arguments were settled with fists and All Star Wrestling moves. Sarcasm and barbed comments were the realm of his mother and his sister. An exchange like the one he'd just heard would have resulted in a snarling match within minutes.

He held his breath as the two women stared each other down.

Nicole snorted. Janet laughed out loud. The older woman reached over and mussed the younger woman's hair. The fondness they felt for each other was palpable. Aaron realized he was smiling, too.

"So tell me, Nicky, what brings you

down here on the run?"

"Oh, right." Nicole shoved her hair away from her face in an absent gesture Aaron remembered so well. He didn't know her, not really, but there were times when he almost felt like he did. "Actually, I'm glad you're here, Aaron."

A warm, foolish glow spread through him at her words. From the moment he'd arrived she'd been telling him to go. Now she was glad that he was here.

"I'm glad I'm here, too, Nic."

Her eyebrows pulled together, and his foolish glow faded. He was no good at charming women. Never had been. Probably never would be. The question was: Why did he suddenly want to?

"I keep thinking about the phone number," Nicole mumbled.

"What phone number?"

"Yours. In my Bible."

He winced. "You kept my number in the Bible?"

"Where else?"

"Anywhere," he muttered.

"I didn't think anyone would look in there. Not even me."

Janet sighed. "You might find something useful one day if you try."

Aaron glanced at the older woman as a

flicker of sadness crossed her face, erasing the earlier laughter. It had to eat at her to know that Nicole had no use for God.

"I think I did find something," Nicole said slowly. "The day Rayne disappeared I thought the Bible had been moved, and I certainly hadn't moved it. I found Aaron's number stuck in Revelation."

"So?" Janet asked.

"I could swear I left the note in Genesis."

Aaron smiled. "The beginning."

Nicole shot him an unreadable glance.

Janet scratched her head. "You think Rayne found the note then put it back in Revelation?"

Clever girl, Aaron thought. The more he discovered about his daughter, the more he liked her.

"I think Rayne may have found the note and called the number."

"But I talked to Dean," Aaron interjected. "No one else called for me but you."

"How many people live in your house, Aaron?"

Aaron sighed. *Too many.*

"Hell." He crossed the room, picked up the phone and dialed.

Nicole followed and hovered near

enough to touch. As the muted *brrring* filled his ear, her scent teased him again. But coconuts no longer made him think of sand and sun and sex. Instead he thought of cream pie, the flicker of a candle's flame, warm against the chill of the night, and he had to resist the urge to pull her close and never let her go.

The receiver was lifted. As if to prove his earlier thought, the jumble of too many voices traveled over the line before his brother growled, "Yeah?"

"Hey. It's —"

"All right!" Aaron tensed. Dean was far too happy to hear from him. "Hold on."

Nicole sidled closer, peering into his face with a frown. "What?" she whispered.

He shook his head as the phone was picked up again in Illinois. "You are so busted, young man!"

The volume of the shout made him pull the phone away from his ear. He could still hear every word his mother said. So could Nicole.

"I just put your daughter to bed."

Nicole's quick intake of breath was filled with joy. "She's safe!"

Tears filled her eyes and without thought, Aaron reached out and pulled her to his chest.

His mother's voice went on. "Your *daughter!* She's thirteen. *Thirteen!*"

"Mom, you don't have to repeat everything. I can hear you." *Boy, can I hear you.*

"I *do* need to repeat everything since I must be dealing with a half-wit. Where on God's green earth are you?"

"Vegas."

That shut her up. "What? Why?"

"My daughter. I thought we established that."

"You knew about her?"

"Of course not."

An exasperated sigh flew hundreds of miles. "You'd better get your butt on the next plane so we can sort this out."

The thought of returning to Illinois put a damper on his joy at finding Rayne. He wanted to walk the streets of Las Vegas with Nicole, help everyone that they could, watch the sun set behind the mountains and the neon light the sky. He did not want to go back where he had merely existed; he wanted to stay here and live.

He sighed. "We'll be there tomorrow."

"We?"

"Nicole will be coming with me."

He glanced down at the bright blond head resting against his chest. His shirt was damp with her tears. His skin was warm wherever they touched. She felt good there. Real good.

"You think that's a good idea?" his mother asked.

"The best one I've ever had."

"I don't like this, John."

The clock in the hall chimed midnight. Thankfully Eleanor's days of crawling out of bed before the sun shone were a thing of the past. A thing of John's past, too, since his heart attack over a year ago and subsequent semiretirement.

Dean was in charge now, with a little help from Evan and Aaron, and a lot of help from his new toy — the robotic milking machine. It had taken a lot of time, and a lot of shouting, before John had agreed to a trial run of what he'd seen as creepy science fiction. But now he was as proud of the new machine as Dean was.

"What's the matter?" John turned to Eleanor and his hand slid over her hip. "Need a sleeping pill?"

She laughed and put her hand on top of his to keep it from creeping any farther north. John's idea of a sleeping pill was sex. Always had been.

"Not tonight."

"Got a headache?" He tugged her close.

"I got something for that, too."

"Not a headache." She sighed. "More like a heartache."

He pulled back and peered into her face. "Your chest hurts?"

Men. They were so literal.

She kissed his chin. "No. I'm thinking about Rayne."

He grinned. "Isn't she something?"

"Mmm.

"What does that mean? You don't like her?"

"Of course I like her. I'd have liked her for the last thirteen years, if I'd known she was alive."

Suddenly Eleanor couldn't sit still. She disentangled herself from her husband's arms and climbed out of bed. John gave an aggrieved sigh, which she ignored, and sat up, propping his back against the head-board. He crossed his arms and watched her pace.

"I have a thirteen-year-old grand-daughter I just met today. It makes me angry, John. Very, very angry."

"Have you been keeping up with your medication?"

She stopped pacing and scowled. "Every swing in my mood does not have to do with my hormones. I may be in menopause, but that doesn't make me crazy."

"Could have fooled me."

Eleanor resisted the urge to throw something, which would only prove his point. She *had* been a bit crazy a few years back. Her body had betrayed her with early menopause. She'd figured her husband would trade her in for a younger model — something he did with the cows, and sometimes she thought he liked them a whole lot better than he liked her.

She'd felt old and useless, cold and then hot, itchy, sad, on the verge of insanity. Coming on the heels of John's heart attack, and the return of the prodigal daughter, their lives had been in turmoil.

But they'd learned a new way of dealing with each other. They talked about their feelings. What a concept. And as a result their marriage, and their love life, had never been better.

Still, John was of the old school. Nothing could make him a girlie man or a bleeding heart liberal — the two worst things on the face of the earth in his opinion. He was a guy's guy, a man's man — a fool. So even though she loved him, that didn't prevent her from wanting to shake him half the time.

Eleanor took a deep, calming breath.

"I'm going to let that one pass," she murmured.

John shrugged, oblivious to what he had done to offend her. But he'd learned when to speak and when to just agree with anything she said and move on.

"We've lost so many years with Rayne," she continued. "Aaron lost them, too."

"Be happy we have her *now*. You worry too much, Ellie. You always have."

"I've always had plenty to worry about. My daughter runs off and doesn't come back for eight years. Only then do I find out she lost a baby and has been agonizing over it ever since."

"Kim's fine. She and Brian are married and Zsa Zsa is adorable. Your worries are over."

Ellie made an aggravated sound. "I shouldn't worry about Colin, off in some underdeveloped hellhole, getting dysentery because of his devotion to the people's right to know? I shouldn't get overly excited about Bobby's choice of profession? The Special Forces are sent where no one else wants to go. *I* don't want him to go."

"Bobby's serving his country. I'm proud of him."

"So am I. But we haven't heard from him in —" Her voice broke.

"Hey," John murmured. "If there was bad news, someone would have called."

She cleared her throat and blinked away the tears. "I know. I just —"

"Worry."

"A mother's prerogative."

The distant, muted thud of footsteps on the stairs made her glance at the door and frown. "Dean doesn't sleep."

"He never did. Even when he was a baby."

"He stayed up once for thirty-seven hours straight."

"And when you called the doctor he said, 'He should sleep more.' " John chuckled. "I thought you were going to make the doctor sleep. Permanently."

"I should have. The first rule of medical school ought to be Never get smart with a sleep-deprived new mother."

John smiled. "Or at least *this* sleep-deprived new mother."

She sighed and the sadness in the sound amazed even her.

"What else?" John asked.

"Evan will never settle down. He's got itchy feet and an even itchier —" Ellie broke off. "You know what I mean."

"He likes women. Better than not liking them."

Ellie rolled her eyes. John wasn't a

homophobe. Not quite. He just didn't understand people who were different from him.

"I want them all to be happy," she said. "To find someone to love, have a family, make a home."

"That's your idea of happiness. It might not be theirs."

"Aaron hasn't been happy since he came back from college."

"And now we know why."

"Do we? Was he unhappy because he left her? Or because he left God?"

"Hell if I know." She shot him a dirty look and he sighed. "They're all grown-up. You need to put the worry beads away."

"I can't. They're my children. They always will be."

"Things happen, Ellie. You suck it up and move on."

"Maybe *you* do. I want to know what she was thinking."

He patted the breast pocket of his pajamas, forever searching for cigarettes that were no longer there. For a while after he'd quit he'd kept a spare available at all times. Until she'd caught him with the spare in one hand and a match in the other. Since she'd torn that cigarette into itty-bitty pieces and threatened to make him eat it, she hadn't seen another.

"Who?"

"That woman."

He glanced around the room. "What woman?"

"Rayne's mother."

"What did she do?"

"Kept our granddaughter from us. And a daughter from our son."

"I'm sure she had her reasons."

"What reason could possibly explain thirteen years of silence?"

"You can ask her tomorrow."

"Rayne said her mom was angry when Rayne found out about Aaron. That after keeping her away from us all those years, suddenly she sent her off alone."

"Not alone." He smirked. "There's the Timinator."

"Who she kept in a storage closet."

"She did not. I have a feeling Rayne picked him up and sneaked him in."

"Like a stray puppy?"

"She's Aaron's daughter, remember?"

Eleanor smiled. Aaron had always brought home every stray in town — not that there were so very many in Gainsville. But if there were, they ended up at the Luchettis' for dinner.

She shook her head. "It's still odd for her

to send Rayne halfway across the country to strangers. Does that sound like the behavior of a rational woman to you?"

"*Rational* and *woman* do not go together in the same sentence."

"Har-har."

"A lot of what Rayne said doesn't add up."

"Are you saying that she's lying?"

"I'm saying we'll find out the truth tomorrow." He patted the mattress. "Now come to bed before you make yourself crazier."

She tilted her head. "Crazier?"

"Crazy," he said quickly. "I said crazy."

Eleanor sat down on the bed. "I'll just bet you did."

Dean stood on the porch and listened to the cows lowing in the pasture, watched the stars wink brightly at the night and waited for the peace such things had always brought him in the past to arrive.

He waited in vain.

The farm was everything to him. From the moment he could walk he'd followed his father — to the barn, the pigpen and the fields. He'd learned to gather eggs at the age of four, feed the cows before he was ten, drive a tractor by the time he was twelve. He could milk at dawn, make hay all day and milk again at dusk without complaint. Because he belonged here; he'd always known it. Still did.

In the past whenever he couldn't sleep, all he'd had to do was come outside and breathe the fresh air — for several hours. Dean sniffed.

It was fresh all right.

He scrubbed a hand through his close-cropped hair. What was the matter with him? He should be as happy as a pig in shit — one of his father's favorite sayings, and a darned good one if you knew any pigs. Dean had updated the farm. He was running it his way. The Luchetti place was the most modern facility in three counties.

So why did he feel so empty?

Dean fished a cigarette out of his pocket, then glanced around the empty yard. If his mom caught him his ass would be grass. She'd just gotten his father to quit after a love affair with nicotine that had lasted over forty years. If she saw her son taking up the habit, she'd lose what was left of her mind.

Shaking his head, Dean struck a match. He was twenty-nine years old and worried that his mommy might catch him smoking. No wonder he was miserable.

The screen door opened behind him, and he blew out the match, then sneaked the cigarette back into his pocket. No reason to beg for trouble.

But when he turned, Tim stood behind him dancing in the moonlight. "Take it to the end of the porch, kid, before you wet your pants."

He did. Seconds later the sound of liquid hitting the bushes made Bull, or was it Bear, yelp and start up from the shadows beneath the porch.

"Sorry," Tim whispered, or at least attempted to. A true whisper appeared beyond him.

The dog leaped up the steps and butted Dean's hand with his head. "Hey, Bull," he murmured. "Where's your pal?"

Dean's gaze searched the darkness. He gave a sharp whistle. But Bear did not appear. He cursed lowly.

"Whassa matter?"

Tim patted Bull on the head and received a face full of saliva as a reward, before the dog curled up at Dean's feet and closed his eyes.

"Bear's gone again."

"So?"

He wasn't sure how to explain to a kid of five or six that when a boy dog made a habit of disappearing it often meant there was a girl dog in the vicinity. With Bear, that was what it always meant.

There were enough puppies with spots in and around Gainsville to fill a small pet shop. One of these days, if he wasn't careful, Bear was going to get a butt full of buckshot. Maybe then he'd stay home. Then again, maybe not.

"Never mind," Dean told Tim. "He'll come back eventually."

Dean expected the boy to head up to his bed, but he didn't appear tired at all. In fact, he appeared as if he could dance all night, and he was going to.

"Relax, kid, you're makin' me nervous."

Tim froze. His smile fell. "Sorry," he repeated.

Dean cursed again, but this time in his head.

He put his hand on Tim's shoulder. The boy's skin was twitching beneath the thin cotton of the old T-shirt Dean had given him to sleep in. For an instant he wanted to pick Tim up and cuddle him close until he stopped shaking. But Dean had a feeling that no amount of cuddling was going to do any good. What was making Tim dance and twitch went a whole lot deeper than a hug could fix.

Instead he punched Tim lightly on the arm, as guys do, and winked. "Hey, don't let anything I say upset you. I talk first and think never. I don't mean to be mean, I just am."

Tim's eyes went round and he shook his head. "I've met mean and you're not it."

Dean frowned. "Who was mean to you?"

"People don't like me." Tim nodded sagely. "I'm annoying."

"Yeah? I get that all the time."

"You do? I never thought people would tell a grown-up he was annoying."

"You'd be surprised."

"There's somethin' wrong with me," Tim said in the lowest voice he seemed able to manage. "Everyone says so."

Sympathy tugged at Dean. He'd heard the same about himself, many times. He was not as charming as Evan, as patient as Aaron, as exciting as Colin or Bobby; he'd never be as smart as Kim.

But he was a big boy, and he didn't give a damn what people thought anymore. He was who he was and folks could like him or kiss his ass. However, he didn't feel that was a motto to be shared with the kid.

"You look fine to me," Dean said. "Nothing growing out of your nose." Tim giggled. "You don't smell — anymore." He squinted against the navy-blue night. "No body piercings where the sun don't shine, right?"

Tim's smile widened to an all out, toothy grin. "Nope."

Dean shrugged. "What's not to like?"

The boy sidled closer and leaned against Dean's leg. Dean gave in to the urge and ran a hand over the messy hair. "Tired yet?"

"No." Tim sighed. "I'm almost never tired."

"Me, neither."

"Drives people nuts."

Dean sighed, too. "I know."

They watched the moon and the stars until Bear came trotting home his mouth open in a lolling, idiotic doggy grin. Dean could have sworn he smelled French perfume.

"You're in trouble, mister." Bear snapped his mouth shut.

"Where were you?" The dog bowed his head.

"Stay in the *yard.*" Dean pointed at the ground for emphasis.

"*Bad* dog!" Tim announced, getting into the spirit of things.

Bear slunk under the porch.

"You think he'll stay now?" Tim asked.

"No."

Bear needed to be fixed. Dean winced in sympathy at the thought, but there was no alternative anymore. He'd given the dog a chance to reform, and Bear had been unable to. Sooner or later he was going to get hit by a truck as he went out on the prowl. Dean would rather have the dog lose his manhood than his life — though Bear would probably disagree.

"Come on, kid. I'll put you back where you belong."

"With Social Services?" Tim's voice wavered.

"In your bed. If my mom catches you awake you'll find out what annoying really is."

They climbed the stairs and Tim crawled into Bobby's old bed without argument. Dean went to his room. He didn't fall asleep right away, but when he did he slept better than he had in years.

When he awoke, he discovered Tim asleep at his feet, thumb firmly tucked into his mouth.

He stared at the boy and he wondered. Where did this kid belong?

For once, having a sister who was an almost lawyer might come in handy.

Chapter Ten

The plane banked over Chicago, the morning sun sparking brain-piercing beams off the windows in the high-rise buildings. The terrain in Illinois was so much different than in Nevada. Flat land instead of mountains, amber and green fields instead of sand.

They'd left Las Vegas in the wee hours of the morning. Nevertheless Nicole's last sight of the place had been filled with blinking neon. The city that never slept, until the sun rose anyway.

Nicole had never been on an airplane. She never wanted to be again. She'd spent the entire flight staring out the window, waiting for the ground to come up fast to meet them.

Aaron had tried to talk to her as they lifted off. He'd attempted to hold her hand as they climbed to their altitude. Nothing helped. She couldn't stop staring out the window.

"A lot of people feel more vulnerable since September 11," the flight attendant murmured when she delivered their complimentary bag of nuts. Her gaze went to Nicole's white-knuckle grip on the arms of her chair.

But Nicole's panic had nothing to do with the horrific images of that day. Rather they were a direct result of the belief that it was not a natural state for a human being to hurtle through the sky at thirty-five thousand feet. She wanted to be back on solid ground. Immediately.

As soon as possible after they landed, Nicole made a beeline for the door. Her fellow travelers, after one look at her drawn face, cleared the way.

She stepped off the plane. The gangplank swayed. Her stomach lurched. She walked faster, ignoring the bright lights in front of her eyes and the wobbling beneath her feet.

Her first step onto the carpet of the terminal was pure bliss. She stood there and let the other passengers stream around her as she soaked in the secure building and the firm floor.

Aaron was the last passenger to appear. His arms were filled with packages and bags that weren't his. Nicole sat down on a blessedly solid seat and waited as several older ladies and one frazzled mom with three young children, retrieved their carry-on baggage from him.

He glanced around the terminal, caught sight of her and smiled. That smile went straight to her heart and made it flutter. She wanted to kiss him right here and now.

Honestly, would the lust ever go away? It didn't appear likely.

"Sorry," he said as he hurried over. "I was —"

"Helping," she interrupted. "I saw. Did you pick up trash on the floor and any left-over soft drink cans with your teeth?"

He frowned at her sarcasm and it was Nicole's turn to apologize. "Never mind me. Jet lag."

She brushed her hair out of her face. Aaron cursed and grabbed her hand. "You're shaking, Nic, and your skin's ice-cold."

He tugged her from the seat and wrapped her in his arms. She knew she had to pull away, but she couldn't make herself go.

"You should have told me you were afraid of flying. We could have driven."

"I didn't know I was afraid until I saw the ground far, far away." She shuddered and his arms tightened.

"You've never flown before?"

"No reason to. And I hope I never have reason to again."

He chuckled and the movement rubbed his chest against her cheek. The fresh scent of soap on his skin and detergent on his clothes made her want to burrow closer, but she refrained.

"Never mind," she said. "If I have to be shaky and sick for a little while it's worth it to get to Rayne today."

Aaron inched back, keeping his arms around her, letting her decide when she felt well enough to step away. Since clinging to him wasn't going to help her get past the continual urge to slip her hands beneath his shirt and trace the muscles he'd refined over the last several years, she forced herself to release him.

At the loss of his warmth and support, she swayed. Aaron frowned. "You okay?"

Nicole gave a sharp nod. She needed to be strong. The sooner she stayed on her feet, the sooner she would see Rayne.

"How do we get to your farm?"

He eyed her a moment longer before replying. "My truck's in the remote lot. Since we've got a two-hour drive ahead of us, maybe you should sleep."

"I should, but I won't."

He raised a brow as he took her carry-on

and led the way through the terminal with long, brisk, confident strides. "Nervous?"

Nicole nodded. "Rayne's been unpredictable lately. Janet says she's thirteen, as if that explains everything."

"From what I hear, Janet's right."

"Rayne could be thrilled to see me, or refuse to speak to me at all. I have no idea what she'll say to you. And —" She broke off.

"And?"

"I have to meet your family."

He laughed. "They're nice. Really."

"How nice are they going to be to the ex-stripper who seduced their son."

Aaron snorted. "I seduced you, Nic, not the other way around."

She stopped dead in the middle of the terminal. Someone bumped into her from behind, muttered an uncomplimentary term and kept on going. Aaron was several feet ahead of her before he realized he was alone. He glanced back.

"You wanna keep up here?"

She hurried to join him. "You think you seduced me?"

"I know I did."

"How?"

"Don't you remember? We were watching the clouds one afternoon. You said you'd never seen anything so beautiful. Then I said I had and kissed you."

"You call that seduction?"

"For me it was."

"For me it was nothing I hadn't heard a hundred times before."

He didn't appear convinced. "If I didn't seduce you, then why did you sleep with me?"

She couldn't let him know how in love she had been. Or how in love she *thought* she had been.

"Because I decided I was going to have you the first time I saw your face."

Now it was Aaron's turn to stop dead and get bumped. He glanced at the hundreds of people swirling by them. "Maybe we better talk about this in the car," he said.

"Maybe we'd better."

They didn't speak again until they were ensconced in his blue pickup and had navigated the many twists and turns necessary to remove it from captivity and head southwest toward home.

The day was unseasonably hot for Illinois. If Aaron had been alone, he would have opened the windows and let the high speed breeze cool him down. But if he and

Nicole were going to talk, and they were, they had to, they'd never be able to hear each other inside the cab with the swirl of the wind and the squeal of the semi trucks on I-55.

Aaron punched a button and seconds later the neglected air-conditioning unit spurted cool air from the vents.

"Comfortable?" he asked.

Nicole shrugged. "I doubt I'll be comfortable until I have Rayne safely back at Mercy House."

"I meant the temperature."

"Oh. Yes. Thank you."

Silence settled over them once more. He wasn't sure how to begin, but Nicole didn't let him.

"When you said you'd betrayed my trust, I thought you meant by leaving."

He winced. "I guess I betrayed you twice."

"Aaron," she said gently. "You didn't betray me at all. I was a big girl. I knew what I was doing. Much better than you did. If anyone should be agonizing over betrayal, it should be me."

"No —"

"Let me finish."

He let out a breath, shut his mouth and nodded.

"I wanted you. I took you."

"You make me sound like a prime cut of beef."

She raised a brow. "Join the club."

He colored. "I suppose you've been treated like that all your life."

"Yes. Which only means I should have known better than to treat you the same. If it's any consolation, I felt bad. I tried to make up for what I did by keeping Rayne a secret. I truly didn't want to ruin your life by ruining your dream."

"As long as we're being honest here . . . can I ask you something?"

"Of course."

"How did it happen? Your getting pregnant?"

"You don't remember? I certainly do."

He hadn't thought he could blush anymore. But he was wrong. "I remember." *Everything. All the time.*

"I mean . . ." He lifted a shoulder. "You know."

"How did I *let* it happen?"

He nodded. "I know I should have asked, or done something, or gone out and bought something. I was —"

"Naive. Innocent. Seduced. You're right. I should have known better." She glanced out the window, her face dreamy, as if she were peering into the past. "You charmed me, Aaron. When I was with you I almost believed I was special."

"You were. You are."

Her wan smile said she didn't believe him, but she held up her hand when he started to argue. "I wanted you to touch me, but I didn't think you would. It's a tired excuse, but it's the only one I have. That night, there was only us. Birth control never entered my head. Until the morning after."

He sighed. "Well, it never entered my head period. Some Lothario I was, hey?"

"You did all right."

Though he knew it was foolish, he was unreasonably pleased with her comment.

Aaron continued to drive. The road was straight. The land on either side flat. He could see in every direction for miles. The terrain had always made him edgy — nowhere to run, nowhere to hide when disaster threatened. He'd been born here, but he'd never truly belonged. The only place he had was Las Vegas — both then and now.

Aaron glanced sideways. "There's something else that's been bothering me."

She raised her brows.

"Janet said you don't like men."

"Janet has a great big mouth," she grumbled. "I like men fine. But when I stepped foot inside Mercy House I promised myself no sex without love ever again. It makes me feel like that piece of meat you mentioned."

Though he should keep his mouth shut, Aaron couldn't help but ask. "There's been no one? Since . . . me?"

She hesitated, then shook her head. "No. No one. I haven't found anyone worth loving — except Janet and Rayne."

Why did he find that far too intriguing?

Despite her words to the contrary Nicole fell asleep. It was almost as if the conversation with Aaron had been cathartic. She hadn't told him the whole truth. He could never know that she'd believed herself in love with him and him with her. But she'd told him a hell of a lot. She felt less guilty. She hoped he did, too, but she doubted it.

Unfortunately, she dreamed of Aaron in ways she should not dream. Of sex without love, seduction, temptation and more.

She awoke with a start as his truck slowed, her skin humming with awareness, her body aching with need. When she felt like this, she had a hard time remembering

why she'd vowed never to have meaningless sex again.

"Welcome to Gainsville," Aaron murmured when he saw she was awake.

"Don't sound so excited."

"I'm not."

Nicole rubbed the sleep out of her eyes,
but they were still gritty. Her blouse was
wrinkled, her jeans creased. She wished
she could take a shower before she met his
family, but she'd just have to make do with
what she had — a comb and a stick of
gum.

"You don't like it here?" she asked.

"I'd rather be in Vegas."

"Ugh." She popped the gum into her
mouth and chewed ferociously.

He cast her a surprised glance and
turned a corner, then slowed even more as
they passed a modern hospital on the out-
skirts of town. The tall, gray monstrosity
seemed out of place in contrast to the
quaint main street of Gainsville.

"You don't like Las Vegas?"

"Loathe it."

"Then why do you stay?"

"Where else would I go?"

His gaze flicked over the town and he
sighed. "I hear you."

"What's the matter with Gainsville?"

"Not a thing. Gainsville is perfect. Everyone's happy."

"Somehow I doubt that."

"That everyone's happy?"

"And Gainsville is perfect. You don't have a few street people hiding somewhere?"

He snorted. "The last person who tried to sleep on the street was Freda Lallenheimer. Her husband locked her out after she came home from the Daughters of the American Revolution meeting at 3:00 a.m. singing selected offerings from the soundtrack of *Moulin Rouge.*"

Nicole giggled. Aaron slid a glance her way and his lips twitched. "Seems the daughters had broken out the peppermint schnapps in an attempt to cure the common cold."

"Does that work?"

"No. But you no longer care that you have a cold."

She laughed. "Then what happened?"

"The chief of police found Freda setting up housekeeping right about there." He pointed to a grassy green in the middle of the town square. "She'd stripped down to her slip and was brushing her teeth in the water fountain. The chief took her home, where his wife was already sleeping off the effects of her own cold medicine."

"Then Freda's husband picked her up in the morning?"

"Actually Fred said the chief could keep her."

Nicole choked. "Fred and Freda?"

"Uh-huh."

"And did the chief let her stay?"

"For about two weeks. Then he couldn't stand one more rendition of 'Diamonds Are a Girl's Best Friend' and dropped Freda off at home. She and Fred pretended that nothing had ever happened."

Nicole couldn't stop smiling. "I take it no one goes hungry here, either."

"Are you kidding? That's what the ladies' auxiliary is for. Word gets around that a family is having tough times and food magically appears on their doorstep, attributed to the food fairies, of course. Illinois farmers have their pride."

"Of course." She sighed. "Gainsville does sound perfect."

They reached the far side of town, and Aaron accelerated onto the highway. "Nothing's perfect."

"No?" She drew the word out long enough to be sarcastic. "Do tell."

He shrugged. "There are recreational drugs. They're everywhere these days. The biggest problem is alcohol. Kids are bored. They have parties on someone's back forty, then get in the car to drive a long way home on single-lane roads that have never seen a streetlight. Rural communities lose more kids to drunk driving than you'd expect."

"I guess every silver lining has its cloud."

Aaron didn't answer, and Nicole glanced his way only to find him staring intently through the windshield. "There it is," he whispered.

She followed his gaze to the three silver silos reaching for the sky. Her heart gave a sharp, painful thud.

"You think she'll like me?" Aaron asked.

"I was going to ask the very same thing."

"Rayne loves you."

Nicole released a long, wavering sigh. "I was talking about your mother."

Chapter Eleven

The truck turned into the long, winding gravel lane that led to a three-story stone farmhouse surrounded by fields and white outbuildings. As they got closer Nicole saw that the porch was filled with people.

Her heart, which had already been thundering pretty fast, increased in pace. She began to get a headache behind her right eye. "Who are all those people?"

Aaron cursed — a rarity, which only revealed his agitation.

"That's about half my family."

"Only half?"

Her voice squeaked and Nicole cleared her throat. She would not meet his family sounding like Minnie Mouse. She would not lose her cool with Rayne. She would be a calm, mature adult. She had to be.

Aaron parked the truck next to several others just like it — their only variation the color. Anxious to see Rayne, though her daughter didn't appear to be a member of the welcoming committee, Nicole opened her door before the engine died.

Two Dalmatians shot from underneath the porch, barking like slavering hell-hounds. She shrieked and dived back into the car. The dogs hit the door with a thud. Everyone on the porch laughed.

"They're harmless," Aaron said.

Nicole glanced out her window where the animals continued to leap and bark as if trying to get inside and devour her. She shrunk toward Aaron. "They don't look harmless to me."

"You're afraid of dogs?"

"I guess so."

"Guess?"

Her nervousness and fear got the better of her and she snapped, "How should I know, Aaron? These are the first ones I've been around for more than a minute."

Instead of getting angry, too, and snapping right back as she no doubt deserved, he patted her knee. "Stay here."

He climbed out. "Would someone put the dogs in the barn, please?"

One of the men, clothed in work boots and muddy jeans, separated from the others and whistled to the Dalmatians. They followed obediently. Nevertheless, Nicole stayed inside the cab until the barn door closed behind them.

"Nic?" Aaron leaned back in through the door. "Ready?"

"No."

He smiled. "I'll be right next to you."

Sighing, she got out of the car. As they walked toward the house together she noticed so many things. The smell of grass and dirt, the bellow of something big and angry behind the barn, the heat of the morning sun on her head a sharp contrast to the coolness of Eleanor Luchetti's gaze.

She felt completely alone, until Aaron stepped closer and took her hand. Eleanor's eyes narrowed. Nicole tried to tug free, but he wouldn't let her go.

"Where's Rayne?" Aaron asked before he even said hello.

"Upstairs." His mother continued to stare at their joined hands. "She's upset. She didn't want to talk to her mother, and she didn't want to meet her father for the first time in the front yard."

Nicole winced. Aaron tightened his fingers around hers, and she found the courage to speak. "Mrs. Luchetti, I'm glad to —"

A small boy erupted from the house, leaped off the steps and ran full speed in their direction.

"What the — ?" Aaron muttered.

The kid stopped in front of Nicole and grinned. "Hi. You're Rayne's mom. I'm Tim. I hear you took your clothes off for money. Sounds like fun to me. I take my clothes off every day and no one pays me for it."

Her face flamed. Her eyes burned. She raised her gaze to Aaron's family. They all appeared as shocked as she was.

"Where did this kid come from?" Aaron demanded.

The boy slapped his hand over his mouth and scooted across the lawn to hide behind the man who had incarcerated the Dalmatians.

Eleanor crossed her arms over her chest and stared at Nicole. "He came with Rayne."

"What?" Nicole yelped.

"His name's Tim, and Rayne has been keeping him in your storage room."

A near audible click sounded in Nicole's head. This was what Rayne had been hiding before she'd disappeared. Not a boyfriend or drugs or a failed math test. But another stray.

"I want to see her," she said.

Nicole thought she saw a flicker of interest in Eleanor's cool blue eyes, but it was gone the instant the older woman shrugged. "She's upstairs." Eleanor glanced at Aaron. "In Kim's room."

"Let's go." Aaron led her toward the house.

"Aren't you going to introduce your . . ." Eleanor's voice trailed off and she frowned. "Uh, your, um. Well, *her* — to your family?"

A petite young woman, who resembled Rayne enough to be her sister, and therefore must be Aaron's, stepped forward, jiggling a darling baby girl on her hip. "Sheesh, Mom, you'd think you were born in a barn."

Eleanor turned her attention to her daughter, and Nicole was glad to have the force of those eagle eyes off her for a moment.

"Watch it," Eleanor snapped.

The girl ignored her mother, which made Nicole wonder. Did mothers and daughters behave the same, generation after generation?

"I'm Kim Riley, Aaron's sister." Kim jerked her head at the tall man with the sun-kissed skin and sun-streaked hair who stood at her side. "My husband, Brian." He winked. The pressure in Nicole's chest eased a little.

"And this is Glory." Kim wiggled the baby's funky straw hat.

The little girl scowled and yanked it firmly back on her head. She kicked her feet, became interested in her purple sandals and leaned over to pat them and coo. The band around the crown of her hat perfectly matched the shade of the shoes and the material of her sundress.

"We call her Zsa Zsa," Brian added. "It was Dean's idea."

He nodded at the man who had put the dogs in the barn. Dean flicked his index finger off the top of his head as a greeting. Nicole smiled, though the expression felt forced. Everyone was being friendly, trying to pretend the embarrassing moment with Tim hadn't happened. Nicole wanted to pretend that, too, but she was too busy trying to pretend Eleanor wasn't still staring at her.

The need to say something, anything, overwhelmed her. "Why Zsa Zsa?"

"Dean thinks our place is a lot like *Green Acres*," Kim explained.

That sounded intriguing. But a puzzle tickled the back of Nicole's mind and she frowned. "Wasn't that Eva Gabor?"

"So sue me," Dean muttered. "I'm not the king of classic television. She looks more like a Zsa Zsa anyway."

Nicole glanced at the baby, who was still

talking to her purple shoes. "I agree," she murmured, and earned a grin from Aaron's gruff brother.

Someone cleared his throat. Nicole peered up at the tall, lanky man with eyes just like her daughter's. She liked him instantly.

"I'm John. Aaron's dad. Welcome."

His smile was warm, very much like Aaron's, and actually made her feel welcome. "Thank you."

"Knock, knock," he said.

"Not now," Eleanor barked.

John ignored her, as Kim stifled a laugh.

"Ahem." John lifted a brow.

Nicole shrugged. "Who's there?"

"John."

"John who?"

"John with the wind."

Kim choked, snorted and started to laugh. Brian chuckled. Zsa Zsa clapped her hands as she bounced up and down on her mother's hip. Everyone else just rolled their eyes.

John stared at Nicole expectantly. She gave a wan smile. "I'm sorry. I've never really understood knock-knock jokes."

John's shoulders slumped. "She's one of yours," he informed his wife.

Eleanor scowled but didn't comment.

Nicole glanced at Aaron and spread her hands helplessly.

"Never mind," he muttered. "I don't get them, either."

He urged her up the porch steps and the crowd parted. They went through the screen door. It banged behind them and made Nicole jump.

At the foot of the staircase, she hung back. He understood immediately and placed a hand on her shoulder. "It'll be all right."

She stared into his eyes, and for the first time in a long time, she didn't feel alone. Having Aaron at her side gave Nicole the courage to climb the steps, then pause at the bedroom door and do the right thing.

"I need you to wait here a minute."

"What? No. I want to see her."

"You will. But she's going to be angry. Let her get it out at me. I don't want your first meeting to be a bad memory."

"I don't want you to do this alone. You've done too much alone already."

She touched his face. He was so sweet, so damn *nice* she wanted to shake him. "I *have* done too much. So let me fix it as best I can. Please?"

She could tell he didn't want to let her

go, but he did. Because she asked him to. And for that alone, she adored him.

Rayne paced from one end of Kim's room to the other. From the moment she'd gotten out of bed that morning things had gone downhill.

When she'd come into this room last night, she'd been happy. She was safe. Her grandparents loved her and she loved them. She was a thousand miles away from her mom, and she didn't have to deal with meeting her dad. Yet. Life was good.

Then at seven this morning, Ellie had knocked on the door and woken Rayne from the best sleep she'd had in a week with the words, "Your dad and your mom are on their way from Las Vegas."

After her initial surprise at hearing her father had gone to Vegas and was returning with her mom, Rayne got nervous. Now she would have to deal with meeting him and getting yelled at by her mom at the same time.

Topping off her lousy morning was the absence of Tim, who had suddenly become Dean Luchetti's shadow. He'd even slept with him last night instead of her. Though the break from his chatter was welcome, Rayne had to admit she felt abandoned and just a tiny bit mad.

The tiny bit had grown larger as the morning wore on. Her aunt Kim, uncle Brian and cousin Zsa Zsa had arrived before eight. People around here seemed to get up with the sun — and they enjoyed it.

Though Rayne liked her aunt — Kim was irreverent enough to be fun — she soon tired of hearing the remarks about the uncanny resemblance between them. All the Luchettis seemed to think it was wonderful. Rayne just found it spooky.

She became quieter and quieter as the hours passed. Zsa Zsa fell asleep right in the middle of the living room floor. The baby just laid her head down, closed her eyes and crashed. Since she'd been woken at what to Rayne was practically the middle of the night, she wanted to lie down and crash, too.

After a glare from Kim when they became too loud and nearly woke Zsa Zsa, the men had dragged Tim outside to observe Dean's pride and joy, a robotic milking machine that Rayne secretly thought of as "cows in space."

Her gramma was showing Rayne yet another photo album filled with pictures of her father at every stage of life, though there were far more of him in his first year than in any year thereafter.

"Baby photos are a casualty of too many children," Ellie explained.

Rayne's attention wandered and was brought back when Kim whispered something to her mother. Ellie glanced at Rayne.

"Why don't you go on up to your room, honey, and rest until you mom comes."

Right. Like she could relax knowing the father she'd thought dead was going to show up at any moment.

But the opportunity to be alone with her churning, whirling thoughts was too great to resist, so Rayne escaped upstairs. She'd been hiding here ever since.

She was not only scared but furious. Her stomach burned; her chest hurt. She was getting a headache.

She'd heard the truck drive into the yard fifteen minutes ago. The barking of the dogs had been followed by the slamming of car doors, then the murmur of voices. One loud and high pitched revealed that Tim was down there meeting her dad before she could.

Rayne kicked the bed, then hopped around as pain ricocheted through her toe.

Didn't her mom miss her? Wasn't she worried? Didn't her dad want to see her?

Rayne grew angrier and angrier so that when she heard footsteps on the stairs at last, she was ready to erupt.

And erupt she did, the moment her mother opened the door and stepped into the room. That her father was nowhere in sight did not help Rayne's disposition.

"I am *not* going home!" she shouted.

Nicole stared at Rayne as if she'd never seen her before. Of course she hadn't seen *this* her. Insane Rayne was a new character development courtesy of the last few months.

"We don't have to make any decisions right this minute." Her mom spoke low and calm. She didn't make any fast movements.

That she was treating Rayne like a rabid animal — even though she deserved it — only made Rayne madder. She had a right to be mad, she told herself. No one was going to talk her out of it, not even her mom.

"Decisions? You can't make a decision. Or at least not a right one. Whose idea was it to keep my father from me? Obviously not his. He never even knew I existed. Did he?"

Her mother rubbed her forehead. For a minute Rayne felt bad. She had never gone hungry. She had never been hit. She knew she was loved. Tim would give his right toe for a mom like hers. However, the way Rayne felt right now, Tim could have her.

She glanced at a picture of all six of the Luchetti children, which sat on Kim's dresser. Her gaze zeroed in on the man her gramma had pointed out as her father. Rayne's anger returned as hot and as uncontrollable as it had been moments before.

Her mother had lied to her for thirteen years and that was something Rayne could not forgive. Not yet.

"How could you?" Rayne didn't shout, but it was close.

"I did what I thought was best."

There seemed to be another person inhabiting her body. A screaming, furious, nasty girl who bore no resemblance to the Rayne she had believed herself to be.

Lately, any little inconvenience could overwhelm her and make her cry. Any unkind word she took to heart and agonized over. She no longer knew herself and it scared her. Because she was scared, Rayne lashed out.

"I don't want to be with you. I don't want to see you. Go away."

Nicole didn't cry. She didn't shout. If Rayne had been in any condition to think clearly, she would have admired her mom's courage. As it was, her calm goaded Rayne to further heights of nastiness.

"I hate you," she shouted.

The door opened. Aaron Luchetti stepped into the room. Rayne wanted to swallow her tongue, melt into the floor, anything to be gone from here and the knowledge that her father's first impression was of her being a brat.

But he smiled pleasantly and said nothing at all. As he closed the door behind him, Rayne observed the end result of her daddy quest.

He was older than he appeared in any of the pictures Rayne had seen. Shorter than she'd expected, too, although he wasn't exactly short. The sun had streaked his hair and darkened his skin, making his eyes shine neon blue. Tiny white lines streaked out from the corners where he'd squinted against the glare.

Rayne took all this in, even as anger replaced her mortification. She glared at her mom. "He was listening to the whole thing?"

Nicole shrugged. "I wanted to talk to you first. I needed to explain."

"There's no way you can explain what you did."

"She did what she thought was best," Aaron repeated.

"For who? Her?"

"If she'd been interested in the easy way out there were several other paths she could have chosen."

"You're saying I'm lucky to be alive?"

Rayne couldn't believe how belligerent she sounded. Her mother stared at her as if an alien had invaded her body. Funny, because Rayne felt as if something ugly and evil just might burst from her chest. She wanted to calm down, be charming and sweet, but she couldn't.

"We're all lucky to be alive," he said. "What I meant was, your mother could have had a much easier time if she'd called me or my family. But she chose to raise you on her own, to make my life easier."

The gaze he turned on Nicole was full of admiration and Rayne frowned. What was going on here? If he liked her mom so darned much, why had he left her behind?

Before she could ask, Aaron continued. "In my opinion, your mom made the wrong decision, but she did it for the right reasons."

"Thank you," Nicole whispered.

Rayne snorted, breaking the warm and fuzzy mood. Aaron sighed. Her mother headed for the door. "I think I'll leave you two alone for a while."

"Good idea," Rayne muttered, though a part of her wanted to cry out for her mother to stay, not to leave her with this calm and reasonable stranger. But Nicole never gave Rayne a chance to agree or disagree. She just opened the door and slipped outside.

The room went silent. Rayne glanced at her father. He stared at her as if he were observing one of the seven wonders of the world.

"What?" she asked. "Do I have spinach in my teeth?"

Why she was taunting him, Rayne had no idea. But he didn't appear angry. Instead, he laughed. "No. You're the most beautiful thing I've ever seen."

Rayne's face heated. She shuffled her feet, shifted her shoulders, glanced away, then back. He was still gazing at her with an expression she could only describe as fascinated. No one had ever looked at her like that before. That he could look at her like that now, after the scene she'd just made . . .

"I — I'm usually not such a . . ." Her voice tailed off. She didn't know how to describe her behavior.

"Disagreeable young lady?" he suggested.

That was putting it mildly. She'd been thinking more along the lines of snotty little bitch. Of course she'd only met him five minutes ago, and Rayne already knew Aaron Luchetti would never think anything so rude, let alone say it.

Rayne shrugged. "It must suck to discover you have a daughter like me."

"Like you? What do you mean by that?"

He appeared confused. As if her outburst had been nothing uncommon, and her nasty words to her mother were already a thing of the past. Too bad Rayne could still hear them echoing in her head.

"I think I'm losing my mind," she blurted. "One minute I'm angry, the next so excited I can't sit still. Little things make me sad. Big things make me insane." She took a deep breath and expressed her newest fear. "Do you think I'm crazy?"

"I think you're thirteen." He smiled. "I've heard all this before, watched a perfectly good sister turn into a raving lunatic. As awful as you're feeling, as badly as you're behaving, you're normal, Rayne."

"*This* is normal?"

"As normal as thirteen gets."

"Swell," she grumbled. "I was hoping I

could take a pill and it would all go away."

"No such luck. You're just going to have to live through it like the rest of us did." He paused. "You want to go downstairs with everyone else?"

She shook her head. She didn't want to share him. Not yet.

"How did you find out about me?" she asked.

Quickly he explained how he'd ended up in Vegas while Rayne had ended up here.

"Fate," she muttered.

"God," he returned.

"You believe in God?"

"Why wouldn't I?"

"You didn't become a priest."

"Not because of any failing in God. It was a failing in me."

"Because of me." She looked down.

"No." Aaron waited until she raised her head and met his eyes. "I didn't know about you, so you had nothing to do with it."

"Mom —"

"Your mom, either. My failings are my own." He tilted his head as if listening to another voice. "Someone told me once that a wrong turn can become a right."

"You've been talking to Janet."

"How did you know?"

"I've been living with her for thirteen years. I can quote the woman in my sleep."

"She's a very wise lady."

"She likes to think so."

Aaron grinned. "And do you let her?"

"Of course."

Silence descended again. The low rumble of John's voice drifted from downstairs, punctuated by Tim's high-pitched chatter. Zsa Zsa laughed and Rayne found herself smiling.

"You like it here?" Aaron asked.

"Yeah. A lot. I don't want to go back yet."

"All right."

All right? Just like that? He hadn't even asked her mom.

She liked her father more with each passing moment.

Aaron couldn't take his eyes from his daughter. She truly was the most beautiful thing he'd ever seen. She was dressed in bell-bottom jeans and a tie-dyed T-shirt. Her feet were bare, her toenails, too. She wore no makeup and her hair was held back with a headband that matched her shirt. Though she resembled Kim, she reminded him very much of his mother.

Aaron wished that for just an instant he

could shrink her back to babyhood, listen to her babble, hold her close against his chest and rock her to sleep. He wanted to see her first smile, watch her first step, buy her first bike.

Frustration bubbled in his belly. He had missed so much. There was no getting it back.

Life wasn't fair. But then who had ever promised it would be?

Regardless of what he'd missed, Aaron couldn't be angry at Nicole. Rayne was angry enough for them both.

Though they should join the others, he couldn't make himself go. He wanted to have more time with her, just the two of them.

Rayne sat on the bed, her face open and curious. She was as easygoing now as she'd been tense and awkward before.

Sudden changes in mood were to be expected at her age. Not only did she bear an uncanny physical resemblance to his sister, but it appeared that Rayne was going to have the same trip through the hormone minefield that Kim had endured.

"You like school?" he asked, then cursed himself for the typical, stupid adult question.

She shrugged. "Not really."

He frowned. "Why not?"

"I get teased."

His hands curled into fists automatically. What had gotten into him? A man who detested violence, he had suddenly become mighty violent.

Aaron forced himself to release his fingers and speak calmly. "What about?"

"I dress funny. I live in a halfway house." She pressed her lips into a tight line and glanced out the window.

"You've got no dad?"

She shrugged again, then nodded.

"These days I'd be surprised if that was a novelty."

"It's not. But that doesn't mean kids won't make fun of you for it."

"I suspect kids are just as nasty now as they were when I was young."

Rayne glanced at him with interest. "You got teased?"

"All the time."

"Why?"

"I did all my homework. Got straight A's. Never misbehaved."

"Geek-o-rama," Rayne said dryly.

"You bet. I didn't have many friends."

"I don't, either. I never fit in. The stuff the girls talk about is so stupid. Who cares if your lipstick is tea rose pink or scrumptious peach when there are people sleeping in alleys and starving in the richest country in the world?"

Aaron found himself staring again.

"What?" she asked, a hint of annoyance creeping into her tone as she swiped a palm over her nose. "Something sticking out?"

He shook his head. She was so blunt, honest, original. He was fascinated with everything about her.

"This is just so strange," he murmured.

"I know I'm weird," she snapped. "I don't need *you* to tell me something I've heard a hundred times before."

"No." He moved closer and laid his hand on her shoulder. He figured she'd jerk away. When she didn't he left his hand right where it was.

"I had the same problem when I was your age," he said. "I was worried about the starving masses in Africa while everyone else was concerned about losing the football game, even my brothers. They could barely tolerate me, either. I was the family embarrassment. I liked to take up collections in the lunchroom and send the money to Southeast Asian orphanages."

Instead of laughing, Rayne's eyes widened. "Great idea," she breathed.

"You like that one? I got quite a few others."

Before Aaron could list the many geeky things he had done to embarrass his family all of his life, his mother started ringing a cowbell downstairs.

Rayne shrieked and leaped off the bed.

Aaron grabbed her shoulders. "It's okay. That's just my mom calling us to lunch."

"Sheesh," Rayne muttered. "Is everyone deaf around here?"

"They are now."

She snickered. Aaron squeezed Rayne's arms and released her. She hesitated, as if she wanted to hug him but she didn't know how. He took a step toward her, but she headed for the door.

Aaron sighed. Despite the connection they'd established in the last hour, they were still strangers. He couldn't rush the relationship. He couldn't force her to love him.

He'd be patient. They'd have time. He wasn't going to let Rayne walk out of his life now that he had found her.

Chapter Twelve

Eleanor couldn't stop staring at Nicole. Not even when John kicked her under the table and glared.

Nor when Tim piped up, "Whatcha starin' at Rayne's mom like she's a bad girl for?"

Even her son's pleading expression, his mouthed plea of "Mom!" did nothing to keep her eyes from returning to Nicole Houston as if she were metal and Eleanor the magnet.

So this was the woman who had ruined her son's life.

She knew she was being unfair. In fact, she was being downright unreasonable. From what she'd gathered in bits and pieces of the conversation over lunch, more mistakes than just Nicole's had gone into the making of this mess.

Eleanor Luchetti had never been one to hold a grudge. Life was too damn short. So what was the matter with her now?

It wasn't as if she'd wanted Aaron to be a priest. She'd wanted him to be happy.

And he hadn't been.

But the question remained: Had he been miserable because he'd left God or because he'd left Nicole?

Did Aaron know the answer? Was he aware of the question?

Eleanor muttered beneath her breath. Everyone ignored her. Even Nicole.

She had to say the girl was a cool one. No matter how hard or how long Eleanor glared, Nicole kept her attention on her plate.

Of course she'd danced naked on a stage, so she'd probably learned to ignore a lot worse than the stares of an old lady.

But what had Aaron seen in her? Oh, Nicole was beautiful. She should be on the cover of a magazine, or perhaps in the center. Eleanor understood why most men would throw themselves on the ground at Nicole's feet and beg. But she would never understand why Aaron would.

She'd always figured her son's taste would run toward a plain, passive, pious woman. Someone who needed help and needed him. Nicole didn't appear to need anyone — except her daughter — the only thing she and Eleanor seemed to have in common.

"How long can you stay, Nicole?"

John's question had Eleanor leaning forward in her chair. Nicole frowned, glanced at Rayne, who was *not* looking at her mother as hard as Eleanor *had* been.

"I don't want to leave Janet on her own at Mercy House any longer than I have to. It wouldn't be fair."

"What would you know about fair?" Eleanor muttered.

"Ellie," John snapped.

Aaron gave her his "I'm so disappointed in you" glare.

Nicole faced her. "You seem to be angry with me, Mrs. Luchetti. I'd like to know why."

A flicker of admiration for the girl's guts made Eleanor hesitate, but only for an instant. "I missed thirteen years of my granddaughter's life. Aaron missed them, too."

"I'm sure you'd have been thrilled to have a stripper show up on your doorstep with a baby."

"I'd have been thrilled to have my grandchild show up any time. And by the way, what possessed you to put a child on the bus and send her halfway across the country to strangers?"

Nicole tilted her head. "I what?"

"Oh, oh," Rayne muttered.

Everyone looked at her. She shrugged sheepishly. "I — uh — well, you see, I kind of —"

"Lied," Ellie stated.

"Yeah. I'm sorry. I know I shouldn't have. But I was afraid if you knew I'd run away, you'd call my mom."

"In a heartbeat."

Rayne stared down at her lap. Ellie shifted her gaze to Nicole. The woman must have been frantic. A wave of sympathy washed over her, but Ellie shoved it away. She needed to remember that Nicole had kept Rayne from them for far too long.

"I'm so disappointed in you, Rayne," Nicole murmured.

Rayne's head came up and her face wore a belligerent expression. "Just like I am with you."

"That's enough," Aaron interjected. "We're not going to waste time blaming each other anymore. What's done is done. Now we deal with it."

"I'm the *it* you're dealing with." Rayne stood and glared across the table at her mother. "And I'm not leaving. You can't make me."

Nicole's mouth opened and closed like a fish in polluted water. She didn't seem to be able to get any air. Hadn't Rayne ever talked back before? Eleanor was shocked and more than a little bit impressed. If she were being honest, Nicole had to have done something right for Rayne to have become the capable, empathetic young woman she was. Not many thirteen-year-olds would have taken responsibility for Tim or would have cared for him as well as she had despite his problems.

"Why should I have to make you?" Nicole asked. "Your home is in Las Vegas."

"My family is here."

"But —"

"I'm not leaving!" Rayne shouted and ran from the room.

The silence was broken by the slamming of Kim's bedroom door.

"Ah, just like old times," John murmured.

A burst of laughter lessened the tension.

"Should I go and hug her now?" Tim asked, his lower lip trembling.

"Nah," Dean said. "She wants to be alone, and believe me you want to leave girls alone when they're like that. Right, Princess?"

He glanced at Kim. She stuck out her tongue. Zsa Zsa giggled and did the same.

"Nice," Eleanor muttered. "Excellent example."

Kim rolled her eyes. Brian distracted his daughter with a cracker.

Tim didn't appear convinced, but Dean patted him on the back, then kept his hand there just in case. Her son seemed to understand just what Tim needed, a miracle in compassion considering Dean's usual lack of care for anything that didn't go *moo.*

"I apologize," Nicole murmured. "Rayne's never been like this before."

Eleanor shrugged. "She's going to be like it again. And again and again. Girls stomp and shriek." She gave Dean and Aaron a pointed glare. "Boys grunt and mutter."

"I remember thirteen." Kim plucked the cracker from Zsa Zsa's hand before the baby could throw it on the floor. "Everything's a tragedy."

Nicole frowned. "It is?"

"Weren't you ever thirteen? Nothing goes right. Your parents are idiots." She threw Eleanor an impish grin and winked. "Your friends are the only ones who understand."

"I never had any parents. Or too many friends, either."

Kim's smile faded. "Sorry," she said. "My mom drove me nuts. Which, now that you've met her, I'm sure you can understand."

Nicole choked and focused on her hands, tearing her napkin into tiny pieces in her lap. Eleanor almost felt sorry for her. This couldn't be easy.

"No parents?" Dean asked. "How did you manage that?"

"I got dumped," she said flatly.

"Just like me," Tim announced. "Did you have ants in your pants, too?" He bounced up and down on his heels in the chair as if to illustrate.

Nicole shook her head. "No. I was too little for them to know much about me."

Tim quieted at the thought of being dumped for no reason at all. He climbed down from his chair and into Dean's lap.

Eleanor tensed, expecting her cranky, impatient son to say something rude, then shove Tim away. Her eyes widened when Dean shifted so that the boy could snuggle against his chest.

"I guess I should be happy I had a mom." Kim glanced at the ceiling as Rayne stomped across the floor and —

A thud, which sounded very much like a foot striking against the bedpost, came through loud and clear. Silence followed.

Eleanor contemplated her son and

his . . . what was she? Not wife, not girl-friend. Lover? Well, not anymore.

This was too complicated. She had to do something.

"You should stay a few days," she blurted.

Nicole's head came up so fast Eleanor feared she might get whiplash. "Ma'am?"

"Ellie," she said, sighing when Aaron and John both beamed at her. She'd given the woman permission to use her name not be her everlasting pal.

Nicole nodded but didn't repeat the name. "Won't our staying be too much trouble for you?"

Eleanor shrugged. "Trouble seems to be the order of my week."

"Mom, could you be more rude?" Aaron asked.

"Yes. But I'm trying not to. Nicole can stay in Bobby and Colin's room." She took a deep breath to fight the usual sense of panic any mention of her two wandering sons brought to her heart. "It isn't as if either one of them will be using it any time soon."

Aaron, always sensitive to every nuance of her voice, gave Eleanor a sharp glance. "No word?"

"None," she sighed. "From either one of them."

"My brother, Bobby, is in the Special

Forces," he told Nicole. "We haven't heard from him in several months."

"Is that unusual? Don't the Special Forces get sent out on secret missions and —" she shrugged "— stuff?"

Eleanor snorted. "All kinds of stuff."

Aaron narrowed his eyes but didn't say a word. "We usually hear from Bobby more often. To top it off, my brother Colin, who's a foreign correspondent, is covering a story in the Middle East. We haven't heard from him, either."

"I'm sorry," Nicole said. "That must be very difficult for all of you."

The compassion in her voice was genuine, and Eleanor experienced a tug of camaraderie. Nicole would understand exactly what Eleanor was feeling, having just spent several days as the mother of a missing child. Be they thirteen or thirty, your child was always your child.

In an attempt to lighten the mood and banish the softer feelings she suddenly had for Nicole, Eleanor brushed her hands together and stood. "Aaron, get your . . . friend's bag and take it upstairs."

He tugged his gaze away from Nicole with obvious difficulty. "Right this minute?"

"Please."

"Why?"

"Because I said so."

"I've never understood why that's a reason for anything."

"It's always made perfect sense to me."

Eleanor couldn't be sure, but she thought she heard Nicole stifle a giggle.

There just might be hope for her yet.

Nicole's attempt to help clear the table was shot down before she lifted the first plate.

"You're a guest." Ellie snatched the dish out of her hand. "Go upstairs and rest."

"I'm not tired," she said, but the swinging door to the kitchen had already closed behind Aaron's mother.

"She likes to do things herself." Kim's hands were full of plates. Nicole gave them a pointed stare. Kim shrugged. "She likes me to do things, too. Probably revenge for all the times I didn't do anything when I was a kid."

Even Tim was helping, dragging anything that wasn't breakable from the dining room back into the kitchen. The men had disappeared, along with Zsa Zsa, who, after shrieking and throwing everything from her plate onto the floor, had fallen asleep with her face in the gooey mess she'd made of crackers and applesauce.

Nicole sighed and trudged upstairs. She paused outside the room formerly known as Kim's and listened. But she heard nothing from Rayne — no tears, no mutters, no thumps or kicks. Perhaps she was sleeping. A nap might do Rayne as much good as it would Zsa Zsa.

She hovered outside the only open door, saw her bag next to the bunk bed and walked into a place that had been frozen in late adolescence. Except for the bed, everything else had been split down the middle with military precision. When Nicole looked closer she could swear she saw a fading Magic Marker line across the floor.

One side of the room could only be described as a montage. The pictures on the wall depicted faraway places, many she didn't recognize. They'd been torn from magazines and taped everywhere. The desk held a typewriter, dictionary and thesaurus, as well as dozens of magazines haphazardly strewn across the surface. Nicole strolled over and read the titles.

National Geographic, US News and World Report, Time, Newsweek. She picked one up. *Sports Illustrated?* Nicole shrugged. "Boys will be boys."

From the toy soldiers marching across the shelves attached to the wall and the camouflage shade on the desk lamp, the other side of the room appeared to have been inhabited by G.I. Joe. Janet would love the place.

Nicole jumped at the thought. *Janet!* She'd promised to call her as soon as they got in.

She hurried to her carry-on and retrieved her phone from the depths. One button turned the thing on, another speed dialed her best friend's cell phone.

"One-nine-hundred ask a nun," Janet answered. "Tell me all your troubles."

"She hates me," Nicole responded, not bothering to identify herself. Janet would have known her voice, even if she hadn't had caller ID.

"Rayne doesn't hate you."

She flopped onto what must be Bobby's bed, considering the pea-green comforter and crisp tan sheets. "I wasn't talking about Rayne, though right now, she hates me, too."

"Explain."

Nicole glanced at the door, but she'd closed it tight. Nevertheless, she lowered her voice. "Aaron's mom. She hates me."

"I doubt that she hates you."

"You haven't met her."

"That bad, huh?"

Nicole could hear the amusement in Janet's voice. "You think this is funny? I'm hundreds of miles away, sleeping in a room only you could enjoy, my daughter looks at me as if I'm Hannibal Lecter and Aaron's mom looks at me like I'm . . . I'm . . ."

Nicole frowned, thinking back to some of the stories Janet liked to tell whenever the television failed to amuse her, which was often.

"Who's the one who seduced somebody who was perfect until she got a hold of him?"

"Satan's sister?"

"Would you be serious?"

"I'll try. Run that clue by me again. You know how I love Bible trivia."

"There was this guy who was chosen of God. Then he met some woman and she ruined everything."

"Not much of a clue."

"He had long hair. She cut it."

"Oh, Samson and Delilah."

"Yeah. His mom looks at me like I'm Delilah. Because of me, Aaron was ruined."

"You're overreacting. I'm sure Aaron's mom is just angry because you kept her granddaughter from her."

Nicole sat up so fast she smacked her

head on the underside of the top bunk. "Ouch! How do you *do* that?" she demanded.

"What?"

"She did say she was mad about losing time with Rayne."

"See? I doubt she hates you. She's angry. She'll get over it."

"She doesn't seem like the get-over-it type."

"Chin up. Show her what you're made of."

"Which is?"

"Stronger stuff than anyone she's ever met before."

"I don't feel very strong. I feel tired and sad and completely alone."

"You're never completely alone."

Nicole's answer was a growl, which only made Janet laugh. "So tell me, what's the girl done now?"

The question was exactly the same one Janet had asked a hundred times before and made Nicole more homesick than she already was. She never would have believed she'd miss Vegas at all — definitely not so soon.

"She hates me, too. Refuses to come home. Said I couldn't make her."

"Uh-oh," Janet murmured.

"Exactly. What do I do about that?"

"Make her."

"I can't drag a thirteen-year-old girl kicking and screaming all the way back to Las Vegas."

"She comes pretty quickly if you yank on her ear hard enough."

"Rayne is not a dog."

"I wouldn't do that to a dog!" Janet sounded offended.

"Quit goofing around and give me something I can use here."

"You never let me have any fun." Janet sighed. "Stay awhile. Help it might, hurt it can't."

"Swell. Yoda *and* psycho babble. I'm so glad I called."

Nicole could have sworn she heard a snicker quickly stifled. She chose to ignore it. "If you need me, I'll be staying at the Luchettis' house."

"That sounds like fun."

"Not," Nicole said dryly.

"Play nice, Nicky."

"I'm not sure I know how."

"Learn. Hurt it —"

"Can't, help it might. I got that already."

"Then I'm fulfilling my mission."

"To be the most annoying woman on the planet?"

251

"That, too." Janet hesitated. "What about Aaron?"

"What about him?"

"How are he and Rayne getting on?"

"Better than Rayne and anyone else, except her gramma. They seem to be two peas in a pod."

"Jealous?"

Nicole considered. "Maybe a little. Rayne and I were always pals. And now . . . I'm not sure what we are."

"Mother and daughter. It's complicated."

"I'll say."

"Be glad she has someone to talk to. Better than no one."

True. Nicole had had no one, and it had been a very bad thing.

"What about you and Aaron?" Janet pressed.

Nicole stiffened. "There is no me and Aaron."

"Why not?"

"You know why not. He wants me, he doesn't love me. I can't go there again, Janet. I just can't."

"But you love him."

"I thought I did. I don't know anymore."

"You want him?"

A sudden and intense memory of their

kiss shot through her mind so fast she shuddered. She'd dreamed about that kiss and so much more. She remembered their single night together when she least expected it. Whenever he touched her, however casually, she wanted to yank him into her arms and kiss him all over.

"No," she answered.

"Liar."

Nicole gave a mental shrug. Add it to her list of sins. She had a million. Lying was the least of her worries. She wasn't going to discuss her sudden and inconvenient journey into the world of lust with Janet. No way, no how.

"One more thing?" she asked.

"I live to serve."

Which, with Janet, was not merely sarcasm but also the truth.

"Can you call some of your friends in the system? See if there are any missing little boys. About five or six, light-brown hair, blue eyes, missing teeth."

"Oh, that narrows it down."

"Name's Tim and he appears to have a raging case of ADHD."

Janet sighed. "Where did she find this one?"

"Not sure, but apparently he's been living in our storage closet."

"What?"

Nicole had to laugh. She had at last surprised Janet. "That's what I said."

"Anything else in there that I should know about?"

"I think you'd better have a look."

"Me, too."

Chapter Thirteen

"Why do I have to take the kid to the doctor?" Dean demanded. "It's not like he's mine."

His mother had cornered him on the far side of the barn, where he'd gone to get away from all the people. He'd even managed to send Tim on a wild Dalmatian chase. Tiny dog- and boy-shaped dots frolicked in the far pasture.

Dean scowled. Trust his mother to follow him out here and ruin perfectly good peace and quiet. Furtively he tucked the cigarette he'd been about to light back into the pocket of his pants.

"It's not like he's anyone's," she countered. "So we'll just have to help him as best we can while he's here."

"Isn't that Aaron's department? Helping the helpless? Why can't he take him?"

Eleanor's lips tightened. "Aaron has his hands a little full right now."

"Sounds like he had his hands full about fourteen years ago, too."

He ducked before his mother's palm

could connect with the side of his head. He'd gotten very good at ducking during his teen years, and he hadn't lost the talent since. Probably because he got so much practice.

"Just do what I ask for a change, would you?"

The desperation in her voice made Dean bite back a sarcastic retort. Once his mom had been the calm in every storm. Then, about two years ago, she'd lost her mind. Turned out to be menopause.

She'd gone to the doctor, gotten some meds and improved considerably. But she was still a helluva lot more excitable than she had been before.

He didn't mind taking Tim to the doctor. He just didn't like doctors. The last one he'd seen had said Dean was healthy as a horse. But he needed a psychiatrist.

Dean was overworked and underpaid, lonely and sexually frustrated. What man wouldn't be depressed about that? He'd get over it — without the consultation of a head doctor and the use of little white pills — or whatever the hell color they were these days.

Dean's mood softened when his mother's shoulders slumped. "Hey," he murmured, and awkwardly patted her shoulder.

He'd never been any good at comforting women. He was much better at making them cry.

Eleanor reached up and took his hand. "Thanks," she murmured. "I knew you'd help out."

His mother released him and disappeared around the corner of the barn. Once again she'd weaseled him into doing what she wanted without him realizing she was doing it.

"How does she *do* that?" he muttered, pulling the cigarette out of his pocket and sticking it into his mouth.

"Do what?"

Dean started and the cigarette fell into the dirt. Tim and Bull danced all over it. By the time Dean shoved the dog away and guided the child to another patch of dirt, the cigarette was mush.

The things were getting to be more trouble than they were worth.

"Never mind," he said. "Where's Bear?"

"Took off thataway." Tim pointed north. The direction Bear had been returning from far too often lately.

"Son of a bitch," Dean muttered.

"Yeah! Son of a bitch!" Tim repeated,

then latched on to Dean's leg and peered into his face with a grin. "You're the best guy there ever was," Tim announced. "I like you lots and lots."

A warm, peaceful feeling spread through Dean, similar to the one he got when he had five minutes alone to stare at his farm and partake of a cigarette, but without the smoky aftertaste.

Dean ruffled Tim's hair. His rough fingers caught in the strands and pulled.

"Sorry." Dean tugged them loose.

"Thas okay."

"I've got some errands to do in town. Wanna come?"

"Can I look for a daddy?"

The thought of Tim walking up to every man in Gainsville and asking, "Are you my daddy?" made Dean's desire for nicotine return.

"No," he said shortly.

"But —"

"Tell you what, kid, I'll find you a daddy. You leave it to me."

"Really?" Tim stared at Dean as if he were this Angel of Light superhero the kid kept harping on. "Thanks."

An hour later they entered the office of Dr. Maxwell — Pediatrician. The place was packed with crying, snuffling, sneezing children. Dean grimaced and glanced at Tim. The boy's face held the same expression.

He started to slink back out the door. Dean grabbed his collar and held on. "Nuh-uh," he said. "My mom will have our hides."

"Ellie likes me. She said so. She wouldn't want me to stay here."

"Ellie's not as nice as she seems," Dean said. "Believe me."

He led Tim through the herd of kids and their mothers. What had happened to sharing the load, equal opportunity and paternity leave? He was the only man in the room. Obviously the twenty-first century hadn't reached Gainsville quite yet.

He nodded to the receptionist who was beaming at him with far too much joy for the situation. "Mr. Luchetti, I presume?"

Dean grunted. Her perky smile faded. He had that effect on a lot of women.

"Fill these out." She handed him a clipboard full of forms. "As best you can."

He turned, searched the room desperately for a quiet corner, and finding none headed for the single empty seat. Tim clung to him like a barnacle on the hull of a ship.

"Aren't you Evan's brother?" the woman to his right asked, bouncing a feverish-looking blond boy on her knee.

"Yeah."

"He fixed our roof last summer. Nice young man."

Dean nodded. He heard that a lot. Evan could fix anything and he did so with a smile, unlike Dean.

He turned his attention to the clipboard as Tim pressed against his right arm so hard he wouldn't have been able to write if he wasn't left-handed.

Last name?

None.

First name?

Tim.

Middle initial?

Got me.

"How's Bobby?" murmured the woman to his left.

"Fine," he said shortly, then glanced her way to discover a drooling baby on her lap and two in the double stroller between her feet.

"Holy hell," he muttered. *Triplets.*

"Holy hell!" Tim announced joyfully.

The babies scrunched up their faces and began to cry. Their mother appeared ready to join them.

"Quit repeating everything I say," Dean told Tim.

"Maybe you should quit saying things he shouldn't repeat," a third woman interjected from across the aisle.

Maybe you should mind your own business, Dean thought. But he kept his mouth shut and nodded.

"Colin back?" she asked.

"Not yet."

"How's Aaron?" This from an older lady who appeared to be bringing every grandchild she could claim in for a checkup.

"Swell," Dean muttered.

He'd heard the office of the OB-GYN was gossip central. Everyone must come to the pediatrician's office to discover how the Luchetti brothers were doing.

He should be used to the questions by now. The five brothers looked very much alike. Dark hair, blue eyes, they resembled their mother. The only differences were their heights, their weights and their personalities — or lack of one.

"What was your name again?" the first lady asked.

"Dean."

"Dean?" She frowned. "Funny, I don't remember you."

"Why am I not surprised?" he muttered

as he returned his attention to the clip-board.

His brothers had all been more social than he. Bobby and Colin had no doubt gone to school with the two young women who had asked about them. Evan had probably dated everyone in the room, twice. Even Aaron knew most of the folks in town and spent a lot of time talking to them. Dean's main interest had been cows. It still was.

"Mr. Luchetti?" The receptionist beck-oned. "You can come back now."

Tim and Dean followed the woman to an empty room. "What are they gonna do to me?" Tim asked.

"No clue, kid. None." Tim's lip trem-bled. "Tell you what, anything they do to you, they can do to me, too. Okay?"

" 'Kay."

The door opened and the doctor en-tered. Frowning at the clipboard and mumbling to himself, he reminded Dean of a chemistry teacher he'd had in high school. A man so brilliant in science he'd had little room left in his mind for any-thing as mundane as real life.

Dr. Maxwell's glasses slid down his nose, his hair stood on end as if he'd repeatedly yanked on the ends, and he'd forgotten to tie his tie that morning. The strip of material decorated with Mickey Mouse icons hung around his neck like a limp spaghetti noodle.

He raised his gaze to Dean and scowled. "Mr. Luchetti, I hardly think 'got me' is a sufficient response to nearly all these questions."

Tim snickered and kicked the leg of his chair in syncopated rhythm. He'd start to bounce any second now.

"I'm afraid it's the only one I have."

"You don't know your son's middle name."

"He's not my son."

Dean glanced at Tim to discover he'd gone completely still and his smile had faded. Dean sighed. What was he supposed to do? Lie?

"You'd better explain," the doctor said.

So Dean did, as quickly and as thoroughly as he could while Maxwell made notes on a fresh new chart, and Tim began to bounce higher and faster as the moments ticked by.

"Well, that's quite a story. One I'm going to have to repeat to Social Services later today."

"Social Services," Tim shrieked and made a dash for the door.

Dean caught him by the collar and hauled him back. He gave the doctor a disgusted look. "Nice one."

Maxwell ignored Dean and focused on Tim. "Have you dealt with Social Services before?"

"Nope. Every time I hear the word, I run." Tim jogged in place while Dean continued to hold on to his shirt.

"Hmm." Maxwell made a note on his chart, then glanced up at Dean. "We'll start with a physical. Take some blood. See what we can figure out about his immunizations." He stared at Tim for a long moment, his chin going up and down in time with Tim's bounce. "And then I want you to step over to Dr. Harter's office where he'll do a diagnostic for ADHD."

"Who's Dr. Harter?"

"A psychiatrist."

Dean frowned and Maxwell held up one hand. "That's common practice, Mr. Luchetti. He'll also do an IQ test and check for a few other common disorders. As a favor to me, he'll fit you in today."

"What's the rush?"

"Don't you think Tim's been ignored long enough?"

"Definitely."

"In an ideal world, Tim would have rec-

ords we could consult about his past behavior — from another doctor or a teacher
or a relative. However, Tim's world appears to be far from ideal. So let's fix that,
shall we?"

Without waiting for Dean's answer the
doctor stepped into the hall and called the
nurse. Tim crawled into Dean's lap and
proceeded to wiggle. "Why does everyone
keep callin' me those numbers?"

"Numbers?"

"ADHD?"

"Letters," Dean corrected automatically.

"Whatever. What does that *mean?*"

"I'm not exactly sure, but I guess we'll
find out."

The nurse came in with a basket of bot-
tles and needles and bandages. "This
won't hurt a bit."

"That's what they all say," Tim muttered. "You first."

He grabbed Dean's arm and held it out
in front of them. The nurse blinked. "Uh,
not you."

"You said you'd do everything I did,
didn't ya, Dean? Huh?"

"I did." He wiggled his arm at the nurse.
"Me first."

She frowned. "It'll cost double."

Dean sighed. Why was everything always about money?

"Bill me."

"I intend to."

Several hours later Dean and Tim had been stripped, poked and prodded. They'd been questioned and queried. Dean was exhausted. Tim was still bouncing. Together they sat in Dr. Maxwell's office and waited for the results.

The doctor read his chart and nodded slowly.

"Nothing I didn't expect here, Timothy."

"Tim-inator," Tim sang.

"Excuse me?"

"I'm the Timinator. No one messes with me."

The doctor smiled indulgently. "All right." He turned his attention to Dean. "We'll need to update his immunizations. That's minor and can be taken care of before you leave today."

"What's he sayin'?" Tim whispered loudly.

"Shots. Later."

" 'Kay." Tim shrugged. "I'm not a girlie man."

The doctor cleared his throat and his lips twitched. "He does have classic symptoms of ADHD."

"In English?"

"Attention Deficit Hyperactivity Disorder."

"We know he's hyper. I didn't need an M.D. behind my name to figure that out."

"I'm sure you didn't. But there's more to ADHD than just . . ." He glanced at Tim who was happily kicking the desk. "That."

"What else?"

"Inattentiveness."

Together they watched as Tim jumped up and wandered over to the window, ignoring them as they discussed him like a bug.

Dr. Maxwell raised his eyebrow. "Also impulsiveness. Does he run headlong into trouble?"

The incident with Herby came quickly to mind. "You might say that. But don't a lot of kids?"

"Of course. That's why it's so hard to diagnose ADHD at a young age. Many of the symptoms are common to children in general."

"So what makes Tim different from every other goosie kid on the block?"

"The combination of symptoms and their intensity."

"How did he get like this?"

"No one really knows. We have learned genetics play a part in ADHD, as does improper prenatal care and malnutrition in the first year."

Dean shifted his gaze to Tim, who had lost interest in the window and turned his attention to the books on Dr. Maxwell's shelf.

Three strikes and you're out, kid.

"It's also quite common to have a learning disability or anxiety and conduct disorders along with ADHD. These lead to feelings of inferiority, a lack of confidence, low self-esteem. Children with ADHD are often depressed. Tim isn't. They also throw temper tantrums. Tim hasn't. I'd say he has a relatively mild case, but one we're going to want to treat before he develops the problems I've mentioned."

Dean's head spun with all the information. But he did his best to focus on what the doctor was telling him. His mom would want to know every detail later.

"I'll give you a prescription for a low dose of Ritalin. If that doesn't help him focus, we can increase it a bit."

"Does everything warrant a pill these days?" Dean demanded. "Can't I just make him run around the pasture twenty times an hour and keep him off the sugar?"

The doctor shook his head. "Those are common myths associated with ADHD. In reality, exercise doesn't help and sugar, in moderation, doesn't hurt."

"What's he saying?" Tim dropped back into his chair with a thud.

"You don't have to jog and you can eat some candy."

"I *like* you," Tim breathed, making the doctor smile again.

"I don't want him to be a zombie," Dean insisted.

"Neither do I. That's why I'm starting him out on the lowest possible dose of Ritalin. Soon he'll be able to sit still. Focus on a task. Sleep at night. He won't be a zombie. I promise."

Tim burst into tears and threw his arms around Dean's neck. Dean glanced at the doctor with wide eyes. The doctor shrugged.

"What's the matter?" Dean awkwardly patted Tim's heaving, skinny shoulders.

"There's somethin' the matter with me. I'm broken. No one's gonna want to be my daddy now."

"Sure they will. The doctor's going to fix you right up."

"I am." Maxwell scribbled something

unintelligible onto a prescription pad.

Dean stood, taking Tim with him since the kid was clinging to his chest like a baby monkey. "Thanks, Doctor."

He held out his hand for the paper, but the doctor didn't give it to him. Dean frowned.

"Perhaps you'd better sit down again, Mr. Luchetti."

"There's more?"

"I'm afraid so."

Tim hiccoughed and tried to catch his breath. Absently Dean rubbed his back, then sat. Tim wasn't heavy, but he was as wiggly as a worm.

"It's a good thing you took the same tests as Tim did today." The doctor pulled a second chart from beneath the first. "We need to discuss what I found."

Aaron was at loose ends. Rayne was still in her room, and she didn't appear to be coming out soon. Nicole had gone into her room with the same results. Kim, Brian and Zsa Zsa had decamped to their farm. His parents were taking a nap.

Aaron snorted. Right. He hadn't fallen for that excuse even when he was a kid. He should be happy they still loved each other enough to partake in a little afternoon delight. He was. It was just mortifying to realize his fifty-three-year-old father had a better sex life than he did.

Aaron went to the barn and checked the milking apparatus and the cows. Everything was as it should be. With the robotics in place, he was becoming obsolete.

Returning to the front yard, Aaron climbed the porch steps and sat in the rocker. His attention was caught by a cloud of dust blowing in from town. From the bright-red shade of the truck in the middle of the dust ball, Aaron figured Dean was just about home.

Bull, lonely without his brother, who appeared to have another date in a string of far too many, ran out to meet the truck, barking loud enough and dancing fast enough to make up for the missing Bear.

Tim hopped out of the cab and, after waving at Aaron, chased Bull toward the back of the house. Dean approached more slowly.

"Where were you?"

His brother started, frowning at Aaron as if he hadn't known he was there. "Mom made me take the kid to the doctor."

"Is he sick?"

Dean blinked. "Huh?"

Aaron flicked a finger at the prescription

package Dean clutched in his hand. "Medicine? Sick? Kid?"

Dean shook his head, climbed the steps and sat in the other chair. Then he stared at his boots and said nothing at all, which was very unlike Dean.

Not that his brother couldn't be spacey. He was. They'd always chalked it up to his being more into cows than people. Which was just fine because then the rest of them didn't have to be.

"Dean? What's up?"

Dean jumped again. "Huh? Oh. The kid's got ADHD."

"No surprise there. It could be worse."

"It is."

"How?"

Dean shook his head. "Never mind." He started to stand. "I've got to check —"

Aaron motioned him back into his seat. "I already did. Everything's running smoothly. None of your cows have exploded. They've all been milked according to their own personal schedules, and the machine is chugging along just fine."

"Great." He sat back down. "Uh, thanks."

Thanks was unlike Dean, too. What was the world coming to? Before Aaron could ask, Dean spoke.

"So you've got a kid."

Aaron raised his eyebrows. Conversation, too? Life just got stranger and stranger.

"Looks that way," he answered.

"And, uh, how do you feel about that?"

Aaron gaped. His brother wanted to know how he felt? The world must have stopped turning while he was otherwise occupied.

"Quit staring at me like I've lost my mind," Dean snarled. "I'm just trying to be friendly. If you don't want to chat, I've got stuff to do."

That was more like Dean. Aaron relaxed. "I'd love to chat with you."

"Then —" Dean waved his hand "— chat."

"All right. How do I feel?" Aaron thought about it. "Shocked. Scared. Embarrassed. Guilty."

"Huh?"

"I never considered I'd left a child behind."

"Duh," Dean muttered, tactful as always.

"Hence my embarrassment," Aaron said dryly.

"Ah." Dean nodded. "Okay. But what's to be scared about?" He tilted his head. "Except her rants. Teenage girls. Sheesh,

273

remember Kimmy? What a nutcase."

Aaron smiled. Dean and Kim had always butted heads. Especially when Kim was in the throes of adolescence. Dean had delighted in tormenting her. He still did.

"I remember," Aaron murmured.

"So what are you scared of?"

He hesitated, getting his thoughts in order. "I'm scared I'll never be able to be a father to her. I'm scared she'll get hurt. I'm scared she'll get dead. I'm scared she'll never love me."

Dean shrugged. "What's not to love?"

Aaron coughed to clear his suddenly tight throat, then glanced at the setting sun. "I think that's the nicest thing you've ever said to me."

"Just don't let it go to your head."

Aaron laughed and the tension in his throat disappeared. They sat on the porch in companionable silence as Tim's laughter warred with Bull's bark. Fireflies danced at the edge of the yard. The grass smelled fresh and clean.

"Why guilty?" Dean asked.

"For years I thought of Nicole as a test I failed. I'd been tempted, and I'd fallen right into Satan's trap."

Dean snorted. "She doesn't look like Satan to me."

"Me, either," Aaron said ruefully. Nicole looked more like heaven.

"Please tell me that you don't think Nicole is the devil in disguise. Because I'm not in the mood to haul your ass to town and put you in a little white room for the rest of our life."

"Don't worry. I don't believe the devil is inhabiting the earth. Yet."

Dean slid a suspicious glance his way. Aaron laughed. "I'm *kidding.* Lighten up."

"Hardy-har-har. Next thing I know you'll be spouting knock-knocks, and then I'll have to hurt you."

"Not in this lifetime."

They shared a smile of commiseration over their dad's love of knock-knock jokes and their bafflement with them. Aaron had tried to humor his father, but no one understood how those jokes could be funny except John, Kim and now Rayne.

"Let's get back to why you feel guilty," Dean said. "I still don't get it."

"Nicole got pregnant. I blame myself."

"Correct me if I'm wrong, but I think she was there, too."

Aaron stiffened. "She wasn't at fault, it was me. My mistake, but she's the one who paid."

"You always were a martyr," Dean muttered.

"What?"

"Mar-tyr," he said slowly. "Do you want me to spell it for you?"

"I know what a martyr is."

"Then quit being one. It got old about twelve years ago."

"I should never have —"

"You did. Get over it. I'm not much of a churchgoer, but I seem to remember something along the lines of no one's perfect. God forgives. Blah, blah, blah. If he can, why can't you?"

Aaron blinked. God forgives. How many times had he said that to others? Why hadn't he ever said it to himself?

"You think you're special?" Dean asked.

"Uh . . ." Aaron wasn't sure what the appropriate answer was. "No?"

"Bingo. You deserve to be forgiven just as much as the next idiot. Maybe more so, because you're a bigger idiot."

His smirk took some of the sting out of his words. Though Aaron did feel more and more like a fool with each passing moment.

He couldn't ever recall having a deep conversation with any of his brothers. He would never have dreamed he'd have one with Dean. Or that Dean would be giving him advice, and the advice would be worth taking.

"Now explain how Nicole paid for your mistake," Dean continued. "She seems fine to me. In fact, your daughter probably saved her from herself."

"My sin was her salvation," Aaron whispered, remembering his conversation with Janet, which already seemed like a lifetime ago.

"Whatever." Dean smooshed a mosquito. "You told me once that everything happens for a reason. You still believe that?"

"Yes."

"Then what are you whining about? This was all supposed to happen."

Aaron frowned. "But —"

"No, buts. You made a mistake. Your mistake knocked on the front door, and now she needs a father."

Aaron bristled. "She's my daughter, not a mistake."

"Really? I couldn't tell that from the way you've been acting."

Aaron stared at his brother. "You know what? I am an idiot."

Dean leaned back in his chair. "You'll get no argument from me."

Chapter Fourteen

Aaron left Dean on the porch, watching Bull and Tim play tag. None of them appeared tired. Aaron was, but he had something to do before he could sleep, so he climbed the stairs and knocked on Kim's old door.

"Go away!" Rayne's voice was choked with tears.

Aaron hesitated. What was the proper etiquette? He'd knocked, could he go in? Or did he have to wait for permission? From the sound of Rayne's voice, he might be waiting a long, long time.

Suddenly the door was jerked open. "I said —"

Rayne clamped her mouth shut at the sight of him.

"Hi," Aaron murmured. "Can I come in?"

She blinked and the teardrops shimmering on her eyelashes dropped onto her cheeks. As she swept them away, her mouth trembled.

Aaron's chest hurt. She was so miserable. He wanted to protect her from every harm, take all her troubles away, make her life as smooth as the surface of a lake at dawn. He couldn't, but oh, how he wanted to.

She spun about, stalking across the room and flopping onto the bed. Since she left the door open, Aaron took that as an invitation and stepped inside. Then he wasn't sure where to start.

"You — uh — you've been crying?"

The look she sent his way made Aaron want to smack himself in the forehead. Why was he so lame when it came to talking to his daughter?

He tried again. "What's the matter?"

"Nothing. Everything."

Well, that narrows it down.

He took a step closer and she burst into tears. Aaron sat next to her and she threw herself into his arms. He sighed. Their first hug and his daughter was hysterical.

"There, there," Aaron patted her back, smoothed his hand over her braid and let her cry.

"You — you — you —" her breath hitched; she couldn't get the words out.

"Me?" Aaron encouraged.

"You'll n-n-never love me now!" she wailed.

Her words and her manner were so melodramatic he wanted to laugh. But he knew better. To Rayne, the world was coming to an end.

"I already love you."

She lifted her head from his shoulder. Aaron's shirt stuck to his skin, soaked with her tears. Rayne squinted at him with swollen, miserable eyes. "What?"

"I love you always, no matter what."

"You do?" Her misery turned to suspicion. "Why?"

"You're my child."

"That's not a reason. All I've done is scream and rant and kick things. Why would you love me?"

"You don't have to earn my love, Rayne. I'm your father. I just love you."

"That makes no sense."

"It does to me."

And amazingly it did. So many things that had been confusing or unbelievable to him were becoming clear since he'd discovered he had a little girl.

He'd spouted the doctrine of forgiveness and of God's infinite love, but he hadn't believed it. Not really. Because he hadn't understood that if you loved with all your heart, as a father loved a child for no other reason than that they existed, then you could forgive anything, too.

"I don't believe you." Rayne slid out of his embrace.

Aaron caught her hand before she could run away. "Believe me. I love you, Rayne, and there's nothing you could do that would make me stop."

"But I was a mistake!" she wailed.

"I used to think so. But not anymore."

She pulled her hand from his and crossed her arms. "Well, I certainly wasn't on purpose."

Aaron laughed. "I'm starting to think there are no mistakes in this life."

"You talked to Janet *way* too much when you were in Vegas."

"Or maybe not enough. Did you ever do something that you thought was a mistake, but it turned out to be the right choice all along?"

"No."

"You're young yet." He winked. "Let's take a glance at me, for instance. I broke an important promise, betrayed someone's trust, acted like a fool for a long, long time."

"And then what happened?"

Aaron brushed a stray teardrop from his daughter's cheek and smiled softly. "Then my mistake turned into a miracle."

Nicole heard Aaron and Rayne talking. She was just glad she no longer had to listen to her daughter crying and know she could do nothing to comfort her because she was the cause of Rayne's misery.

She wasn't used to being at odds with Rayne. It had been the two of them and Janet against the world for so long. Now it was Rayne against Nicole, and she didn't know what to do about it.

Nicole drifted off, still dressed and lying on top of the military quilt. A tiny tap on the door had her coming awake with a start. Disoriented she called out, "Come in," before she remembered where she was.

The light from the hall revealed the silhouette of a man. Despite the overabundance of them in the house, Nicole knew immediately that the man was Aaron.

"You were asleep." He started to leave the room.

"No. I mean yes. Just drowsing really."

She sat up and shoved her tangled hair from her face. "What's going on?"

He hesitated, then stepped back inside. As soon as he shut the door, a tiny glow appeared from a night-light stuck into an electrical outlet. There was just enough illumination for her to see his face.

He looked happy.

Aaron pulled a chair away from the nearest desk and straddled it. "I talked to Rayne."

"From your expression, that went well."

"I think so."

"Well, at least someone's having some luck with her." She sighed and even to her the sound was pathetic and needy.

"She'll come around, Nic. She's a kid. She's been hurt."

"And lied to."

"It happens."

"Shouldn't have."

"But it did. We need to quit worrying about what we should have done and figure out what we need to do now."

"Do?"

"About Rayne."

Her heart started to beat faster. Her skin went clammy in an instant. "You want to keep her, don't you?"

He blinked. "What?"

"Keep her here with you."

"For a while. Don't you think it would be better if she was here, at least for the summer?"

Nicole's eyes burned. The years stretched before her — every summer, every holiday, every vacation — Rayne would be here and she would be there. But she couldn't be selfish; she had to learn to share.

"As long as she's back for school in the fall, I guess that's all right. Can you drive me to the airport tomorrow?"

"No."

"The next day?"

"No. I want Rayne to stay. That doesn't mean I want you to go."

"You don't need me here."

He'd never needed her, anywhere. That was the problem. Nicole pushed aside the self-pity. They were discussing Rayne, not her.

"Rayne needs you."

"Rayne hates me. So does your mother." Aaron actually laughed. "That's not funny."

"Rayne doesn't hate you. And my mother doesn't hate anyone."

"Except me."

"You're being ridiculous."

Nicole didn't answer. Instead she hugged herself. No one else would.

Aaron got up. She thought he was going to leave. Instead, he sat on the bed and put his arm around her shoulders. "Cold?"

"Not really." She leaned against him. He felt so good — strong and warm. She should pull away, but she couldn't. It had been far too long since anyone had held her.

"Why do you think my mother hates you?"

"I'd hate me if I were her."

"Then you'd be foolish."

"You want to tell your mother she's foolish? Can I watch while you do?"

He chuckled. "She's not that scary, is she?"

"Yes."

"All right. Why would you hate you if you were my mother?"

"As she so kindly pointed out, I kept her granddaughter from her."

"You didn't do it on purpose."

"I'm sure that gained me points."

"It should."

Aaron rested his cheek on the top of her head. Nicole relaxed into the embrace.

"This is nice," she whispered before she could stop herself.

"Mmm-hmm," he agreed.

His breath brushed her hair. His chest rose and fell next to her cheek. The pulse in his wrist beat slow and steady against her shoulder. Nicole felt connected to Aaron more deeply than she ever had before, so she asked the question that had been bothering her for a while now. "Why aren't you angry with me?"

He took a deep breath, let it out slowly. "I was at first. But then I realized it didn't do me any good to be angry that I'd missed her first step, her first word."

Nicole closed her eyes against the pain his words caused. She couldn't give him back what was already gone, no matter how much she might want to.

"Those things are done," he continued. "I need to look ahead."

He didn't sound angry. He didn't sound sad. In fact, he sounded hopeful. Nicole opened her eyes. "To what?"

"Her first prom dress, her first car, graduation, walking her down the aisle."

Nicole tilted her head back so she could see into his face. His joy soothed her soul.

"You're a good man, Aaron Luchetti."

"I think I'm just starting to figure that out."

Eleanor rose with the sun. She had a houseful of people. There was work to do.

She cleaned the kitchen, fed the chickens, grabbed some eggs and began to cook. As she did, she sang to herself. It had been a long time since she'd had more work than she had time for.

Funny how things changed. She used to pray for an hour to herself. Now she had hour after hour and she had to admit, she was bored.

A lifetime of being frantically busy did not a good retiree make. Her husband wasn't much better. Though he was supposed to be semiretired, he often got up in the dark and went out to watch the cows being milked all by themselves.

Rayne walked into the kitchen. "Hi," she chirped. Though Eleanor could see traces of last night's tears in her red-rimmed, swollen eyes, she chose to ignore it.

"Morning." Eleanor smiled. It was good to have children in the house again — especially when they weren't hers.

She'd been waiting for grandchildren she could spoil and then send home. Within the last year she'd suddenly been blessed with two — a baby she could cuddle and a young girl she could talk to. How lucky could one woman get?

"Hungry?" She pointed her spatula at the platter of scrambled eggs. "Help yourself."

"Thanks." Rayne dished up a large portion and snatched two pieces of toast from the plate next to the toaster. "I never ate dinner last night."

Eleanor glanced over her shoulder with a frown. "I put out sandwiches. You were supposed to help yourself."

"I know. But I wasn't hungry."

"Oh." Eleanor didn't ask why. She'd learned a few things while raising Kim — the main one being, the less you said the more you heard. Moments later her tact was rewarded.

"Mom and I don't get along anymore."

"No?"

Rayne snorted. "No. She makes me so mad."

"I can understand that."

"You can?"

"Of course."

Nicole made Eleanor mad, too, though she wasn't going to say so out loud.

"I want to live here forever."

A warm glow started up in Eleanor's chest. Someone actually wanted to live with her forever. "Well, we'll have to see what we can do about that."

A choked sound came from the doorway and Eleanor spun around to discover Nicole. The accusatory expression in the woman's eyes made Eleanor bristle. But before she could speak, Aaron stepped into the room and attempted to make peace as he always did.

"You'll be staying for the summer, Rayne."

Rayne jumped up from the table and threw her arms around Aaron. "Thank you!"

Eleanor took in the delight in Aaron's eyes and the happiness in her granddaughter's voice. The warm glow increased.

Rayne released her father and sat back down. "See ya, Nicole."

Nicole blinked. "Excuse me. What happened to Mom?"

"I'm not comfortable calling you Mom right now."

Eleanor raised her eyebrows and turned back to the stove. Boy, did she remember arguments like these with Kim, and she did *not* miss them.

She flipped a few pancakes and kept her ears tuned to the conversation. How would Nicole handle this? Eleanor had never handled Kim well at all.

"Fine," Nicole said. "I understand how you feel. But I'm not leaving."

"Why not?"

"We have things to work out. It wouldn't do either one of us any good to be separated right now."

"It'd do me a lot of good," Rayne muttered.

Nicole ignored her. Eleanor had to say she admired Nicole's calm. By now she and Kim would have been at each other's throats.

"I agree that you need to get to know your father and his family, but you and I also need to talk."

"I don't want to talk."

"I'm sure you don't, but we will."

"Why do you get to tell me what to do?" Rayne cried.

"Because I'm your mother, even if you don't want to call me that."

"I can take care of myself. I don't need you."

Eleanor winced. *That had to hurt.*

"You may think you can take care of yourself but you can't."

"You did when you were my age."

"And I'm not recommending it. Be a kid for as long as you can."

"I don't have to listen to you."

"Actually, you do."

"Why should I take advice from someone who got pregnant when she was sixteen?"

Eleanor's hand froze midflip. "What was that?"

She turned and her gaze went straight to Aaron. He stared at Nicole, eyes wide in his white face.

"What did she say?" Eleanor demanded.

Nicole appeared confused, Rayne smug. "Didn't you know? Mom was sixteen when she had me."

Eleanor reached out and smacked her son in the forehead with the spatula.

"Ouch!" Aaron pressed his palm to his face.

Nicole wanted to go to him, but John, Dean and Tim chose that minute to crowd into the kitchen. She was shoved to the back of the room.

Tim began to dance. "What happened?"

Eleanor grabbed Tim by the shoulders and pointed him toward the hall. "Bathroom."

" 'Kay!" He ran off, banging the door behind him.

"Ellie, what the blazes are you doing hitting our son with a cooking utensil?"

"He deserved it. Nicole had Rayne when she was sixteen. *Sixteen!*"

Everyone looked at Nicole. She wanted to crawl off into a hole and die.

Aaron sat in the nearest chair and put his head into his hands. "Oh, my God. Oh, my *God.*"

"Praying isn't going to help you now."

Dean slapped Aaron on the back. He seemed amused.

Eleanor turned off the stove and laid the spatula on the counter carefully, as if afraid she might use it again for more than cooking. "Aaron, how could you? She was a child."

At last Nicole found her voice. She stepped between Aaron and his mother, put her hand on his shoulder and straightened her own. "He didn't know."

"He should have asked."

"Why? Strippers are supposed to be older than sixteen."

"Sin city," Eleanor muttered. "I can see why."

Nicole shrugged. Vegas had changed in the last decade. Become more classy, a playground for the new millennium. But it still had a trashy underbelly, which was why she still had a job.

Aaron raised his head and Nicole caught her breath at the pain she saw on his face. Just last night he'd been smiling, agreeing that he was a good man. Now the guilt was back. She wasn't going to let it stay.

Ignoring the rest of the family, she went down on her knees so they were face-to-face. "Don't start agonizing over this. Aaron. The past is still the past. How old I was then has absolutely no bearing on now."

"But Rayne —"

"Has known for years how old I am."

Nicole glanced over her shoulder. Rayne appeared as worried about her father as Nicole was.

"Yeah," Rayne put in. "I learned subtraction in second grade. This isn't news to me."

"Just to me," he muttered.

"It doesn't change anything, Aaron."

"Ever heard the term jailbait?"

"Oh, please!" Nicole lost her temper. "You didn't do anything wrong. If we'd been in high school, no one would have blinked an eye at an eighteen-year-old and a sixteen-year-old together."

"I might have," Eleanor muttered.

Nicole shot her a glare. She'd had enough of Aaron's mom for one lifetime. The woman could hate her all she wanted, but she wasn't going to make the sadness return to Aaron's eyes. Not while Nicole was around.

"He did *nothing* wrong."

Eleanor's eyebrows shot up.

"Uh-oh," Dean muttered. "Gotta find Tim."

He escaped.

"Ellie," John said in a warning tone and inched closer.

Nicole refused to be intimidated. Eleanor Luchetti might rule this roost, but she didn't rule Nicole. Nicole had faced down dragons big enough to eat Midwestern farmwives for breakfast.

The two women continued to stare. Everyone else in the room watched. At last, Eleanor's lips twitched. She very nearly smiled before she spun back to the counter and grabbed her spatula. Both Aaron and Nicole got to their feet, tripping in their haste to stand in front of each other. But Eleanor calmly flipped the rest of the pancakes onto a plate.

"I think Nicole and Rayne should stay at Evan's for a while," she said.

Nicole wasn't surprised Eleanor wanted her out of the house, but —

"Why Rayne?"

"You two need some time together."

"No, we don't," Rayne muttered.

Aaron frowned. "But what about —"

"Evan's gone for a month or so. I got a letter yesterday. Why that boy can't just pick up the phone and dial I have no idea."

The thought of a house just for herself and Rayne, without everyone else's input, was too good to pass up. "All right," Nicole agreed.

"Wait a minute." Aaron glanced back and forth between the two of them. "I'll come, too."

"I don't think so," his mother said.

Aaron didn't even look at her. "I don't care what you think. I'm spending as much time with my daughter as I can."

Eleanor shrugged. "Suit yourself." She placed the platters of food on the table. "But eat first."

"I'm going to get my things." Nicole slipped from the room.

The low murmur of voices was punctuated by the scrape of serving spoons and forks against plates as she hurried upstairs.

Nicole was glad that she and Rayne would have time to work things out. Although with Rayne's behavior lately, it would probably take much longer than they had. Rayne might be staying for the summer, but Nicole certainly couldn't. A few weeks, if that.

She was also thrilled she wouldn't have to stay in the same house with Eleanor any longer. The woman made her crazy.

But what really bothered Nicole, what made her run into her room and lock the door, then stand with her hot forehead pressed against the cool wall as she tried to stop her heart from racing, was the thought of herself, Rayne and Aaron tucked into a cozy little house all alone.

Just like the family she'd always wanted.

The table was cleared; the kitchen was empty, except for Eleanor and her dishes.

She liked this time, when everyone was fed and she could contemplate the rest of her day. Lazily, she dipped her hands into the warm water, sniffed the lemon-fresh scent of the suds and watched dust motes chase each other across the stream of sunlight through the window above her sink.

"Pretty proud of yourself, aren't you?"

She smiled at the sound of John's voice but didn't bother to turn around. "Uh-huh."

"I didn't realize you were so sneaky."

"You don't realize a lot of things."

He crossed the room and leaned against the counter, staring at her with an amused expression. "You set him up."

"Who?"

"You know who. By sending Rayne and Nicole to Evan's, then telling Aaron not to go, you made certain he would."

"Aaron?" She rinsed a dish. "He's not that contrary."

John snorted. "They're all that contrary."

Eleanor lifted one shoulder, then lowered it. "So what if I did?"

"That's like putting oily rags, gasoline and a box of matches into an old shed in the middle of summer."

"You think?"

He narrowed his eyes. "Ellie, you know there's going to be an explosion. Are you prepared to put out the flames?"

"Why do we have to put them out?"

"If Nicole and Rayne behave like you and Kim, we're going to need a high-powered fire hose."

"It wasn't that bad."

"Yes, it was."

Since he was right, she let the matter drop. "We'll have Rayne come over here a lot. That'll help keep the temperature from getting too high."

"And what about the coming conflagration between Aaron and Nicole?"

"They don't seem ready to argue to me."

"No, they seem ready to jump each other's bones as soon as they're alone."

Eleanor calmly rinsed another plate.

"I thought you didn't like her."

"I didn't."

"So what changed your mind?"

Eleanor remembered the determination in Nicole's eyes when she'd stepped between mother and son, the tension in her body as she'd watched Aaron come apart, the way she'd touched his face and told him it wasn't his fault.

Not only was she a caretaker, she was a fighter. She protected those who needed protecting, and she didn't back down from anyone.

A lot could be forgiven of a woman liked that. A woman very much like Eleanor herself.

She had thought Aaron needed a quiet, prayerful, peaceful woman, but she'd been wrong. What he needed was Nicole.

And Eleanor planned to make sure that he got her.

Chapter Fifteen

Aaron, Nicole and Rayne took up residence in Evan's cottage that same afternoon. With only two bedrooms and one bath, it was a tight fit.

"I'll sleep on the pull-out sofa," Aaron announced, placing Nicole's carry-on in one room and Rayne's backpack in the other.

"That's okay —" Nicole began, thinking it would be better for everyone if she and Rayne bunked together. Her daughter couldn't very well ignore her forever if they slept in the same bed.

"Thanks, Daddy," Rayne sang and disappeared into her room. The lock on her door clicked home.

Nicole and Aaron stood in the hallway blinking. "She called me Daddy," he said.

His face was so sweetly dazed and his voice so filled with wonder Nicole stifled her irritation that he had become Daddy while she was now Nicole.

She took a quick tour of the cottage.

Aaron's brother wasn't much of a house-keeper.

"Evan appears to be between maids," Aaron observed.

"He has maids?"

"More like girlfriends. A lot of them."

"His girlfriends clean his house?"

"And do his wash and his shopping and his cooking. It's pathetic."

"You're kidding, right?"

"No. In fact, they fight over the privilege."

"I gotta meet this brother."

"No, you don't."

Nicole glanced at him in surprise, but he'd already turned away. For an instant he'd almost sounded jealous, and she wasn't sure what to make of that.

"Nic." Aaron leaned against the counter and stared out the window. "We should talk about this morning."

Though she couldn't see his face, she could tell from the set of his shoulders that he was upset. How was it she had spent less time with this man than she'd spent with most anyone else, yet she felt like she knew him inside out?

"There's nothing more to talk about, Aaron. It never occurred to me to tell you how old I was."

"It never occurred to me to ask. To be honest, I thought you were older than me."

She sighed, remembering how it had felt to be her back then. "I was."

The only sign that he'd heard her was the clenching of his fists. "I'm glad I didn't know," he blurted. "If I'd known you were sixteen, it might have stopped me. Then we wouldn't have Rayne."

She crossed the room, laid her hand on his shoulder and when he turned, she lifted that hand and cupped his cheek with her palm. "Now you're starting to think like me."

He pressed her hand tighter against his skin. Her pulse leaped. Their gazes held and heated. She wanted to kiss him, even leaned forward until her thigh brushed his.

The scrape of Rayne's lock had them leaping apart. But their daughter didn't even glance their way as she went down the hall and into the bathroom.

When the door closed behind her, Nicole took a deep breath. "I'd better start cleaning up."

"I'll help you."

"You will?"

"I've got nothing pressing to do."

They cleaned the place from top to bottom. Rayne conveniently disappeared while they were in the basement searching for cleaning supplies. The note on the table said she'd gone to her grandparents'.

"Let's drag her back." Nicole crumpled the note in her fist.

Aaron laughed and pulled her fingers open one by one, removing the paper and tossing it into the trash. "Leave her be."

And because he asked it of her, she did.

They went grocery shopping in the quaint, family-owned store in town. The ancient clerk with a bleached-blond beehive hairdo, which threatened to topple sideways whenever she leaned too far in one direction, quizzed them unmercifully.

"I hear tell there's a youngun come to town with Kim's face."

"Better let Kim know it's missing," Aaron said.

"Don't get smart with me, sonny. I was working here when you were a gleam in your papa's pretty green eyes."

Aaron winked at Nicole and she had to stifle a giggle. She'd heard small towns were like this — everyone knowing everyone else and their business — but since she'd never been in one she hadn't really believed it.

"Who's she?"

Nicole blinked at the finger waving in her face.

Gently Aaron reached out and lowered the woman's hand. "This is Nicole Houston, Annabelle."

"I mean who *is* she?"

"Ma'am?" Aaron waved off the equally ancient bag boy and bagged his own groceries.

"Cousin? Long-lost half sister?"

Aaron glanced around the grocery store with an exaggerated expression of terror. "*Shh.* My mom can hear for miles."

The woman cackled. "And none of us wants to get on Eleanor's bad side."

"I'll say," Nicole muttered.

"Hmm." Annabelle's gaze swung back to Nicole like a hawk with a mouse. "Girlfriend," she pronounced. "But whose?"

She tapped a finger against her lip, causing the excess amount of neon-red lipstick to spread past the confines of her mouth, before she proceeded to ask questions and then answer them herself. "Bobby back? Nope. I'd have heard. Colin? Same deal. One of Evan's many? I don't think so. Dean?" She looked Nicole over from top to bottom and clucked her tongue. "No way."

Nicole scowled. "Why can't I be his?" she jabbed her thumb in Aaron's direction.

With the same infinite patience, he reached over and lowered her hand, too, then continued to pack the groceries.

"Are you?"

Nicole opened her mouth, then shut it again.

"Nice one," Aaron murmured and lifted matching grocery bags onto his hips.

He turned and headed for the door. Nicole hurried after him, anxious to be out from under the scrutiny of what must be the town's greatest gossip.

"Aaron Luchetti!" Annabelle shouted.

He glanced over his shoulder, sighed, then shrugged. "Annabelle, meet the mother of my child."

The woman goggled. "Child? What child?"

"The one with Kim's face."

While Annabelle puzzled that out, Nicole followed Aaron onto the sidewalk. "Are you nuts?" she asked.

"No."

"She's going to tell everyone."

"Precisely."

"You want her to?"

"Why not? They'll all find out eventually. Might as well get it over with."

"Your mother is going to have a conniption."

"I know." He grinned. "Won't that be fun?"

As the days passed, Rayne did not forgive Nicole; she barely spoke to her. Nevertheless the tiny cottage became the home Nicole had dreamed of during a long, lonely childhood without one.

Despite the tension between mother and daughter, or perhaps because of it, father and daughter flourished. When Rayne wasn't escaping to her grandparents' to be with Tim — who had moved right in and made himself at home, becoming as much a part of the Luchetti family as anyone else — she was spending time with Aaron.

The two of them took walks, played cards, watched television. Nicole made meals and cleaned the house, she read books, did the laundry, hovered around the edges of their lives and listened to them laugh. She missed the closeness she and Rayne had shared, but she marveled at the relationship developing between Rayne and her father. Nicole couldn't think of a greater gift she could give either one of them than each other.

Her favorite time of the day was early morning. She rose when the sun spilled through her bedroom window and across her bed, across her face. The rest of the house remained silent as she tiptoed to the doorway of Rayne's room and watched her daughter sleep. During those few moments, Nicole could convince herself that Rayne might someday forgive her.

After making coffee, she headed for the porch. Passing the living room, she was unable to stop herself from peeking in and watching Aaron as he slept, as well.

His hair tousled, his chin shadowed, the sheet trailed over his waist, resting half on the couch and half off. His chest was bare, his long, strong legs, too. She hurried outside into the coolness of the morning before she gave up every principle she'd found and crawled in next to him.

The cows on the other side of the cornfield lowed a mournful serenade to the dawn. A rustle through the tall grass to her right announced the daily arrival of one of John's Dalmatians. The animal slunk through the yard, glancing over his shoulder as if he feared she'd throw her cup at him if he took his eyes off her for a minute.

Nicole knew just what he was up to, carousing all night long, and it made her remember Aaron's chest, made her wonder if he slept with anything on at all.

Outside in the still of the morning, Nicole thought of other men she had known. She couldn't recall a single one of their names. No one had ever touched her as deeply as Aaron had in one short night. She doubted anyone else ever would.

Once she'd believed herself in love with him. She'd been a child, longing for affection. A lonely, desperate young woman in need of a hero.

Then he'd returned and her fantasy had faltered. For Aaron she'd been nothing more than a mistake, their night together a sin for which he'd paid over and over again. She'd discovered that lust wasn't love, but that hadn't kept her from lusting.

The best way to get over an addiction was to cut it out of your life — but she couldn't cut herself free of Aaron. Their daughter only bound them more closely together.

If he'd remained the same defeated man who had returned to Las Vegas, she might have been able to get over him. But since losing their daughter, then finding her again, Aaron had changed. He reminded her of the young man who had once had the entire world at his feet and his whole future ahead of him.

He joked and he laughed. He touched

people with affection and ease. He walked with his head held high. He took Rayne everywhere and introduced her to everyone. Nicole, too.

The first few times he'd dragged her into the VFW or the post office, she expected questions, even rude comments, but the residents of Gainsville greeted Nicole and her daughter with the same warmth and affection they obviously felt for Aaron himself.

The conniption fit they'd expected of Eleanor never materialized. In fact, Eleanor took Rayne wherever she went and introduced her as proudly as Aaron did. Nicole's daughter was having the time of her life. She doubted Rayne would ever want to go back to Vegas.

But sooner or later the days of playing house would have to end. Then what? Would she drag Rayne back kicking and screaming and hating her still? Or would she do the right thing and leave her only reason for living in Illinois to enjoy a better life than Nicole could ever give her?

As Rayne would say, *That was a no-brainer.*

In finding her father, Rayne had found a new life, a new family, a new home.

One that didn't include Nicole.

The wind rustled through the corn, bringing with it the scent of . . .

"Eau de farm."

Nicole jumped, spilling coffee all over her hand. The sharp burn was forgotten when she saw who had arrived for an early-morning visit.

Aaron's mother was already dressed for the day. Nicole glanced down at her pajamas and felt even more inadequate than she already did.

"Sorry." Eleanor sniffed, once, twice. "I never realized this cottage is directly in the wind pattern of our barn."

"I don't mind," Nicole said.

What were they going to do, move the barn?

"Okay if I join you?" Eleanor didn't bother to wait for an answer before climbing the steps and taking a vacant chair.

"W-would you like some coffee?"

"No, thanks. I've already had enough for one day."

Eleanor had probably fed the chickens, slopped the hogs, done the laundry and mowed the lawn before Nicole had even hoisted her lazy ass out of bed.

She took a sip from her cup to steady her nerves. What *was* Aaron's mom doing here?

"I suppose you're wondering what I'm doing here."

Nicole blinked. Aaron had mentioned his mom was a bit spooky — knowing things she shouldn't and able to read guilty minds with a single piercing glance.

Instead of answering, and stuttering again, Nicole shrugged and drank more coffee.

"Was one of our dogs over this way?" Eleanor appeared to be stalling, too.

"He walked through, but he came from . . ." Nicole pointed north.

"Son of a —" Eleanor pursed her lips. "That dog is a hound."

Since Eleanor was stating the obvious, Nicole didn't comment.

"I mean that in the worst sense. There's a French poodle over there." She shook her head. "I just know she's already pregnant. Her mistress is going to drop those puppies on our doorstep, mark my words."

Nicole winced. The conversation was hitting too close to home for her.

Eleanor winced, too. "I didn't mean — I was just . . . making conversation. Sorry. I'm never sure what to say to you."

"That makes two of us."

Silence fell between them, more uncomfortable than the conversation had been.

"So how's it going over here?" Eleanor asked.

"Fine."

"Rayne and Aaron seem to be doing well."

"They are."

"What about you and Rayne?"

"We aren't."

"That child sure carries a grudge."

"She has a right to. I was always a stickler on the subject of lying. Practice what you preach is a good rule to live by."

"And sometimes pretty hard to follow."

Her words, her manner, her tone — it almost sounded as if Eleanor understood why Nicole had done what she had done.

"Kim and I didn't get along, either."

Nicole hesitated. Aaron had told her all about his mother and sister's relationship. It hadn't been pretty. However, Nicole wasn't sure if she was supposed to know the family secrets, or let on that she did.

"But once she was all grown-up with serious problems of her own, I suddenly became a whole lot smarter than dirt."

Nicole discovered herself smiling. "Don't tell me I have to wait until Rayne is all grown-up before I lose my position as village idiot."

"Hope not." Eleanor's expression was

wistful. "Just remember the relationship you have with your daughter once she's an adult is worth all the trouble you have with her when she's a teenager."

"Really?"

"No. But we like to tell ourselves that. Cuts down on the Valium."

Nicole laughed. "I was always afraid she wouldn't grow up normally because of where she was raised, who she was raised by."

"You seem pretty normal to me."

Eleanor appeared to be serious. Nicole wasn't sure what to say, except the truth. "That might be the nicest thing anyone's ever said to me."

"Then people need to be nicer."

The two women stared at each other and understanding passed between them. Together, they smiled.

"I still worry," Nicole admitted. "Rayne's been exposed to things that kids her age are not usually exposed to."

"Might not be a bad thing. Despite her behavior over the last few weeks, she's a good kid. Empathetic, sympathetic. Look what she did for Tim."

"I suppose. She's just so edgy and unpredictable."

"It's the hormones. Believe me, I understand. I went through menopause not quite two years back. I felt like I was losing my mind. Everything was a tragedy. Laugh, cry, shriek all in one day."

"Then she hasn't gone off the deep end because I was a bad mother?"

Eleanor laughed. "We all think we're bad mothers. It's part of being a mother. If you *didn't* think you were awful, I'd be worried."

"It never said anything about the worry and the guilt in the books I read."

"What books?"

"The parenting books."

Eleanor snorted. "Burn 'em."

"Pardon me?"

"You read books about being a mother?"

"I never had a mother of my own."

Eleanor's face softened. "That must have been tough."

"I didn't know anything else. Which was why I needed something to go by when Rayne came along."

"Every kid's different. Every family. Every home. You're her mom. Just be her mom. Love her no matter what and do the best that you can. Everything will be all right."

It was nice to talk with another woman about something they both understood. So nice, Nicole almost forgot that Eleanor didn't like her, and Rayne couldn't stand the sight of her face.

Almost.

"I never meant to keep Rayne from you."

Eleanor waved the apology away as she did so many other things. "I've had time to think. You were a kid. You made a mistake. If I had to explain all the stupid choices I made at sixteen, we'd be here a while."

"Thanks," Nicole said dryly.

"Don't mention it. I came over this morning to ask you something."

Nicole tensed. Eleanor probably wanted to know when she was leaving.

"You were in love with him, weren't you?"

Nicole gaped, then shot a quick glance at the house.

"The door's shut, so are the windows," Eleanor stated. "We'll hear either one of them coming long before they're here. And you know as well as I do that they aren't going to be up at this hour. So talk to me, Nicole. I'd really like to know."

"Wh-why would you think I was in love with him? I barely knew him."

"You knew him well enough to have his child."

Nicole closed her eyes. She did *not* want

to have this conversation with Aaron's mother.

"Accidents happen. I was a kid and kids are stupid. You said so yourself."

"Nicole." Eleanor's voice was soft but nonetheless demanding. Nicole opened her eyes. "I know you were in love with my son."

She considered denying it, but from the expression on Eleanor's face there wouldn't be much point. "How did you know?"

"You kept the baby for starters. I'm sure your life would have been a whole lot simpler if you'd gotten rid of it."

"No. My life would have been empty without her. Meaningless. She saved me."

"You didn't know that then. You kept her because you thought it was all you'd ever have of him."

Aaron was right. His mom was damn spooky. Nicole had never told that little tidbit to anyone, not even Janet.

"A lot of women would have called the number he left," Eleanor continued. "To hell with his life, what about yours? But Aaron's dream was more important than your comfort. That's the kind of love most men never find and few deserve."

Nicole had been agonizing over the question of love since she'd seen Aaron again. She'd persuaded herself that she hadn't loved him. That she'd been blinded by lust, just as he had been. But now his mother had convinced her otherwise, and it hurt.

She *had* loved him then. She loved him now. But it didn't matter. Because he hadn't and didn't love her.

"Don't tell him," Nicole blurted. "Please. Don't tell him that I loved him then. He'll only feel guiltier than he already does."

Eleanor shook her head. "That boy — he took the whole Catholic guilt thing to heart. But he seems to be moving on with his life now. Maybe you should try it."

"Don't worry. I'll be leaving soon."

Eleanor blinked. "What?"

"I'm going back to Las Vegas. And leaving Rayne here."

"Why?"

"She wants to be with her father. She deserves to be."

"And you?"

"I deserve Las Vegas. That's where I belong."

Eleanor stared at her for a long moment, then sighed. "If you believe that, then maybe it is."

Eleanor returned to her house, a woman with a mission. She was going to get her family straightened out if it was the last thing she ever did. And knowing them, it just might be the last thing she ever did.

Her talk with Nicole that morning had been both good news and bad. The girl had loved Aaron then. Eleanor was certain she loved him now. However, Nicole planned to be as much of a martyr about her dreams as Aaron had once been about his.

Honestly, sometimes she wanted to grab everyone by their ears — as she had in the good old days when they were young — and *make* them do what she thought was best.

But the good old days were gone. More's the pity.

"Morning, Mom."

Dean, coming in from the barn, paused to give her a kiss on the cheek as he passed through the kitchen. The gesture was so unexpected, she grabbed his hand and held on tight.

"You okay?" she asked.

"Sure. Why wouldn't I be?"

She didn't think it was a good idea to point out that he'd been in a good mood all week, which just wasn't like him. Such an observation would no doubt end the mood immediately.

But he was snarling so much less and cursing hardly at all, he and his father hadn't raised their voices to each other in days. Something wasn't right.

"Where's Tim?" she asked.

"He was chasing the dogs through the cornfield for about an hour. Now he's practicing his letters on the porch."

"He's still full of energy, isn't he?"

"I'll say. But I'm glad he isn't a zombie. I was worried."

Eleanor had been, too. She'd raised five boys, and she knew that they wiggled and ran and got into things. That's what boys did — and most of the girls, too. She didn't want Tim to be deprived of the opportunity of being a kid on a farm because the doctor thought he should be medicated.

But he was fine as far as she could tell. He was able to sit still long enough to learn the alphabet and practice writing the letters. He'd even stopped sucking his thumb, though that was probably more a result of being safe and happy than being on Ritalin.

He appeared to be a very bright little boy. His energy and precociousness reminded Eleanor of Dean. Her fourth son had been impulsive and curious — until he'd gone to school. He'd done so poorly there his confidence had suffered. Eleanor had never been able to convince him he wasn't dumb, because Dean believed that he was.

However, Tim seemed to take to new information and the promise of new opportunities with a vengeance. Eleanor liked him, and she wanted to keep him around.

"Anything from Kim?" she asked.

Dean shook his head. "No one she's contacted knows anything about a missing boy matching Tim's description."

"Now what?"

"I'm not sure. I promised I'd find him a daddy."

Eleanor gaped. "You did?"

The Dean of a week ago would have been more likely to say, *Go away, kid, you bother me.* Eleanor couldn't imagine him promising to find the little boy a father.

"I did." He shrugged. "Guess I'd better get to it."

Eleanor wasn't sure what to make of the changes in Dean. But since they were for the better, she'd relegate him to the bottom of her to-do list for the moment.

Right now she had to deal with her number-one item.

"John!" she shouted.

She followed the mumbled "What?" up the stairs.

Chapter Sixteen

For the first time in . . . Aaron couldn't quite recall, he awoke with a smile on his face. Even with the constant crick in his neck from sleeping on the sofa, each day was a gift.

If he could live forever in this little house with his daughter and his . . .

Nicole.

Aaron sat up too fast and hissed as pain shot from his neck straight into his brain. He hated when that happened.

He stood and walked to the bathroom, rubbing at the tight muscle and pondering the biggest question in his life.

What was he going to do about Nicole?

Aaron stared into the mirror over the sink and realized he had no idea.

Some of his happiness faded. As much as he'd like to continue to live the life they'd been living for the past few weeks, he knew he could not. Sooner or later decisions would have to be made — not the least of which was what he was going to do with the rest of his life.

A distant tap on the door had him stepping into the hallway and listening. No footsteps raced across the wood floor to indicate Rayne was home. No call of "come in" sounded in Nicole's husky, arousing voice.

Aaron shoved a hand through his messy hair, then glanced down at his cutoff sweatpants. He winced at the early-morning hard-on he hadn't yet lost, and wouldn't lose if he kept thinking about Nicole's voice and how she'd once whispered his name.

"Who's there?" he called.

"Me."

Aaron gave a rueful laugh. He'd recognize his father's gruff growl anywhere.

"Come in. I'll be right out."

He stepped back into the bathroom, dropped his shorts, turned on the cold water full blast and shoved his head, then the rest of him underneath the spray until he was fully awake and no longer fully aroused. Thankfully it didn't take long.

Still, by the time he'd dried off, brushed the sleep from his teeth and found a clean pair of shorts, his father had made coffee.

"What's up?" Aaron filled a cup.

His first sip left him blinking. This stuff was going to stand up and walk out the door it was so strong.

"Not much." John sipped. "Ah, nothing like the perfect cup of coffee. Now if I had a cigarette —"

"You gave those up a long time ago."

John patted his shirt pocket. "Gone but not forgotten. No matter how long I've been smoke free, I still want one." He sighed. "Guess that'll never change."

"Guess not." Aaron frowned as his dad continued to drink the coffee and stare at his boots. "Is everyone all right?"

"What? Yeah. Sure. Why wouldn't they be?"

"No reason. Just wondering what you're doing here."

"Can't a dad want to see his son? You've been gone. I'm not used to it."

"You've been telling me to get the hell out of your house for years now."

"That was just kiddin' around."

Aaron knew his father loved him, knew most of his gruff chatter was just that — chatter. He also knew this wasn't just a social call.

"Rayne sure is special," his dad observed.

"That she is."

"A bit snarky at times. Like her gramma and her aunt."

"Must be a family trait."

"Noticed her mom's not that way. Interesting woman, Nicole."

Aaron sighed. "Speak your piece, Dad."

"I'm tryin' to. Let me work around to it. I'm not one of those Jerry Springer types. Even though your mom and I have been working on the talking, I still don't like to blab my feelings." He shuddered. "Or discuss anyone else's."

"Then why are you here?"

"Because your mom shoved me out the door. You know how she is."

"Mom sent you over here?"

"You think I'd be here otherwise? I got fields to plow."

"And sons ready, willing and able to do it for you."

John looked Aaron over from the top of his damp head to the tip of his bare toes. "Yeah, I can see that."

Aaron just grinned. "You know you want to plow the field yourself. Why not just say it?"

"I want to plow the field myself."

"Don't you feel better now?"

"No. I got to talk to you or your mom will have my hide."

"Since when do you listen to her?"

"I've always listened to her, boy. It saves

me a lot of aggravation."

"Uh-huh." Aaron wasn't going to point out that his dad had dealt with the farm and the cows, his mom with the house and the kids for as long as he could recall. The two of them hadn't listened to each other because they hadn't really talked to each other until after his father's heart attack. The relationship they shared now was as new as Dean's robotic milking machine.

Aaron took a deep sip of coffee, then nearly sprayed it all over the floor. He braced himself, swallowed and could have sworn the caffeine shot through his bloodstream and straight to the backs of his eyes, making them bug out like a cartoon character's.

"What are we supposed to talk about?" he choked out.

Aaron figured his father wanted to discuss the farm. There was really no need for Dean, John, Aaron and sometimes Evan to work there anymore. Aaron didn't mind giving up his chores. He'd never liked them anyway.

He'd come to the conclusion over the past few days that he couldn't stay here. But where he would go, what he would do, was anyone's guess, and he had Rayne to consider now.

Aaron opened his mouth to tell his father he already knew what he wanted to say; however, John surprised him.

"We're going to talk about Nicole."

"Sir?"

"Don't *sir* me. What's going on over here?"

"Nothing!"

John shook his head. "Boy, sometimes you worry me. A beautiful woman you're obviously interested in. A little cottage past the cornfield —"

"And my daughter in the next room."

"Which is no different than a thousand other homes between here and Bloomington."

"Except I'm relatively sure those other homes consist of a family."

"You've got a family. Or you could have, if you wanted one. Do you?"

Aaron didn't even have to think before he answered, "Yes."

"Then what are you waiting for?"

Now Aaron hesitated. He'd never spoken to anyone about his shortcomings — his inability to understand his own feelings, his lack of knowledge about male-female relationships. He didn't particularly want to discuss them with his dad. But since John was here, he wanted to talk, and

Aaron had no one else to talk to, he shrugged and plunged forward.

"I'm not sure if I love her."

"Your own daughter?"

This was one of the reasons he didn't talk to his father about serious issues. John Luchetti had a hard time focusing on anything but the cows.

Annoyance slashed through Aaron. An unusual occurrence for him and one that made him speak more sharply and sarcastically than usual. "Dad! Try to keep up. Of course I love Rayne. We were talking about Nic."

John frowned harder. "Whaddya mean you don't know if you love her?"

"How do you know if you're in love?"

"Hell," his dad snapped. "You just do."

"Is that how it was between you and mom? You just knew?"

"I guess. All I could think about was her. Us." John shrugged. "You know — us. Together. I wanted her the first time I saw her. I still do."

Aaron's face heated. "Sheesh, Dad, that's lust, not love."

"It's done us fine for thirty-odd years. Tell me somethin', boy, did you ever feel for anyone else what you feel for her?"

Aaron thought back to the way things

had been between him and Nicole once, how it was now. He thought of the women he had known in between. What were their names again?

"No," he whispered.

"There's something to be said about everlasting lust."

Aaron didn't know what to say. He should have known his father wasn't finished.

"Ack, I'm no good at giving advice. I can only tell you what I think."

"Which is?"

"Marry the mother of your child, Aaron."

"Because I want her?"

"Because a man takes responsibility for his actions. Marry for the good of your daughter. Make a family and a home for her."

"Isn't that a bit 1950s? Even for you?"

His father glared. "You're beginning to take on Dean's smart mouth, and just when he was losing it, too."

"Sorry."

"I'm not saying that two people who loathe each other should stay together and make everyone around them miserable. But when did staying together for the children become a bad thing?"

"In 1975?"

"Hippie time bullshit," John growled. "Family is what's important. If you don't do something, and do it quick, Nicole's going back to Vegas."

Aaron's heart gave a hard, painful thud. "What?"

"She told your mother this morning."

"But what about Rayne?"

"Leaving her here. For you."

Aaron frowned. He didn't want Nicole to be miserable so he could be happy. But he didn't want Rayne living on the other side of the country, either. What *did* he want?

He already knew the answer. He wanted things to stay the way they were right now, and his father had just handed him the way to make it happen.

After Eleanor left, Nicole took a walk and had a nice long talk with herself. If she was going home, she'd best get going. Prolonging the agony wasn't going to do her or anyone else any good.

The thought of telling Rayne she was going back to Vegas, and hearing her daughter say, "Good riddance," brought tears to Nicole's eyes.

As a result, when she neared the house and saw John leaving, she hung back, skulking in the tall grass until he disappeared into the cornfield.

Nicole glanced at her watch. She needed to pack, stop by the main house, where her daughter had no doubt already gone to get away from her, and beg a ride to town. There had to be a way to rent a car — even in Gainsville.

She might be going home, but that didn't mean she had to hurry. She'd had enough flying for one lifetime. Maybe by the time she drove to Las Vegas, she'd be able to stop crying.

Eyes burning, nose stuffed, she ran up the steps, into the house, down the hall and straight into Aaron, who was coming out of the bathroom.

"Hey!" He grabbed her forearms to steady her. "I was just going to look for you."

Nicole didn't want him to see her tears, so she stared straight at his chest.

Big mistake. He wasn't wearing a shirt.

All the fantasies she'd had about his body — the ones she'd cultivated over fourteen years and the ones she'd discovered since he'd returned — crashed together. His skin inches from her lips, she could feel his heat caress her face. The scent of him, soap and sleepy male, filled her senses.

Of their own volition her hands reached for his waist. Her palms slid along his ribs. Her thumbs stroked his nipples as her fingers threaded through the soft, fine, curling matt of dark hair.

His breath caught, the movement tightening the muscles beneath the skin, beneath her hands. He was so much bigger, so much stronger, so much sexier than she remembered. Fascinated, she traced the dips and curves and peaks.

His fingers tightened on her shoulders. She glanced up, tears forgotten, uncertain if he meant to push her away or pull her close.

"Nic?" he murmured.

The uncertain tenor of his voice made the past and the present collide. He was both comforting and forbidden, the father of her child and the man she could never have.

She swayed forward, mouth lifted toward his. He hesitated and she wanted to shriek in frustration. She was leaving. She meant to have one last, passionate embrace before she did. If she let him, Aaron would analyze their attraction into oblivion, and she'd have nothing. She went on tiptoe and kissed him.

He moaned, the sound making her mouth tingle. She spread her hands across his chest, curved her fingers over his shoulders and held on tight.

Her tongue played with the seam of his lips for only an instant before his stroked hers in a lazy rhythm. He tasted of toothpaste — bright shiny morning and mint.

He pressed tiny, frantic kisses down her jaw to her throat. His hands cupped her hips, pulled her against him. His arousal pressed against her stomach, and she had to clench her teeth to keep from arching against him.

This was how it had been all those years ago. There had been no stopping them then, how was she going to stop them now? Especially since she didn't want to.

"Where's Rayne?" she managed.

"Gone to Gramma's. Won't be back for hours."

Before she knew what he was about, he swung her feet off the floor and backed into her bedroom. The slam of the door and the click of the lock played along her already screaming nerves.

"We shouldn't," she began as he let her slide down the length of his body until her feet touched the floor.

"I've had a lifetime of shouldn't."

His mouth swooped down on hers, his tongue searching and finding. Though his kiss was rough, his hands were gentle. One strong arm tugged her close as his palm swept beneath her shirt, fingertips across her belly, and his thumb smoothed the skin marred by the underwire of her bra. She shivered, wanting him to go further, yet afraid that he would.

He lifted his head and stared into her eyes. "Marry me, Nicole."

She started and would have pulled herself from his arms, but he held her with the iron band of his forearm at her back. His other hand still up her shirt gave an almost comical bent to the situation. Too bad she'd never felt less like laughing in her life. Instead she stared at him as if he'd lost his mind. She knew she had.

His head lowered. He pressed a featherlight kiss to her brow, trailed his lips past the corner of her eye. Her eyes slid closed as sensations seduced her.

"Marry me." The warmth of his breath brushed her jaw an instant before his mouth did.

"Aaron." She wasn't sure if she was protesting or pleading.

His palm cupped her breast, the heat of his skin seeping through the plain white cotton. His thumb caressed her nipple; his tongue teased her ear. She tried to think and discovered she could not, so she gave up trying.

"Touch me," he whispered. "Please, Nic. No one ever touched me like you did."

Remembering how she had touched him, how he had responded, how she had, made her body clamor for more. No one had *ever* touched him that way? She doubted it. But the thought that he wanted her hands on him, her body beneath his gave her a feeling of satisfaction she could not recall having since the last time they had come together.

Holding his gaze she slid her hand down his chest, across his belly, then cupped him through the slippery material of his running shorts.

He was hard and firm, exactly as she remembered. Back then she had stroked him, then taken him, taught him everything she knew and a few things she'd only heard about.

She ran a finger up his length, and he tensed then placed his hand over hers. But instead of pulling her away as she feared, he pressed her closer, showing her what he wanted, needed, and teaching her that his needs and wants were hers, too.

By the time they tumbled onto the bed, she was breathing as fast as he was. Her mind was still frazzled — had he truly asked her to marry him?

Yes. She was certain that he had.

When had he fallen in love with her? Why hadn't he told her before now?

She pushed aside the questions and let the feelings take control. As she reached for the waistband of his shorts, he grabbed her wrists.

"Not yet. You first."

Nicole glanced down. She still wore every stitch of clothing while he wore hardly anything at all.

He lay back on the bed. "Your hair," he murmured. "Take it down."

She tugged the band from the end of her braid, ran her fingers through the waves, shook her head as she'd learned to do a long, long time ago.

There were a lot of things she'd learned to do long ago, things that hadn't been about anything but money. But now, for him, she wanted to take off her clothes slowly, seductively.

She wanted him to want her again, as he'd wanted her before. She wanted him to want her forever, and it appeared that he did.

She popped one button free, then another. His gaze followed the path of her fingers. She shrugged her shoulders; the blouse slid free. He sat up and held out his arms. Nicole went into them with a sigh.

"Let me," he murmured, tossing the rest of her clothes, then his onto the floor with the others.

"You're so beautiful," he said as he stroked her skin, kissed her face.

But she didn't want to be beautiful, she wanted to be his. She discovered very quickly that what she wanted was what he wanted, too.

She relearned every inch of his body, pressed her lips to scars that had not been there before, caressed with her tongue the muscles that had grown and hardened in the years he and she had been apart.

His fingertips traced the silver tracks across her breasts. She tensed, wondering if the imperfections would remind him of past mistakes, present guilts. Instead he pressed his mouth to the marks, rubbed his nose against her belly, inched his mouth lower still and made her forget everything but him.

While she lay shaking and gasping, he pulled away and she clutched at him.

"*Shh.*" He raised her fingers to his mouth and kissed them. "I'm just going to borrow something from my brother."

The sound of a drawer, the shuffle of a box, the crinkle of plastic and she understood what he was after.

"I might be slow, but I'm not dumb," he murmured when he returned to her.

Smiling, she reached up and tugged on his hair, pulling his mouth back to hers as she welcomed him inside.

He *was* slow. She liked him that way. But definitely not dumb. Not even close.

He knew all the ways to make her gasp, make her moan. Easy to hard, slow and then slower, shallow to deep, her mind and her body strained for completion. She could see something spectacular beyond her closed eyelids, feel it just beyond the reach of her body.

"Aaron?"

Her voice, raspy, desperate, with just a tinge of uncertainty made him still. He leaned on one elbow, raised his head from her shoulder, then his hand to her face.

"Shh, sweetheart." He slid out of her body, then back in. "Come with me. Stay with me."

And she knew he meant for more than just this moment. He meant forever.

She felt him come, the flutter deep inside her body seemed to tantalize her very soul. Their gazes locked as together they found something they hadn't truly lost.

She didn't think there could be more and then there was. What she had felt for him once was nothing in comparison to what she felt for him now. She couldn't keep her joy to herself.

"I love you," she said.

The instant the words left her lips she wanted them back.

He blinked, stunned. Gaped, flummoxed. Spoke and shattered her joy into a million shards of misery.

"Thank you."

How was that for a nightmare come true?

Chapter Seventeen

Aaron wanted to strangle himself. It wouldn't be the first time, nor sadly, the last.

Thank you?

Call him Mr. Smooth.

Nicole shoved at his shoulders and he obediently rolled away. As soon as he did, she jumped up, yanked the sheet from the bed, and left him naked and alone.

"Wait —" He reached for her, but she slapped his hand away.

"Don't touch me." She wrapped the sheet around her shoulders and hunched them as if she were cold. "Just don't."

Aaron snatched his shorts from the floor. He didn't want to have this conversation without them.

"I'm a moron," he began.

"Yes, you are."

"Give me a chance. Let me explain."

"Explain what? You wanted me, I wanted you. We're adults."

Her calm cool words would have worked better if her voice hadn't been choked and her eyes hadn't been damp.

"It wasn't like that."

"What was it like?"

"I asked you to marry me," he floundered.

"I've heard that guys will do that to get in a woman's pants, but you should have known from past experience you wouldn't need to."

She was so cold; she frightened him. How could he have bungled this so badly?

"Nic, please. I'm not good at this."

"On the contrary, you're very, very good. I have no complaints."

Aaron sighed. He deserved her anger, her scorn. He shouldn't have touched her. He should have waited. But he'd been waiting so long; he'd wanted her so much.

"Sweetheart —"

"Don't call me that!"

He blinked at the vehemence in her voice. She hadn't seemed to mind ten minutes ago. Damn, he was hopelessly inadequate in situations like these.

"Fine." He spoke low and slow, as if he were dealing with a skittish animal. "Nicole. I meant it when I said that I wanted to marry you."

"Why on earth would you want to marry me?"

"Why wouldn't I?"

She made an aggravated sound, shoved her hair out of her face and contemplated him for several moments.

"Aaron, tell me the truth?"

"Of course."

"Do you love me?"

He looked into his heart, searched his mind, wished he knew — and didn't.

She sighed. "Never mind."

"Just wait. Let me answer."

She gave a small, sad smile. "You already did."

Nicole picked up her clothes and headed for the door. Aaron sat on the bed. He had to say something.

"I want a family," he blurted.

She paused, turned and shook her head. "You've got a family. You don't need me."

"But —"

She held up her hand and he quieted. "Once upon a time I would have sold my soul for a family." He winced and she laughed. "Don't worry. I didn't."

"Nic —"

"Let me finish. I had a lifetime of being forced on people who didn't want me. No one ever loved me just for being me. I wanted that. I still do." She tugged the sheet closer. "Rayne loves me, or at least she did, for just that reason. So does Janet. I've had a taste of true love now, and I'm not going to settle for anything less. Not even for you. I deserve better, Aaron."

He couldn't argue, because she was right.

"Call me," he said. "If you ever need me."

She paused, leaned her head against the door and sighed, long and sad and deep. "I need you to need me, Aaron. But I know you never will."

Rayne had escaped from the cottage and through the cornfield to her grandparents' as she did every day. She couldn't bear to be in the same house as her mom. She didn't want to forgive her yet. She wanted to hold on to her anger and wallow awhile, which wasn't like her. But then not much was lately.

At the main house, she found very little to do. John was gone. So were Tim and Dean. Ellie was muttering in the kitchen, slamming doors and scribbling things on a piece of paper.

"What's the matter?" Rayne asked.

"Gotta go grocery shopping again. I swear I just went."

Rayne grunted. After living with her

uncle, father, grampa and Tim a while she'd discovered grunting worked on many levels.

"Wanna go to town?" Ellie asked.

"Sure."

An hour later they had transferred half the grocery store into bags. They were nearly done loading them into Ellie's SUV.

"Mrs. Luchetti?" They turned to find a young woman in a nurse's smock standing on the sidewalk behind them. "Hi, I'm Maddy Blake. I went out with Evan for a while in high school."

Rayne stifled a snicker. From what she'd heard, everyone had.

But Ellie just nodded and said, "I remember. How are you?"

"Good. I'm a nurse now. But I guess you know that."

Ellie blinked. "Why would I know that?"

"Because of Dean. All the tests. It's funny how he was diagnosed, but lucky, too."

Ellie glanced at Rayne, who shrugged.

"You mean Tim?"

Maddy's smile faded. "No."

"I think you'd better explain."

"You didn't know?" She clapped her hand over her mouth as if to prevent more secrets from tumbling out. Her eyes, wide and frightened, stared at Ellie over her fingers.

"Know what?"

Rayne swallowed at the tone of Ellie's voice. So did Maddy. The nurse lowered her hand.

"I can't tell you anymore, Mrs. Luchetti. You'll have to talk to Dean."

She turned and practically ran back the way she had come.

"Huh." Rayne continued to move the grocery bags from the cart to the car. "Weird."

Ellie wasn't helping so Rayne glanced her way, only to find her gramma leaning against the car with tears in her eyes and a shaking hand pressed to her mouth.

"What's the matter?" Rayne cried.

Her gramma started mumbling. "He's been acting strange. Too damn nice. Almost as if he's trying to make up for things. I was thinking of looking in the basement for pods."

Rayne frowned. She wasn't making any sense. "Pods? What are you talking about?"

"Huh?" Ellie blinked. "Oh, *Invasion of the Body Snatchers*. A science fiction movie. Before your time I guess."

She shook her head, rubbed her eyes,

sighed. "I was just happy he seemed happy. I thought maybe he'd finally found a reason for living in Tim. God knows they both need someone. But maybe it isn't living we have to worry about."

Rayne glanced down the street where Maddy, the blabbermouth nurse, had run. She thought about what the woman had said. "You don't think — ?"

Ellie slammed the tailgate on the SUV. "I don't know what to think. But I plan to get the truth as soon as I get my hands on Dean."

Rayne laid her hand on Ellie's arm. "It'll be all right, Gramma."

Ellie tilted her head. "That's the first time you ever called me that."

"It won't be the last."

Dean was going over the books in the kitchen. This was the part of being a farmer he liked the least. He had never been very good at sitting down and putting his nose to the grindstone. Which was why he'd barely made it through high school.

No, his talents lay in physical labor. He could work from sunup to sundown, and he liked it. He liked animals. They never talked back. They never stared at him like he was a social outcast or a stupid freak —

as long as he brought them their meals on time.

Dean shuffled the bills into order by date. The barking of the dogs distracted him. He glanced up, frowned. "Sounds like more dogs than we have. Huh."

With no small amount of effort, he pulled his attention back to the stack of paper in front of him, realized he'd lost his place and started all over again.

Dean spent the next ten minutes paying the bills from the top of the pile. The low drone of a vehicle outside the window made him glance up again. His mom and Rayne flashed by. He returned his gaze to the checkbook and wondered what invoice he'd paid for $77.75.

Cursing, he tossed the pen on the table. He still wasn't any good at this.

The front door slammed. The stomp of angry feet headed in his direction. Dean searched his mind for what he'd done to piss off his mother lately and came up empty.

She appeared in the doorway. He braced himself for the shouting that usually accompanied any stomping. Instead, she took one look at him and cried out, "Dean!" then ran across the room and yanked his head against her chest.

"What the hell?" He tried to stand. She hugged him tighter. "Mom, are you all right? Where's Dad?"

"Who cares?" She released him from her stranglehold and Dean stood, then backed up warily, putting the table between the two of them. "What I want to know is — are *you* all right?"

"Peachy," he muttered. "I gotta go check the pigs."

"Freeze, mister."

Dean froze. He might be twenty-nine years old, but he still couldn't stop himself from giving automatic compliance to *that* tone of voice.

"I saw Maddy Blake."

He searched his mind, came up with a hazy, childish face and shrugged. "The one Evan went out with?"

She waved her hand. "Irrelevant."

True. The number of girls Evan had gone out with rivaled the population of a small village.

"You gotta help me out here, Mom, I'm drawing a blank."

"She works at the doctor's office."

"Hell."

"Precisely. Hell is what I've been going through since I spoke to her. What's the matter with you?"

Dean wasn't sure if she was asking the question rhetorically or if she was referring to his physical problem. He chose the latter.

"Same thing that's been the matter with me all of my life, according to the doctor."

"I don't understand." She took a step forward. He took a step back. Her eyes filled with tears and he felt like a jerk. But that was nothing new. "Please tell me you aren't dying, Dean."

"Dying?" He snorted. "Where did you get that idea?"

"Tests. Doctors. The way you've been acting."

"I've been acting nice."

"Exactly. Why?"

Dean sighed. It was an indication of his personality that his mother's first question was why he was acting nice.

He'd always been short-tempered. He'd always had trouble with relationships. He was impulsive, inconsistent — and now he knew why.

"Because I discovered that the things I've been thinking about myself for years aren't true."

"What things?"

"I'm not stupid. I'm not a loser."

"Of course you aren't!"

"What I am is hyper."

"Excuse me?"

"I have ADHD," he said slowly, "Just like Tim."

His mother stared at him, then yanked out a chair and collapsed into it. "I don't understand. You're an adult."

"A lot of adults have ADHD. They just aren't diagnosed until their kids are."

"I — I — I never thought — You were energetic, but nothing unusual. Kids who are hyper climb the walls, don't they?"

"Not all of them. They have trouble in school because they can't focus. Some don't sleep well."

She caught her breath. "You never slept."

"Still don't. Which contributes to my cranky nature."

"But how did they figure this out?"

"Tim was scared to take the tests, so I said I'd take them too and voilà —"

"You matched."

Dean hesitated. They did match — in more ways than one. Since he wasn't sure what to make of that, he pushed the thought aside.

"I'm sorry, Dean. I never considered there was anything physically wrong with you. You were my little boy. Different —"

she shrugged "— but everyone is. We didn't run to the doctor when our kids acted up, we dealt with it in our own way."

Guilt clouded her eyes, and Dean placed his hand on her shoulder. "It isn't your fault. Doctors know what to look for now. Teachers, too. I was diagnosed by accident but that accident turned out to be a gift. I understand why I am the way I am. I can get help. Medication. Behavior therapy. Just knowing that there's a physical reason I can't focus helps a lot in itself."

His mother went silent again. He could tell by the set of her mouth that she was still upset, and that she had more questions.

"What?" he murmured.

"Did I do something to make this happen? When I was pregnant or when you were little?"

"Did you do drugs, smoke or drink?"

"Of course not!"

"Those are the things you could control. They increase the risk. Other than that, genetics, biology, a freak accident during the birth." He shrugged. "Who knows. Everything that happens to your kids isn't your fault, Mom."

"No? Then why does it feel as if it is?"

"Because you're a mom. If you weren't

feeling guilty about one of us, life just wouldn't be worth living."

She snorted. "Smart mouth."

He grinned.

"You going to quit smoking now?"

His heart did a slow roll into his belly. "H-how did you know?"

"Think about who you're dealing with here."

"How do you *do* that?"

"It's a gift."

"Or a curse."

She raised her eyebrows and held out her hand.

Dean stared at her open palm. He *had* been thinking about quitting. After all, he didn't want Tim to get the idea that smoking was okay.

With a sigh, Dean pulled the pack of cigarettes out of his back pocket and gave them to his mother. She dropped them to the floor and smashed them beneath her shoe.

"Ouch," he muttered.

"You'll thank me later."

The barking from the backyard increased in volume and made both of them frown.

"That sounds like more dogs than we've got," she murmured.

Dean had thought the same thing, then forgotten all about it when a more interesting situation came along. The story of his life.

"We'd better take a peek," Dean said.

Together they walked out of the kitchen and onto the back porch, stopping dead at the sight that greeted them.

"Hi, Dean!"

Tim giggled as what appeared to be at least half a dozen spotted puppies tumbled over his legs and tried to kiss him wherever they could reach.

"I'm going to kill him," Eleanor muttered.

Tim glanced at Eleanor with wide eyes, grabbing several puppies and shielding them from her glare.

"Where's Bear?"

The dog in question scrambled beneath the porch with a whimper. Bull followed.

Dean put his hand on his mom's arm before she went after them. "Mom, Bear has no clue what he's done."

"He has the attention span of a gnat."

"Don't we all," Dean said dryly.

Eleanor turned to Tim. "Where did these puppies come from?"

"Some lady drove up. Said they were ours. I said, 'Cool,' and she left. Aren't they cute? Spotted like Bear. And fluffy like —"

"A French poodle," Eleanor growled.

"They're doodles!"

Dean couldn't help but laugh. His mother scowled. "That's not funny."

"Actually it is."

"I told you to get that dog fixed."

Dean shuffled his feet. "You don't know what you're asking when you tell a guy to do something like that."

"You're a farmer for crying out loud. You eat your pig pals."

"That's the entire point of pigs," he pointed out. "They're cute when they're little. When they're no longer cute, they're lunch."

"If you believe that, then why are you squeamish about taking a dog to the vet to be fixed?"

Women just didn't understand. Dean gave up trying to explain. "Calm down, Mom. I'll take care of this."

"How?"

He glanced at the dogs. Tim was right. They were awful cute.

"They were dumped, like me," Tim said, petting first one, then another. "Poor babies. We gotta find 'em daddies."

"Yes." Eleanor fixed Dean with an uncompromising stare. "You do."

When Nicole got out of the shower, Aaron was gone. If his words, or lack of them, hadn't already convinced her he didn't love her, his actions would have. She packed her things and walked to the main house.

Rayne made it easy for her. She was sitting on the porch alone. She took one look at Nicole's bag and stiffened. "I am not going back to Las Vegas!"

"No, you're not." Nicole dropped the carry-on at the foot of the porch steps. "I came to say goodbye."

Rayne frowned. "You're leaving me?"

Nicole sighed. There was just no pleasing her daughter these days.

"You want to stay. I've got to go. It's as simple as that."

"Nothing's simple anymore."

How true.

"You can stay until school starts. But if you want to come home sooner, you can do that, too."

Rayne stared down at her hands. "Are you leaving me because I've been such a pain?"

"I'm not leaving you, Rayne!"

She was leaving Aaron. But she couldn't tell her daughter that.

"What's going on out here?" Eleanor stood on the other side of the screened door.

"It's time for me to head home."

Since she and Aaron's mom had already talked about this, Eleanor had no reason to appear surprised, but she did. Her gaze turned toward the cottage. "Where's Aaron?"

"I have no idea. Can someone give me a ride into town?"

Eleanor tugged her gaze from the horizon and back to Nicole. "Sure that's what you want?"

"Absolutely."

"All right. John can take you. Dean and I have our hands full of the doodles."

She backed away from the door and disappeared.

"What's a doodle?" Nicole asked.

Rayne burst into tears and ran into the house.

Chapter Eighteen

As hours became days and headed toward a week, Aaron's life became emptier and emptier.

He and Rayne lived at the cottage, but his daughter spent most of her time with Tim, helping him take care of Bear's little miracles. When she wasn't with Tim, she was crying in her room. The sound made Aaron want to cry, too.

Every night he'd wake and find himself reaching for Nicole. They'd never slept the entire night together, never lived as man and wife, yet he felt as if he'd lost his soul mate.

The peace that had settled over him in the past few weeks disappeared as fast as Nicole had. The sadness that had lodged in his chest for so many years returned. He felt lonely, guilty, foolish.

He was happy to have his daughter with him, but his daughter was driving him crazy. She hadn't wanted to go back to Vegas, but she didn't want to be here, either.

Aaron tried to immerse himself in work. With Dean spending more time with Tim, the two of them trying to pawn off doodles on everyone in town and having very little luck, there was plenty to do around the farm. But even when he spent an entire day working in the summer sun, Aaron didn't sleep well.

He missed her.

Once again he felt as if he had no purpose, and it was then that he realized his purpose was her.

Eleanor replaced the phone in the cradle and turned to her husband.

"What did they say?"

Her chest hurt. She was dizzy. John reached out and dragged her into his arms. "Ellie." He shook her once, hard. "Breathe."

She drew in some air. The dizziness passed. Her chest still hurt. But she had a feeling it was going to stay that way — until she knew the truth about her son.

"They said he's missing."

"Bobby's MIA?"

"There was no action to be missing from. At least where he was. He's just . . . gone."

"That's impossible."

Eleanor pulled away from John and sat at the kitchen table. "I guess not."

The back door opened. "Where's Rayne?" Aaron asked.

"Feeding doodles."

He hesitated, glancing from her, to his father and back again. "What's the matter?"

"It's Bobby."

Aaron stepped inside and shut the door. "Tell me."

Quickly she filled him in on the phone call she'd received from Bobby's superior. Though Aaron was as concerned as she was, he was also distracted. He carried Rayne's backpack in one hand and his own carry-on luggage in the other.

"You going somewhere?" she asked.

"Vegas."

"About damn time," John muttered. "Thought I told you to marry that woman."

"I'd love to, but she won't have me."

"What?" Incensed, Eleanor stood and put her hands on her hips. "Why not?"

"She doesn't think I love her."

"And why is that?"

"Because when she told me that she loved me I said thank you."

Eleanor's eyes widened. "Idiot."

"Thank you, Mother. I appreciate your support."

She ignored him. "Did she tell you she's loved you all along?"

"No. What?"

"Blabbermouth," John said.

Eleanor plowed ahead. "Of course she loved you. She had your child. Protected your dream. Everything she did, she did for you. Are you blind as well as dumb?"

"How long have you known this?"

"A while."

"And you didn't tell me?"

"Nicole didn't want you to know. She didn't want you to feel any more guilty than you already did."

"But I do," he whispered.

Eleanor glanced at her husband. "What's with Luchetti men and the inability to say I love you?"

"Here she goes," John muttered.

"Hey, we were married over thirty years before you told me that you loved me."

"I showed you."

"Yippee," she sneered.

John scowled and crossed his arms over his chest.

His closed stance only annoyed her more. "Your problem seems to have trans-lated to the kids. I always worried that not hearing you say the words would screw them up. And it did. Now fix him."

"I'm not broken," Aaron grumbled.

"You will be if you don't take your hand off that doorknob."

He complied.

"John . . ."

Her husband sighed and threw up his hands. "Son, what are you planning to do?"

"Take Rayne back to Vegas where she belongs."

"And then?"

"I have no idea."

John just stood there like a lump. Eleanor made a face and stepped into the void.

"What do you feel, Aaron? For Nicole."

Sadly the Luchetti family had never been very good articulating feelings. It had gotten them into no small amount of trouble all of their lives.

Aaron hesitated so long Eleanor wasn't sure he'd answer. But when he did, it was as if he'd broken through a final barrier and everything came rushing out.

"Without her I'm empty." He began to pace the room. "I can't sleep, can't eat. All I can think about is her."

"Why don't you tell her that?"

His face became determined. He picked up the luggage. "I plan to."

He left the way he had come. Eleanor heard him calling for Rayne. John came up behind her and put his big, hard hands on her shoulders. She leaned against him.

"Think we ought to tell him he's in love?" she asked.

"Nah, some things are better if you figure them out for yourself."

Nicole stumbled into Mercy House late on a Thursday night. She'd driven instead of flown — a distance of nearly seventeen hundred miles. She didn't plan on ever doing it again. Since flying was out, she'd just be spending the rest of her born days in Las Vegas.

Where once that might have upset her, suddenly she didn't mind. She'd had to leave to discover the truth. Las Vegas was home.

"Nicky?"

Janet stood at the top of the steps. The sight of her familiar camouflage nightgown made Nicole's eyes water. If Las Vegas was home, then Janet was the closest thing to a mother she'd ever have.

Nicole dropped her bag, ran up the steps and threw herself into Janet's arms. Her friend hugged her tight, then smoothed Nicole's hair away from her face with a gentle touch.

"How was the trip?"

"Awful."

"I bet."

"I miss her already."

"She'll come back."

Nicole's eyes burned as she voiced her greatest fear. "What if she doesn't?"

The doorbell rang. They both frowned.

"Mind getting that?" Janet asked. "I'm a little underdressed."

Nicole ran back down the steps and pulled open the door. Aaron Luchetti stood on the porch.

"I love you, Nic."

She slammed the door in his face.

"Nicky! What's the matter with you?"

The key turned in the lock and Rayne blew inside.

"Mom!" She threw herself into Nicole's arms. Nicole was so shocked all she could do was hold her daughter and stare at Aaron.

"Wh-what are you doing here?" she managed at last.

"I missed you." Rayne didn't seem to want to let her go, and after so many days where Rayne hadn't wanted to see her face, Nicole didn't want to, either.

"I thought you hated me."

"Mom." Rayne pulled back and rolled her eyes in that new way she had which shouted, *Yes, she's a bonehead, but I love her.* "I could never hate you."

"I seem to recall you screaming just that on at least one occasion."

"Sorry." She ducked her head. "I realized something after you left. People make mistakes. And sometimes those mistakes were what was meant to be."

Nicole glanced at Janet over Rayne's head. The older woman spread her hands in a *what can I say?* gesture.

"So what was meant to be?" Nicole asked.

"You lied, and that was wrong. But if I'd known about my dad, I probably wouldn't have been here. I wouldn't have met Tim. He wouldn't have found Dean and everyone wouldn't be happy."

"Everyone's happy?"

"We could be."

Aaron's deep voice made Nicole tense. Rayne tried to disentangle herself from her mother's arms, but Nicole clung.

She didn't want to face him. Not yet. Hell, not ever. The first sight of him had brought everything back. The love, the lust, the pain. What on earth had he meant by *I love you?*

"Janet!" Rayne tore free and ran up the steps to hug the older woman.

In the way of children, Rayne had apologized for her horrific behavior and expected to be forgiven, just like that. And she was.

"Hey, kid." Janet tugged on Rayne's colorful headband. "I've got a whole bunch of new drawings to show you."

"Now?" Nicole squeaked.

Janet glared at her from on high. "Now."

The two disappeared into Janet's room, leaving Nicole and Aaron alone. Nicole fled into the living room.

"Aren't you going to say anything?" Aaron followed. "I just told you that I loved you."

"Thank you?"

His lips twitched. "I guess I deserved that."

"You don't have to say that you love me, Aaron. You don't need to marry me to have a family. Rayne is yours. I won't keep her from you. Other couples share, why can't we?"

"I don't want to share."

Nicole glanced up. He was close enough to reach out and brush his knuckles across her cheek. She was so startled to find him so near, she let him.

"I meant it when I said that I loved you."

"A week ago you didn't know what love meant."

"A week ago I hadn't lost you."

She threw up her hands. "You only want what you don't have. How am I ever going to know if you love me for me, or love me for Rayne, or if you even love me at all?"

"You won't. You're going to have to trust someone sometime. You've been dumped. You've been hurt. You've been lied to. I don't deserve your trust. But I want it. I want you."

"That much I know."

He gave an exasperated sigh. "What I feel for you is complicated. When I was eighteen, I wanted you with a passion I didn't think I was capable of. I labeled it lust because I thought that it was. I mean, how could I fall in love with someone in an instant?"

"You couldn't."

She refused to dwell on the fact that she had.

"But I did. The minute you opened the door tonight I knew. I love you. Maybe I always have. But I know now that I always will."

Nicole gazed into Aaron's eyes. She wanted to believe in miracles, but she didn't know how.

"I need you, Nic. When we're together I see so many possibilities. I wasn't meant to be alone. I was meant to be with you. And I think you were meant to be with me, too."

Nicole looked into her heart and all she saw was love — old love and new, physical love and hero worship, the love of a mother for the father of her child. She had felt each and every one for this man.

Sure she was scared. What if she made the wrong decision? But she'd learned one thing over the past few weeks — a wrong decision was better than no decision at all. She had to trust someone sometime. She wanted to trust him.

"Marry me?" he asked again.

Instead of yes, she said, "When?"

His smile was brighter than the sunshine over the desert sand. "As soon as we can drag my family to Las Vegas."

Epilogue

"You got *your* daddy." Tim scrunched his face into an apple doll frown. "When am I gonna get mine?"

Rayne sighed. "Tim, my parents are getting married in five minutes. Can we worry about your daddy after that?"

" 'Kay. But remember, the daddy quest isn't over with yet."

"How could I forget?" Rayne mumbled.

Since Tim and the rest of the family had arrived in Las Vegas yesterday, he had been bugging her about their quest. She didn't know what she was going to do about finding him a daddy. It appeared he had the perfect one in Dean. However, Dean wasn't volunteering.

"Rayne!" her mother called. "It's time."

"Okay, okay, keep your shirt on."

Her mom, wearing a silk dress the shade of champagne, glanced at Eleanor. "Is she going to be like this for good?"

"And for bad," Eleanor said.

Kim adjusted Zsa Zsa's floppy silk hat. "Or for about three years."

The baby was as dressed up as the rest of them. She even had pink satin slippers, which fell off every time that she kicked her feet. Rayne didn't give them more than an hour before they disappeared.

Her father and her mother were getting married. Rayne had a hard time believing that. A month ago she hadn't even had a father. Now she had an entire family.

The wedding march began. Janet stepped into the room. In deference to her job of giving away the bride, she'd put aside her camouflage and worn a dress. But underneath, she wore pea-green underwear. It was their little secret.

"Everybody get where they belong," Janet ordered.

Kim handed the baby to her mother so she and Rayne could take their places as attendants. Eleanor dipped to the floor and snatched up one of Zsa Zsa's shoes with the absentminded care of a lifelong mother.

Wiggling the shoe onto the baby's foot, she turned to Nicole. "If you hurt him, I'll take you apart and feed you to the pigs."

Rayne blinked, glanced at Janet who scowled. But her mom smirked. "Do pigs eat people?"

Confusion flickered over her gramma's

face. "I'm not sure. Maybe I mean chickens. They eat anything, even chicken. It's disgusting."

"I'll keep that in mind." Nicole winked.

Eleanor laughed, then kissed Nicole's cheek. Everyone relaxed. Eleanor and Nicole had their own way of showing affection.

Rayne smiled. It was kind of nice.

"Ready you are?" Janet asked in her best Yoda imitation.

Nicole took a deep breath. "Ready I've been. For a long, long time."

Dean watched as another sibling got hitched. If he had to stand up in one more wedding, he might as well buy a tuxedo.

What was that saying — always a bridesmaid? He wondered if that applied to groomsmen, as well.

The reception took place at Mercy House. The rule about no men seemed to have fallen into oblivion. Everyone soon discovered why.

Janet lifted a glass of sparkling grape juice. "Congratulations, Nicole and Aaron. It's about time."

Laughter rippled through the room. She handed Aaron a long, legal-size document. "Good luck."

He frowned, then unfolded it. His eyes widened. He handed the paper to Nicole. Her eyes filled with tears.

"Oh, no, Janet," she protested. "You can't give us this place."

"Already did. Me and your husband here were talking one night. This neighborhood could really use a home for runaways."

"What about you?"

"And Reno could really use my help."

As Nicole hugged her friend, Dean's attention was caught by a little voice asking, "Are you my daddy?"

"Hell," he muttered, and let his gaze scan the crowd.

Tim was making the rounds. First the pastor, then Janet's publisher, the caterer, a waiter. As Tim cut a path through the guests, men backed away shaking their heads. Some even left the room — running.

Dean tried not to laugh. What was so frightening about a little boy who needed a daddy?

His laughter died. What *was* so frightening? Not one damn thing.

He stalked across the floor and scooped Tim into his arms. "Hey, kid. How come you never ask me?"

"I did once."

"Try me again."

Tim tilted his head and his smile touched Dean's heart. But then it always had. "Are you my daddy?"

The empty place inside Dean suddenly wasn't empty any more. He hugged Tim tight and whispered, "Yes."

Aaron stared out the window of Nicole's room, but he didn't really see the stars, the night or the neon. All he saw was her — and the way she'd looked at him when she'd said, "I do."

He couldn't believe his good fortune. A wife, a home, a family and a job. He didn't deserve this, but tough. No one did.

The door opened and he turned away from the window. Nicole still wore the dress she'd married him in. He couldn't wait to take it off.

"I love you," he said.

She laughed and crouched to stack a jumble of wedding presents into a corner. "Are you going to make up for not saying I love you by saying it every hour?"

"Got a problem with that?"

"No."

"Good. What do you think about babies?"

She choked. "What am I supposed to

think? They're cute. Sometimes. Then they grow up and they aren't so cute."

"I want what I missed. But only if you want it, too."

"You want night feedings, no sleep, worry, sickness and smelly diapers."

"Please."

"Oh, all right." She winked. "I guess I can manage another one or two."

He sat on the bed. "Now?"

"You don't waste any time, do you?"

"I think we've wasted enough."

She joined him. "I think you're right."

One of the wedding presents started to jiggle, then it started to yip.

"That had better not be a doodle," Aaron muttered.

But it was.

The employees of Thorndike Press hope you have enjoyed this Large Print book. All our Thorndike and Wheeler Large Print titles are designed for easy reading, and all our books are made to last. Other Thorndike Press Large Print books are available at your library, through selected bookstores, or directly from us.

For information about titles, please call:

(800) 223-1244

or visit our Web site at:

www.gale.com/thorndike
www.gale.com/wheeler

To share your comments, please write:

Publisher
Thorndike Press
295 Kennedy Memorial Drive
Waterville, ME   04901